"KATHRYN, YOU HAVE NOTHING TO FEAR FROM ME."

"I mean you no harm. I have no designs on your person. I don't expect anything from you in return for letting you stay here. I've hired a maid and a cook. Starting tomorrow, they'll look after your needs as well as be chaperones to quiet wagging tongues."

She had expected to leave in the morning. "You want me to stay here? With you?"

"Have you anywhere else to go?"

"No." She preceded him into the house, acutely aware of his presence and the fact that she was alone in the house with a stranger. A tall, mysterious stranger. She knew little of men but all her instincts warned that he was dangerous. "I'm tired," she said, not turning around. "If you don't mind, I think I'll retire for the night."

"As you wish." His voice, low and whiskey-rough, sent a shiver down her spine.

"Sweet dreams, Kathryn."

She nodded, then walked sedately up the stairs, afraid that if she ran, he would pounce on her like a hungry cat on a mouse.

Other titles available by Amanda Ashley

A WHISPER OF ETERNITY

AFTER SUNDOWN

DEAD PERFECT

DEAD SEXY

DESIRE AFTER DARK

NIGHT'S KISS

NIGHT'S MASTER

NIGHT'S PLEASURE

NIGHT'S TOUCH

NIGHT'S MISTRESS

NIGHT'S PROMISE

NIGHT'S SURRENDER

IMMORTAL SINS

EVERLASTING KISS

EVERLASTING DESIRE

BOUND BY NIGHT

BOUND BY BLOOD

HIS DARK EMBRACE

DESIRE THE NIGHT

BENEATH A MIDNIGHT MOON

AS TWILIGHT FALLS

TWILIGHT DREAMS

TWILIGHT DESIRES

BEAUTY'S BEAST

A FIRE IN THE BLOOD

Published by Kensington Publishing Corporation

HOLD BACK
THE DAWN

AMANDA
ASHLEY

ZEBRA BOOKS
KENSINGTON PUBLISHING CORP.
www.kensingtonbooks.com

ZEBRA BOOKS are published by

Kensington Publishing Corp.
119 West 40th Street
New York, NY 10018

All Kensington titles, imprints, and distributed lines are available at special quantity discounts for bulk purchases for sales promotion, premiums, fund-raising, educational, or institutional use.

Special book excerpts or customized printings can also be created to fit specific needs. For details, write or phone the office of the Kensington Sales Manager: Attn.: Sales Department. Kensington Publishing Corp., 119 West 40th Street, New York, NY 10018. Phone: 1-800-221-2647.

Zebra and the Z logo Reg. U.S. Pat. & TM Off.

First Printing: September 2019
ISBN-13: 978-1-4201-4739-1
ISBN-10: 1-4201-4739-0

ISBN-13: 978-1-4201-4741-4 (eBook)
ISBN-10: 1-4201-4741-2 (eBook)

10 9 8 7 6 5 4 3 2 1

Printed in the United States of America

For Vicki Crum,
good friend and author.
Thanks for the
inspiration on Chapter 29!

Chapter One

The Mothers of Mercy Hospital was located in what had once been a fashionable part of the town. Age had whittled it down, leaving the place looking as old and worn-out as the dilapidated manor houses that surrounded it. Most of the well-to-do folk had fled the area during an outbreak of the plague some two hundred years ago, though a handful of the wealthy landowners—too stubborn to move on—remained on their estates, closer to what was left of the town.

Roan Cabrera paused on the weed-strewn dirt road that led to the entrance. The air was fetid with the stench of horse droppings, rot, and despair. He didn't know which was worse, the stink outside, or the smell of disease and death that permeated the very walls of the hospital.

Materializing on the third floor, he ghosted past the nurse on duty, unseen, then continued down the hallway until he came to the room at the end of the corridor. A woman lay unmoving on the narrow bed. Maura Single-terry, age twenty-eight, had been badly beaten and left for dead on the side of the road. She was a pretty woman—or she had been. Now, her cheeks were sunken, her eyes shadowed, her hair limp and lackluster. Trapped in a coma for the last three weeks, her prognosis was bleak at best.

Entering the room, Roan closed the door, then glided silently to the side of the bed. He stood gazing down at her a moment; then, taking her limp hand in his, he sat on the edge of the narrow mattress, his mind delving through the darkness that kept her trapped in unconsciousness.

Opening a mental link between them, he murmured, *Hello, Maura.*

Roan?

Who else? Where would you like to go today?

My wedding day, but first . . . I want to know about you.

What would you like to know?

How is it we can talk when I cannot communicate with anyone else? Are you real? Or just a fever dream?

I'm real enough. 'Tis a gift I have, being able to speak with those who are lost in the dark.

I cannot find my way out. She whimpered softly. *I try and try, but I cannot get through the darkness.*

Roan stroked her brow. *I know. That's why I'm here. Put your questions away for now, Maura, and I'll take you back to the day you wed.*

He closed his eyes, his mind searching hers, until he found the memory she wished to experience again. He gave it back to her, not as a dream, not as a faint memory, but as if she were reliving it again . . . She mingled with everyone who had been there, recalled each word spoken that day, each thought that crossed her mind, the love she felt for her new husband, the taste and smell and texture of the food she ate, her nervousness as she and her husband left her parents' home, the carriage ride to the inn where they had spent their first night as husband and wife.

It was a rare gift he had, being able to grant those who were dying a chance to relive their most cherished memories. It cost him nothing, and he took but little in return for the pleasure he gave.

An hour later, Roan kissed Maura's cheek in farewell and left the hospital. He felt a brief twinge of regret in knowing that she had only a few hours to live. It seemed unfair that such a sweet-natured woman should be taken before her time. Unfair, he thought again, that one who had everything to live for should be brought down in her prime while he, a man who had nothing to live for and no one to mourn him when he was gone, had existed for centuries.

Hands shoved deep into his pants pockets, he strolled along the dark streets. Newberry Township was miles away from the politics and corruption of London. The people were mostly peasants and shopkeepers who had no time for anything but providing for their families.

All the shops were closed at this time of the night, with the exception of the tavern at the end of Bayberry Street. The Hare and Hound was one of Cabrera's favorite haunts, a place to while away the long, empty hours until dawn.

He went there now, taking his usual seat in the back, near the window. *Maura Singleterry.* Tomorrow her soul would shake off the pain of mortality and take flight. No doubt she would find eternal rest in heaven, if heaven existed. He had been inside her mind and found no evil there. Would she find peace in the hereafter, knowing she had left a grieving husband and five young children behind?

Roan blew out a sigh. He, too, would grieve for Maura

Singleterry. He had visited her each evening for a fortnight, helping her to relive the happiest moments in her life, always giving her hope that she would recover when he knew it for the lie it was.

He would miss her gentle spirit, but there would be others lingering in the shadow world between life and death. There were always others. He eased their pain, and although they didn't know it, they eased his. It was, he thought, an amicable alliance.

He looked up as Molly Lindstrom sashayed toward him. He had seen her on several other occasions. She was a pretty wench, with a riot of red curls, and soulful brown eyes that had seen too much of the sordid side of life.

"Can I get you something, my lord handsome?" she asked with a saucy grin.

Roan shook his head. The chit had a crush on him. Had he been younger, had Molly been older, he might have taken what she so boldly offered. "Wine," he said. "Red."

She canted her head to the side. "Do you never drink anything else?"

His gaze drifted to the pulse throbbing steadily in the hollow of her throat. "Now and then."

"I'll be going home soon, if you'd care to walk with me."

"Another time perhaps."

She pouted prettily. "You always say that, but you never do."

"Pray that I never say yes."

She looked at him oddly a moment, then turned and flounced away.

"Cabrera, there you are!" George Hampton exclaimed. "We've a game going downstairs. Care to join us?" In his mid-fifties, Hampton had a shock of iron-gray hair.

"That depends on who else is playing."

Hampton braced his hands on the back of the chair across from Roan. "The usual late-night crowd. Westerbrook and Lewiston and Cormac. Flaherty said he might be along later."

"Lead the way," Roan said, rising. After motioning for Molly to bring his drink downstairs, he followed Hampton down the narrow winding staircase that led to the gambling hell.

The rooms downstairs were dimly lit. A layer of thick gray smoke hovered near the ceiling. Hampton's cronies were gathered around a table in the middle of the room. As usual, Walter Cormac was winning. No surprise there, since he frequently cheated, although no one but Roan seemed aware of it. Short and bandy-legged, he reminded Roan of a rooster.

"Looks like your winning streak is about to end, Mac," Henry Westerbrook said as Roan slid into an empty chair.

Cormac snorted softly. "Not tonight, old man. Lady Luck is sitting on my shoulder."

The other men at the table laughed good-naturedly. Cormac always said Lady Luck was on his side, when Roan knew luck had nothing to do with it.

"Well, Lady Luck may be on your side," Frank Lewiston remarked, "but I'd wager my daughter's dowry that Cabrera has the devil's own luck on his."

"Now, gents," Hampton said, "this is a friendly game, remember?"

"Friendly, right," Westerbrook remarked and dealt the cards. Westerbrook had been an officer in the army. He still carried the air of command.

Leaning back in his chair, Roan perused his hand. He had played cards with these men often enough to know how each man reacted when he had little chance of winning the pot. Lewiston folded early, Cormac would bluff, and Hampton, the wealthiest of the lot, would try to buy the hand.

Had he wanted to, Roan could easily have read each man's mind to find out what cards he held, but there was no sport in that. Still, he had done it on occasion.

"So, Cabrera," Hampton said, folding his hand, "have you met Dudley's niece?"

Roan blew out an exaggerated sigh. "We've met."

"Is he still trying to marry her off?" Lewiston asked. "He'd have better luck if he trotted her out in a veil."

Cormac grinned as he raked in the pot. "The doxies all look the same in the dark."

"True enough," Lewiston agreed, "but she does come with a generous dowry."

"Then why don't you offer for her?" Roan asked dryly. Dudley's niece, Clara Beth, was perhaps the plainest woman Roan had ever met. Had she been blessed with a sparkling personality, suitors might have overlooked her appearance, but she was as dull as she was homely, and almost as wide as she was tall. He doubted a king's ransom would entice any red-blooded male to offer for her hand.

Roan passed a pleasant few hours gambling, then bid his companions a good evening and left the establishment.

For a moment, he considered hiring a hack to take him home, but after the smoky interior of the pub, the night's breeze called to him.

He loved the night, the soft sighing of the wind, the salty scent that wafted off the ocean, the earthy smell of soil and damp grass.

Stepping outside, he gazed up at the sky, pitying the poor mortals who glimpsed only a fraction of the heavenly display. Humans. They saw so little of the world around them, missed so much. Each evening, the earth played a symphony they never heard.

There were times when he regretted the loss of his humanity, when he cursed the man who had transformed him against his will.

But tonight wasn't one of them.

Chapter Two

Kathryn Winterbourne crept out of the crowded room she shared with seven other young women at the boarding-house. She had come to the city in hopes of finding a new and better life than the one she had known at home. She had not wanted to leave her mother at her stepfather's mercy. Though her mother denied it, Kathryn knew the man beat her when he was in his cups. Thankfully, he had not yet laid a hand on Kathryn.

Even though it had been her mother who insisted Kathryn must go, it had taken every ounce of courage she possessed to leave everything that was familiar. But staying home had been out of the question, so she had taken the few pounds her mother had stolen from Kathryn's stepfather and run away—away from the poverty of the farm, away from the ever-growing lust in her stepfather's eyes.

To her disappointment, life in the city was little better than life on the farm. The only employment to be had was as a scrubwoman in a bawdy house in the red light district. And now, she was running away again, running from Madam Quinlan's latest paramour. Newberry Township was nearby. Perhaps she could find work there.

And until then, what? She had no money with which to

secure a bed for the night, no way to pay for a room—or for her next meal.

Why was she trying to run away from the fate that would surely be hers sooner or later? She had no education, no useful skills, no hope of a favorable marriage. It was just a matter of time before she was forced to choose between starvation or earning her living on her back in one of the brothels near the docks, perhaps the very house she had fled.

Tears filled Kathryn's eyes as she contemplated such a horrid future. She didn't want to become a doxy, didn't want some fat, uncaring madam to rule her days and nights, or to sell her virginity to the highest bidder. She didn't want to end up old and alone, riddled with the pox.

She dreamed of marrying a man who loved her, preferably a wealthy man who would cherish her, one who would take her to his home and keep her safe from the ugliness of the world. Someone to give her children, but most of all, someone who would love her. But what gentleman of the realm would deign to wed someone like her?

Even though she had never worked above stairs at the brothel, her reputation was ruined. The fact that she had recognized a few of the upper-crust gents who had frequented Madam Quinlan's house only made things worse. None of the eligible men were likely to call on a woman who knew their worst habits. Not that it mattered. She didn't want anything to do with a man—married or single—who would visit such a disreputable place.

She dashed the tears from her eyes, but they only came harder and faster as she looked into an increasingly bleak future.

Lost in misery, Kathryn didn't hear the rapidly approaching carriage until it was too late. When she saw the coach-and-four bearing down on her, she hardly had time to scream.

Chapter Three

Elsbeth Pettibone primped in front of the mirror, admiring the natural curl in her golden brown hair, her perfect figure, the sparkle in her blue eyes as she looked forward to going to the ball at the Hatton's. She loved being young and beautiful, she mused, loved the admiration of the eligible bachelors, the way they competed with one another to dance with her, or sit beside her at supper. She loved the way they tried to steal a kiss when they were clever enough to get her alone.

She laughed softly. Men were such foolish, vain creatures. Didn't they realize it was *she* who decided if and when they would be alone, she who decided whether to grant a kiss? Soon, she would have to choose which marriage offer to accept. Her father favored James, her mother adored young Cameron, but Elsbeth secretly yearned for Roan Cabrera. Roan, with his broad shoulders and hooded indigo eyes. Roan, who could melt her insides with a glance, make her blood heat with just the touch of his hand. She knew her parents would never approve such a match, but she could hope. And scheme. He was, after all, a gentleman. If she could just get him in a compromising situation, she knew he would do the right thing. She had practiced all her burgeoning feminine wiles on him, but thus far, he had remained immune to her charms. It was ever so frustrating.

She put the finishing touches to her toilette, grabbed her wrap, and hurried down the stairs to where her parents waited. Maybe tonight, she thought, her stomach churning with excitement, maybe this would be the night when Roan danced to her tune.

Roan paused outside the Hatton's mansion. Dozens of carriages waited out front. The windows blazed with light. Faint sounds of laughter drifted through the door whenever a new guest arrived.

What was he doing here? He had already fed; therefore, he had little reason to go inside and subject himself to the curious stares of the matrons or the lustful glances of the innocent debutantes who would run screaming from his presence if they knew what he was. Still, it was hours until dawn, and Francis Hatton served the finest wine in the county.

Taking a deep breath, Roan made his way to the door. He had purposely arrived late, thereby avoiding the dinner hour with its elaborate courses and dull conversation. He flashed his invitation at the butler, then stepped inside, where another servant took his hat and coat.

Roan made his way upstairs, wondering again what had prompted him to attend the Hatton soiree.

As usual, Amelia Hatton had outdone herself. The ballroom was aglow with what looked like hundreds of candles, their light reflected on every polished surface. Bouquets of flowers in delicate crystal vases adorned the linen-clad table in the dining room. A number of elegantly clad couples danced to the music of a small orchestra.

Servants moved silently among the other guests, offering caviar and champagne.

Roan was deep in conversation with Hampton and Cormac when Elsbeth Pettibone swept into the room. She stood in the doorway a moment, giving the other women a chance to admire her gown and her coiffure. A smile lit her face as she spied Roan and immediately headed in his direction.

Roan swore under his breath. He had been avoiding Elsbeth's advances for months. He had done everything he could think of—short of giving her the cut direct, something he was loath to do—to convince her that he wasn't interested, but she continued to pursue him.

"Mr. Cabrera," she gushed. "Isn't it a beautiful night? I'm so glad you could make it." Although she acknowledged Hampton and Cormac with a nod, all of her attention was focused on Roan.

He forced a smile. "It's good to see you, too, Miss Pettibone." She was perfectly dressed, perfectly coiffed, and reminded him of nothing more than a porcelain doll, pretty to look at, but not to be touched.

Swaying back and forth in time to the music, she murmured, "I do so love this waltz."

It was a blatant request, he thought, and one not easily ignored. With a sigh of resignation, he offered her his arm. Miss Elsbeth Pettibone was a young woman who knew what she wanted and was accustomed to getting it. Unfortunately, she had set her cap for him.

His gaze wandered over the guests as he waltzed her around the floor. Most of the faces were familiar—women he had flirted with in the past, a few he had seduced. Men he played cards with.

"You haven't listened to a word I've said, have you?"

Roan looked down at the woman in his arms. "How

can I possibly concentrate on conversation when you look so lovely?"

"Why, Mr. Cabrera," she murmured, batting her lashes at him. "You do say the sweetest things."

He smiled at her, wondering if the music would ever end. "It's a bit warm in here, don't you think?"

His gaze lingered on the pulse in the hollow of her throat. "Would you care to go out on the balcony?"

"I shouldn't . . ."

He waited, knowing she would quickly change her mind.

"But I will." Placing her hand on his forearm, she let him lead her outside.

Roan guided her into the shadows at the far end of the balcony, then drew her into his embrace.

"Mr. Cabrera . . ." She voiced a breathy protest even as she tilted her head for his kiss.

"Miss Pettibone." His gaze caught and held hers. When her eyelids fluttered down, he lowered his head to her neck. He drank quickly, all too aware that other couples might also seek a few minutes alone in the dark.

When he finished, he licked the tiny wounds in her throat; then, releasing her from his thrall, he kissed her lightly.

She sighed when he broke the kiss, unaware that they had shared anything more.

"I should get you back inside," Roan said, "before your father comes looking for you."

"Let him find us," she said with a toss of her curls. "I won't mind."

"Perhaps not," Roan said with a grin, "but I have to think of my reputation."

She laughed softly. "You are a scoundrel, aren't you?" Her voice caressed the word *scoundrel,* making it sound like an endearment.

"There are some who think so," he agreed, and taking her by the arm, he led her back into the ballroom.

He had no sooner managed to shake off Elsbeth Pettibone than Arthur Dudley approached him with his niece, the overly plump Clara Beth, in tow.

"Fine evening," Dudley said.

"Yes." Roan took a deep breath. "You're looking quite lovely this evening, Miss Dudley." In truth, she looked extremely uncomfortable, poured as she was into an unflattering froth of bright pink tulle.

Clara Beth's cheeks turned the same shade of pink as her gown. "Thank you, Mr. Cabrera."

"She does look lovely, doesn't she?" Dudley said, beaming with pride. "It'll be a lucky man who wins our Bethy's heart."

"Yes, indeed," Roan agreed. "It was a pleasure to see you again, Miss Dudley. Arthur. If you'll excuse me, I've promised this next dance to Lady Hatton."

After sketching a quick bow, Roan hurried across the dance floor, eager to put some distance between himself and Dudley's niece. He had hoped to enjoy a taste of the refined blood of the city's most eligible maidens as long as he was here, but decided he would rather go hungry than spend the rest of the evening eluding the Misses Pettibone and Dudley.

Retrieving his hat and coat, he left by the back entrance. Outside, he drew a breath of the cool night air, loosened his collar, and headed for home. He was nearing the Crossroads when he noticed the scent of fresh blood in the air. It led him to a body lying facedown along the edge of the road. The tracks in the dirt told him all too clearly what had happened. The girl had been struck by a coach and left for dead. Only, she wasn't dead. With his preternatural hearing, he easily detected the sluggish beat of her heart.

After wrapping her in his coat, he lifted her into his arms and willed the two of them to the hospital. Opening the door, he hurried down the hall to the nurses' station.

"Here, now!" the nurse behind the admitting desk exclaimed. "What's this?"

"I found her on the road, unconscious. She's been hit by a carriage."

"I'll need her name."

"I don't know it."

"Is she kin?"

"No."

"Can she pay?"

"I'll take care of the bill," Roan said impatiently. "You take care of her. Now."

"Very well, Mr. . . . ?"

"Cabrera. Perhaps we can finish our introductions later. In case you haven't noticed, she's bleeding rather heavily."

Moments later, a man in white came with a gurney and wheeled the unknown woman down the hallway into an examination room.

After signing a paper stating he would be responsible for her debts, Roan paced the hall. Though it was nothing to him if the girl lived or died, he found himself unable to leave until he knew her fate. In spite of her shabby dress, she had been a remarkably pretty thing, her skin as fair as fresh cream, her hair a dark golden blond. A smattering of freckles dusted her cheeks. But it was more than her outward appearance that called to him. He had known many pretty women in his time. What was there about this frail lass that set her apart? Her helplessness, perhaps? Or her innocence? Or maybe a combination of the two.

Whatever hold she had on him, he knew he couldn't leave until he'd seen her again.

Two hours later, the doctor stepped into the corridor. "I'm afraid there isn't much hope," the surgeon said after introducing himself. "She's in a coma due to a serious head injury. She has also lost a good deal of blood from a rather deep gash in her leg. In her weakened state, it's doubtful she'll ever regain consciousness. We'll make her as comfortable as we can, of course."

Roan nodded. "Might I see her?"

"If you wish. Last room at the end of the hall."

There were half a dozen women in the room, all sleeping peacefully. The girl he sought lay unmoving in the narrow bed near the window. A thick bandage covered the back of her head. Her hair was dirty and tangled, her skin as pale as the sheet that covered her.

Sitting on the edge of the mattress, he took her hand in his. Her skin was soft, cooler than his own.

Closing his eyes, he sought to make a connection with her. At first there was nothing and then his thoughts brushed hers. His first impression was fear—fear of dying, fear of the unknown, fear of the darkness that held her fast. And then came her stunned realization that there was someone else inside her head.

Who are you? she inquired. *Are you Death?*

A hard question to answer, he mused, for in many ways, death was exactly what he was. But not for her. *No. I've come to help you.*

Help me? How? Where am I?

You're lying in a hospital. Unconscious.

Then I'm dreaming.

It's not a dream. What's your name?

Who are you? she asked again.

My name is Roan Cabrera. If you let me, I can help you pass the time. But first, your name.

Kathryn Winterbourne. You said you could help me pass the time. Do you mean until I die? If you're not Death, are you an angel?

If you wish me to be. Tell me of a happy memory, Kathryn, and I can make it come alive for you again.

A happy memory, she thought. If only she had one.

Not one? he asked. In his experience, every mortal had at least one enjoyable experience. *No pleasant childhood reminiscence? A memorable Christmas, perhaps?*

She did have one happy memory, she thought. *My fifth birthday.* The birthday before her father died. Her parents had taken her to the fair and let her buy whatever she wished—a pretty porcelain doll in a bright blue dress, the sweet treat of her choice, a new red ribbon for her hair.

As she recalled that day, she found herself there again—a little girl with bright green eyes and a brighter future. She relived it all, the sights and sounds of the fair, the animals, the smiles and laughter of her mother and father, her own excitement as they let her choose the gifts she wanted most. It had been a wonderful day, the last truly happy day she had ever known. The last day that the three of them had spent together.

Roan wiped the tears from her cheeks as his mind delved into hers. Her father had been killed by a highwayman the next night. Three years later, her mother, Victoria, had married again. Kathryn's stepfather, Basil Darlington, had seemed a right nice gentleman at first but gradually, his true nature had come to the fore. He spent many a night at the local pub. When in his cups, he tended to be cruel. One night, he struck Victoria. After that night, the beatings grew worse, so that her mother often sported bruises she tried to explain away. As Kathryn began to mature into a young woman, Darlington turned his attention to her. He had taken to giving her fatherly hugs that were far from fatherly, had insisted on kissing her good night, had touched her in unseemly ways "by accident." At her mother's urging, she had run away from home.

"If ever I meet the rogue, he'll beg for death before he draws his last breath," Roan muttered. If there was one thing he despised, it was men who abused their women.

As he brushed a lock of hair from Kathryn's neck, then ran his fingertips over her smooth skin, he wondered if she would consider what he was about to do a form of abuse.

Chapter Four

Elsbeth Pettibone posed in front of her looking glass, hairbrush in hand as she admired her reflection. Last night, she'd had high hopes that Roan Cabrera would fall prey to her charms and come calling on her this morning. But it was past the time for callers and he hadn't made an appearance. She couldn't understand his lack of interest. Every eligible bachelor in the county had offered for her hand. Every one except the one she wanted.

Moving to her wardrobe, Elsbeth frowned as she considered one frock after another. She needed a new gown, she decided. Something less poufy and more mature. Something that would make Roan Cabrera sit up and realize she wasn't a child any longer, but a woman. One who knew what she wanted and intended to have it.

Smiling, Elsbeth rang for her maid.

She had some shopping to do.

Chapter Five

Clara Beth sighed as she looked in the mirror. No man was ever going to offer for her, she thought bleakly. She wasn't pretty like Elsbeth. She didn't have a perfect figure like Mona Williamson. She couldn't sing like Lydia Broadhurst or play the piano like Pamela Symington.

Clara blinked back her tears. She was just a big, fat homely nobody and all her uncle's wealth couldn't change that fact. Last night, at the ball, only Charles Eaton had asked her to dance, no doubt because he was as homely and lonely as she. Still, she had been grateful for his attention. She wondered if he would call on her. Perhaps any beau, even an unattractive one, was better than none at all.

Feeling horribly depressed, Clara Beth went down the back stairs and out into the gardens. If not for her aunt Sadie and uncle Arthur, she would be out on the streets, homeless, penniless.

Sighing, she sank down on the edge of the fountain that graced the center of the backyard. Sometimes she wished she had died in the accident with her parents . . .

Clara Beth's head snapped up as a sudden shift in the wind rattled the leaves on the trees. Overhead, the clouds shifted to cover the moon. Feeling suddenly cold, she hugged herself, overcome by the eerie feeling that she was no longer alone.

"Aunt Sadie, is that you?"

No one answered but the wind.

"Uncle Arthur? Bobby? Bobby, is that you?"

Bobby was her cousin, and a more annoying creature had never been born. He took great delight in teasing Clara Beth or creeping up on her in hopes of making her swoon.

She peered into the darkness, thinking that, in this instance, she would be glad to see her cousin grinning at her from behind the trees.

Shivering, she was about to go into the house when a man appeared out of the shadows, a man wearing a long, hooded cloak.

Fear held her immobile as he glided toward her. In the light of the lamps that lined the path, she could see that his hair was long and black. She opened her mouth to scream, but no sound emerged.

Helpless, she could only stare up at him as he sat down beside her and enfolded her in his arms. His cloak fell across her shoulders, giving her the scary illusion that she was being enveloped in the wings of a giant bat. A bat with glowing red eyes and sharp white teeth.

It was her last thought before he bent his head over her neck.

Chapter Six

At midnight, Roan left his house and headed for the hospital. A bitter wind caused his cloak to billow behind him like Satan's breath. Just as it did with all of the undead, the elements had little effect on him. He felt the power of the wind against his face, but he was impervious to the cold. When it rained, he didn't get wet; when he burrowed into the earth, the dirt didn't cling to him when he rose. He had no idea why such things occurred; they were just facts of his rather bizarre existence, like his aversion to direct sunlight and holy water.

He made his way to Kathryn's room and after assuring himself that the other occupants of the ward were sleeping soundly, he sat beside her. Someone had changed her bandages. They had also washed her hair; it fell over her shoulders in thick golden waves, tempting his touch. Soft, so soft. Her breathing was shallow; her skin seemed even paler than it had the night before. She was losing her tenuous hold on life.

He stroked her cheek, wondering what there was about this woman that called to him. He had seen others near death, felt a moment of sorrow for the young ones taken before their time, but none had truly touched the depths of his heart until now.

"Kathryn?" He spoke her name as his mind sought to meld with hers. He knew a moment of anxiety when he sensed only darkness and then, like a tiny light in the blackest night, he found her. *Fight, Kathryn,* he said. *You must fight.*

No. It's too hard and I'm too tired.

Dammit . . .

Why do you care if I live or die?

I don't know. I only know I can't let you go. Not now.

I'm sorry . . .

Roan cursed softly. He was virtually immortal. He had remarkable powers, yet he could not bring her back from the dead, and she seemed determined to die.

Could you find my mother? Tell her I'm . . . Her voice trailed off in a sigh as her heartbeat slowed.

You will not die, Roan said. *I will not allow it.*

You can't stop it.

She was right and yet, maybe he could. Biting into his wrist, he held his bloody arm to her lips. *Drink, Kathryn.*

When she failed to respond, he stroked her throat. She swallowed convulsively, grimacing at the taste.

He let a few more drops fall onto her tongue, then licked the wound in his wrist.

He sat at her side a few moments longer, wondering what effect, if any, his tainted blood would have on her. Leaning forward, he brushed a kiss across her brow. He would not drink from her this night. She was too weak.

But there were others.

Rising, he moved from patient to patient in the silent ward, thinking it was like a vampire buffet as he helped himself to a taste of each.

When his thirst was satisfied, he went to the tavern.

The Hare and Hound was usually a quiet place, but not tonight. He sensed the tension in the air as soon as he entered the premises, heard the morbid excitement in the voices around him as he made his way down the stairs to the gambling hell. His cronies were gathered around their regular table, all talking at once.

Roan took his accustomed place, his gaze moving from man to man. "What's going on?"

"Haven't you heard?" Cormac said. "Dudley's niece was murdered earlier tonight."

"Terrible thing," George Hampton remarked with a woeful shake of his head. "Terrible."

"Sadie found her in the gardens," Henry Westerbrook said. "Found her lying on the ground, already turning cold."

"Someone ripped out her throat," Frank Lewiston added. "Who would do such a thing?"

Who, indeed? Roan thought.

"Old Dudley's beside himself." Cormac shuffled the deck in his hands again, though he didn't deal the cards. "Can't blame the old sot. She was family, after all."

"No idea who might have done it?" Roan asked.

"No. One of the upstairs maids said she thought she saw a man in the gardens with Clara Beth. The maid thought it was the Eaton boy. He danced with Clara Beth several times last night."

Cormac snorted. "I can't imagine Eaton stabbing the girl, can you?"

Hampton shrugged. "There were other wounds on her neck."

"What kind of wounds?" Roan asked sharply.

Hampton shrugged. "The exact details are being kept

secret, but I heard she lost a lot of blood. Maybe Eaton proposed and she refused him."

"And cut her throat? That's right doubtful," Mick Flaherty said. "He's as squeamish as a girl. Besides, she wouldn't have refused him."

The other men nodded in agreement. Had Eaton proposed, it was doubtful Clara Beth would have turned him—or any other man—away.

"There's a high wall around the gardens of the Dudley estate," Lewiston remarked, "and the gates are always locked. How did the murderer get inside? It's unlikely that he went through the house."

"Sure, and no one went over that wall without wings," Mick Flaherty opined.

"Well, no matter how the blighter accomplished it, the chit's still dead," Westerbrook muttered. "Are we going to play cards or not?"

Hours later, Roan made his way home. Unlike his cronies, he preferred the quiet of country life to living in town. He made his home in a large, rather quaint old manor that some wealthy landowner had built a hundred or so years ago. Situated atop a flat, grassy knoll, surrounded by ancient oaks, it was rectangular in shape, with square turrets at the corners reminiscent of castles of old. A long flagstone path led to the front steps, which were also made of stone. Behind the high manor walls, a pretty little lake sparkled like a rare jewel in the light of the moon.

The inside of the house was sparsely furnished. Living alone, he had little use for the ostentatious creature comforts so prized by his acquaintances and their families, nor did he host lavish soirees or dinner parties. His needs were few and simple—a dark place where he could spend the daylight hours, something to read to pass the time, an occasional woman to warm his bed, a slender throat to ease his thirst.

Entering the manor, he removed his cloak and tossed it on the hall tree. A thought brought the hearth fire in the parlor to life, filling the high-ceilinged room with warmth and light. He kept rooms at one of the inns in Newberry, a place to keep a change of clothes, or entertain a woman from time to time. But the manor was home.

Thoughts of Clara Beth drifted through his mind as he sank down on the high-backed sofa in front of the raised hearth. Why would anyone kill Dudley's niece? She was no threat to anyone. And yet someone had ripped out her throat. Was there another vampire in his territory? Odd that he hadn't sensed the presence of another of his kind.

Reaching for the crystal decanter on the mahogany table beside the sofa, he poured himself a glass of red wine. He swirled the rich red liquid in the glass, wishing that it was Kathryn Winterbourne's blood, wondering what effect his blood would have on her. Would it strengthen her, or steal what little life she had left?

He gazed into the fireplace, fascinated by the flame's deep blues and reds and yellows, the pure white heat where the fire burned the hottest. Save for the sun's light, there was nothing he feared more than the touch of fire.

Sitting there, his thoughts drifted once again to the girl, Kathryn. He had taken her blood; she had tasted his. The exchange had formed a link between them. He sought to open that link now. When nothing happened, he tossed his glass into the fireplace and willed himself to the hospital, praying that he wasn't too late.

Moments later, he was at her bedside. He urged her to

drink a little more of his blood, then took her hand—her icy cold hand—in his.

Kathryn, he pleaded, *come away from the darkness. I'll dress you in satins and silks, give you anything you desire. All you have to do is leave the darkness behind.*

Kathryn woke slowly. Stretching her arms over her head, she gazed at the ceiling. And frowned. Where was she? Not home. And certainly not at her room in the boardinghouse. Her frown deepened as she took in her plush surroundings—the beautiful floor-to-ceiling drapes at the windows, the blue and white striped paper on the walls, the rich mahogany chest and wardrobe, the soft mattress beneath her. Definitely not the shabby accommodations she was used to.

She sat up slowly, surprised to find herself wearing a long, white nightgown with a ruffled hem. She ran her hands over the smooth silk. Never in all her life had she worn anything so fine. Where had the gown come from? And who had put it on her?

Swinging her legs over the edge of the bed, she stood, smiled as her feet sank into the velvety carpet. She wriggled her toes, then moved to one of the windows and opened the drapes, surprised to find that it was dark outside.

A full moon shone brightly on a vast yard enclosed by a high wall.

Where was she? She searched her memory. The last thing she remembered was a coach-and-four bearing down on her, knocking her aside as one of the wheels ran over her. A blinding flash of pain in her head. Why wasn't she in the hospital?

She ran her hands up and down her arms, lifted tentative

fingers to the back of her head. She frowned, surprised that there were no bumps, no bruises. No pain. Nothing was broken.

She had been badly hurt, hadn't she? She couldn't have imagined it.

Why wasn't she dead?

Even though she had been unconscious, she remembered hearing the doctor say there was no hope. But then she'd heard that other voice—low and rough with emotion—begging her to come away from the darkness, promising her a better life.

Frowning, she glanced at her surroundings again, noting the elaborately carved chest of drawers, the matching headboard, the lamps on the bedside tables. Maybe she *was* dead and this was heaven.

She was still contemplating that possibility when she heard the door open. Turning, Kathryn stared at the man looming in the doorway. Tall and dark, with a black cloak falling from his broad shoulders, he looked nothing like an angel. A devil, perhaps, with those fathomless ebony eyes and that penetrating gaze.

"How are you feeling, Kathryn?"

That voice. She would have recognized it anywhere. "Am I in heaven?" she blurted. "Are you really an angel?"

"An angel?" A wry smile tugged at the corners of his mouth. "Hardly." He was captivated by her eyes. They were deep green and heavily lashed. Guileless. Innocent.

"A devil, then?" She clapped her hand over her mouth, horrified at her audacity.

"There are those who think so."

Devil or angel, she thought, the man was obviously a force to be reckoned with judging by his attire and his demeanor. "What am I doing here?"

"You were very near death. I didn't want you to die alone in a hospital." It was partly the truth.

Kathryn pressed a hand to her heart, her eyes wide and scared. "You brought me here to die?"

"Of course not." He had brought her home in hopes of saving her life. To that end, he had given her more of his blood, forced a bit of red wine down her throat to strengthen her, covered her with several thick quilts to warm her.

And then he had spoken to her mind again, promising her a better life, quietly pleading with her to return from the darkness.

To his amazement, her body had healed. The gash in her head disappeared, as did the multiple bruises on her arms, legs, and chest. Now, she stood before him, a beautiful young woman in the prime of life, her expression one of mingled fear and hope.

Damn. Maybe bringing her home hadn't been such a good idea after all. Now that she was here, what the hell was he going to do with her? Remembering the sweetness of her blood, his gaze moved to the hollow of her throat and the pulse beating there.

"I don't understand." She ran her fingertips over her face, up and down her arms. How had she healed so quickly? She had never felt better, stronger. Did Cabrera have something to do with it? But that was impossible. He wasn't a doctor. Was he?

She was about to ask him when her stomach growled. Not a tiny little kitten-like growl, but the deep rumble a hungry lion might make.

Roan lifted one brow. One thing he'd forgotten was her need for nourishment. Clearing his throat, he said, "I'm afraid I've nothing in the house to eat."

She blinked up at him in disbelief. "Nothing?" Surely a man with a manor such as this had food to spare.

"I never dine in," he explained. "If you change your clothes . . ." He swore softly. What was he thinking? She didn't have anything other than what she'd worn in the hospital and the nightgown he had given her, neither of which would be suitable outside the house. "Just sit tight," he said. "I'll fetch you something to wear."

Pivoting on his heel, he stalked out of the room. Once out of her sight, he willed himself into the center of Newberry's business district.

Though her shop was closed, Madame Fontaine quickly opened the door for Roan, a smile of welcome lighting her face. "What a nice surprise!"

He kissed her cheek. "Always a pleasure to see you, Elise." They had met at a ball at Lewiston's two years ago. Though she was twenty years older than he had been when he was turned, they had indulged in a brief, torrid affair and had remained friends when it was over.

"What can I do for you this evening?" she asked.

"I need several dresses for a young woman." His gaze traveled over Fontaine's figure. "She's about your size, I think, perhaps a little shorter."

"Is she fair or dark?"

"She has lots of blond hair and incredible green eyes."

"And young?"

Had he been able, he would have blushed at the knowing look in her eyes. "Yes."

Fontaine disappeared into the back of her shop. When she returned, she carried three gowns and a flat box. "You will find undergarments in here," she said, handing him the box. "I think you will find them enticing."

"It's not like that," Roan protested, his voice gruff.

"But it will be," she said, eyes twinkling with mischief as she packed everything in three large bags.

Shifting from one foot to the other, he muttered, "Thank you, Elise." He paid the bill, adding a little extra for her time and trouble, kissed her again, and left the shop.

When he returned to Kathryn's room, he found her sitting in the chair by the window, her expression pensive.

She stood when he entered, her eyes widening as he dropped a number of packages on the bed. "Are those for me?"

He nodded curtly. "Get dressed and I'll take you out to supper."

"I . . ." She bit down on her lower lip.

"What?"

Embarrassed by her need, she could only stare at him while her cheeks grew hot, hotter.

"What?" Impatience made his voice sharp.

"I can't go out like this. I . . . I need a bath. And a brush for my hair . . ."

Roan grunted softly. Why hadn't he foreseen she would need clothes *and* toiletries? "There's a tub in my room. Wait here. I'll fill it for you."

Kathryn stared after him. Why was he being so nice to her? What did he expect in return? Should she stay? Or make a run for it?

She had just decided to leave when he appeared in the doorway.

He cocked his head to one side, his gaze narrowed.

She had the discomfiting feeling that he knew exactly what she was thinking.

Gesturing for her to follow, he said, "This way, girl."

Filled with trepidation, Kathryn trailed behind him, hands clenched at her sides as they walked down a long carpeted hallway toward a pair of carved double doors at the end of the corridor.

One door stood open.

"You'll find everything you need in there. I'll be downstairs when you're ready." He didn't wait for an answer. Her scent, the sweet siren song of her life's blood, reminded him that he had not yet fed, something he intended to remedy while she bathed.

Kathryn closed the door after him, then stood in the middle of the floor, waiting for her heart to stop pounding. She had never, ever, been in a man's chambers before. The bed was larger than any she had ever seen, covered with a thick black spread. The side tables, the chest of drawers, and the wardrobe were all mahogany. All were massive. Expensive carpets covered the floor. A large painting of an angry sea hung on one wall. Other than that, there was nothing to indicate anyone ever stayed here. No mirrors, no mementos, no knickknacks.

A narrow door opened onto a small room. Steam rose from the claw-footed tub within. Lured by the promise of a hot bath, she stepped inside. A narrow shelf held several fluffy towels. A clean washcloth and a bar of soap had been laid out within easy reach of the bathtub. A long black robe hung from a hook on the wall. Unable to help herself, she ran her fingers over the silk. Then, on a whim, she put on the robe. It seemed to wrap around her, giving her the oddest feeling that she was in his arms.

Shaking off such fanciful thoughts, she quickly put the robe back where it belonged.

After closing the bathroom door, she stepped out of her nightgown and into the tub. Sighing, she closed her eyes. Baths at the boardinghouse were few and far between. She lingered there until the water started to cool, bathed quickly, washed her hair, and climbed out of the tub.

After drying off, she wrapped herself up in a towel and went back into her bedroom.

For a moment, she stared at the boxes scattered on the bed. She couldn't remember the last time she had received a gift. Then, as excited as a child at Christmas, she opened one box after another. The first three revealed gowns— one pink, one blue, one a green and gold print. With each dress was a hat and shoes and gloves to match. And in the final box were delicate undergarments, each one edged with ribbons and lace.

She ran her hands over the blue dress, her trepidation at being alone with a stranger forgotten in the face of such bounty. One gown alone had probably cost more than her stepfather earned in a year.

She carefully lifted the dress out of the box and laid it on the bed. Then, laughing with excitement, she tossed the towel aside, felt herself blush as she put on the scandalous undergarments, which were little more than a whisper of silk and lace. Her hands trembled as she slipped the dress over her head. It fit as if it had been made for her. How had he known her size?

She smoothed the material over her hips. Sitting on the edge of the bed, she tried on the matching shoes, and gloves. Rising, she looked around for a mirror, only there wasn't one. Opening the drapes, she looked at her reflection in the window glass.

"You look beautiful."

She whirled around, shocked to find him standing behind her. "Mercy! You startled me!"

"Forgive me," he said. "Turn around and I'll brush your hair for you."

She stared at him, aghast. Brush her hair? It was a decidedly intimate thing for a gentleman to do for a lady who was not his wife. And even more intimate considering that they were strangers, alone in the house.

Afraid to refuse for fear of making him angry, she turned her back to him.

His touch was gentle as he worked through the tangles. Would his hands be as gentle on her skin? she wondered, then felt herself blush from the soles of her feet to the roots of her hair.

Roan quietly cursed himself. What had he been thinking? He was no lady's maid. He had been a fool to think he could be this close to her, inhale her fragrance, listen to the rapid beat of her heart, and not want to possess her, body and soul. What hold did she have on him, that he had brought her here? Never before had he allowed a woman to enter his lair.

The scent of her blood called to him, sweet and enticing. He had only to lower his head . . .

Abruptly, he put some distance between them, tossed the brush on the bed, turned away from her. "Are you ready?" he asked, his voice almost a growl.

"Yes." Puzzled by his actions, she put on the blue bonnet and followed him out of the house.

* * *

He took her to the Rosemont Inn for dinner. Kathryn stared, wide-eyed, at their destination as he handed her out of the carriage he had rented for the evening. She had often passed by the restaurant, but never dreamed she would be dining there. It was even more beautiful than she had imagined. In spite of her lovely gown, she would never belong in this place. Following the hostess to their table, she felt like an imposter. She might look the equal of the other diners on the outside, but she was quaking on the inside.

She stared at Cabrera when he held her chair for her. No one had ever done that for her before.

He waved away the menu their waitress offered. "The lady will have the pheasant. And we'd like a bottle of your best burgundy."

"Nothing for you, sir?" the waitress asked.

"No, thank you."

With a nod, she went to turn in their order.

"You're not eating?" Kathryn asked.

"No."

Unable to think of anything else to say, she glanced at her surroundings. Blue-and-gold striped paper covered the walls. Sparkling chandeliers filled the room with a soft glow. White linen cloths covered the tables; the napkins were the same shade of blue as the stripe in the wallpaper. The glasses were of fine crystal.

She couldn't believe she was here, mingling with the gentry.

Roan watched Kathryn's face as she watched the activity in the room. Her emotions were easy to read—excitement, trepidation, curiosity. He groaned softly as Elsbeth Pettibone and her parents stopped by their table on their way to their own.

"Mr. Cabrera, how nice to see you!" Elsbeth gushed. "I hope we'll see you at our soiree next week."

Rising, he bowed over the hand she offered.

Eyes narrowed, her smile faltering, Elsbeth seemed to notice Kathryn for the first time. "And who might this be?"

"May I introduce my charge, Miss Kathryn Winterbourne. Kathryn, this is Elsbeth Pettibone and her parents, William and Celia."

"So pleased to meet you," Elsbeth said, her tone frosty.

"Thank you."

"Cabrera, you must bring her to our dinner party Saturday next," William said, smiling. "We're celebrating our anniversary."

Celia Pettibone nodded. "Indeed, we can always use another pretty young woman. Can we count on the two of you?"

Roan nodded.

Elsbeth frowned.

Kathryn looked away.

"Until next week," William said. "Come along, Elsbeth."

"She doesn't like me," Kathryn said as Roan took his seat.

"She doesn't like anyone who's prettier than she is."

Kathryn felt her cheeks warm at his compliment. She darted glances at him from time to time while she ate. Why wasn't he eating? Why were there no servants in his home? What was she going to do when the meal was over? She couldn't stay in his house. It wasn't seemly for an unmarried woman to share a residence with a bachelor, but she had nowhere else to go . . .

"Kathryn."

The sound of his voice brought her back to the present. "What?"

"Are you ready to go?"

She glanced at her plate. She had been so lost in thought, she'd hardly realized she had finished her meal. "Yes." She took the hand he offered, followed him toward the exit, all too aware of the stares that followed them.

The coachman opened the carriage door. Roan handed her inside, then took the seat across from her.

Kathryn's heart pounded as the carriage lurched forward. Was he taking her back to his house? Would he expect her to share his bed in return for dinner?

Roan frowned inwardly as the carriage climbed the hill toward home. Kathryn's discomfort was palpable by the time they arrived at the front door.

She flinched when he reached for the latch. He didn't have to read her mind to know what she was thinking. "Kathryn, you have nothing to fear from me. I mean you no harm. I have no designs on your person. I don't expect anything from you in return for letting you stay here. I've hired a maid and a cook. Starting tomorrow, they'll look after your needs as well as be chaperones to quiet wagging tongues."

She had expected to leave in the morning. "You want me to stay here? With you?"

"Have you anywhere else to go?"

"No." She preceded him into the house, acutely aware of his presence and the fact that she was alone in the house with a stranger. A tall, mysterious stranger. She knew little of men, but all her instincts warned that he was dangerous. "I'm tired," she said, not turning around. "If you don't mind, I think I'll retire for the night."

"As you wish." His voice, low and whiskey-rough, sent a shiver down her spine.

"Sweet dreams, Kathryn."

She nodded, then walked sedately up the stairs, afraid

that if she ran, he would pounce on her like a hungry cat on a mouse.

Only when she was in her room, with the door securely locked behind her, did she let out the breath she didn't realize she'd been holding.

Chapter Seven

The tantalizing scent of freshly baked bread roused Kathryn from sleep. Slipping out of bed, she pulled on her robe, stepped into her slippers, and followed the heavenly aroma down two flights of stairs to the kitchen.

A plump, rosy-cheeked woman smiled at her when she entered the room. "Good morning, dearie. Breakfast will be ready soon. Can I start you off with a cup of tea?"

"Thank you, Miss . . . ?"

"I'm the cook, Mrs. Shumway."

"And I'm Kathryn."

"Right pleased to meet you, I am," the woman said cheerfully. "I'll be fixin' your meals. And this is Nan. She'll be your maid." She gestured at a young woman seated at the small wooden table in a corner of the kitchen.

Kathryn nodded. Nan was a pretty girl, surely no more than sixteen, with curly red hair and mild blue eyes. She flushed under Kathryn's gaze.

"Go on up and have a seat in the dining room," Mrs. Shumway said, placing a number of covered dishes on a tray, "and I'll bring your breakfast straightaway."

Katherine had no sooner made herself comfortable at

the table than Mrs. Shumway bustled into the room. Kathryn watched in awe as the cook laid a feast before her. For a moment, Kathryn could only stare at the sumptuous fare. She wasn't accustomed to being served. Nor was she used to enjoying such lavish meals. Bacon and eggs and ham, rolls warm from the oven, freshly churned butter, a cup of hot chocolate, tea, and toast.

"We weren't sure what you liked," Mrs. Shumway said, "so we made a bit of everything."

"Will Mr. Cabrera be joining me?"

"I don't believe so, miss."

"Have you seen him this morning?"

Mrs. Shumway shook her head. "He informed us that he would not be in residence during the day, and that we were not to expect him at meals. We were told that our main task would be to see to your needs. Will there be anything else?"

"No, thank you."

With a bob of her head, the cook left the room.

Kathryn sampled a bit of everything, her mind more on Roan's peculiar instructions to the cook than what she was eating. He had hired a cook and a maid simply to look after her. Who had taken care of his household before she came? And why didn't he eat his meals at home?

Drinking the last of the hot chocolate, she pushed her chair away from the table, feeling as though she might burst. Everything had been delicious.

She stood there a moment, at a loss as to what she should do with the rest of the day. Then, overcome with a rush of curiosity, she decided to have a look around her new home.

In addition to the room where she had taken breakfast, there was a banquet room, a ballroom, the parlor, a wood-paneled library lined with bookshelves, and what she thought might be a sitting room where visitors waited. All had high ceilings, flagstone floors and walls. And large fireplaces to turn away the chill. Expensive rugs covered the floors; thick drapes hung at the windows. There was little in the way of decoration, nothing to indicate Cabrera's interests or habits, likes or dislikes.

Going upstairs, she counted five bedrooms. Only the master bedroom and the one she occupied were furnished. There were no mirrors anywhere in the house, not even the bedrooms.

She stared at the door to his chambers. Where did he go during the day? He would have had to pass by her room to leave the house. Wouldn't she have heard him?

Walking down the hall, she wondered whom it had belonged to previously, and why none of the other bedrooms were furnished.

Returning to her room, she noted that while she had been exploring, the bed had been made up, her clothing put away, the boxes disposed of. A new day dress of flowered muslin had been laid out on the bed, along with clean underwear and a pair of shoes.

Where had all these new clothes come from?

Curious to see if there were more new garments, she went through the wardrobe and the chest of drawers. She found several additional changes of ladies' underwear, gloves, stockings, and handkerchiefs. The wardrobe held the three gowns he had bought her, plus half a dozen dresses for everyday wear, as well as several pairs of shoes and boots, and a fur-lined, hooded cloak.

Stunned, she sat on the edge of the bed. He was the most generous of men. But, again, she couldn't help wondering what he expected in return.

* * *

The sound of her footsteps treading overhead roused him from his daytime rest. So, she had decided to explore the house. Not that he was surprised. Young girls were noted for their curiosity, and she had much to be curious about. Even here, deep in the bowels of the house, he could hear the steady beat of her heart. Lying there in utter darkness, he relished the warm, womanly fragrance that was hers alone. It stirred his desire, even as the scent of her blood quickened his hunger.

He closed his eyes as the darkness beckoned him.

Only a few hours until sundown.

Kathryn was halfway through supper when Cabrera entered the small dining room.

Inclining his head in her direction, he took the chair across from hers. "Good evening, Kathryn."

His presence seemed to shrink the room, making it suddenly difficult to speak. She was certain he could hear the sudden pounding of her heart.

"Something amiss?" he asked.

"N . . . no."

"Please, finish your meal."

Nodding, she focused all her attention on the remains of her supper. She could feel him watching her as she lifted her fork, and then put it aside.

"Would you rather dine in private?" he asked.

Looking up, she met his gaze. "What?"

"My presence seems to make you uncomfortable."

"Yes, a little."

"My apologies."

"No need. It's your house, after all," she said quietly. "Will you not dine with me?"

His gaze slid momentarily to the hollow of her throat. "It's my habit to dine later in the evening." He rose in a single, fluid movement. "Finish your supper."

She stared at him wide-eyed. "You're leaving?"

"I thought you wished to be alone."

"I . . . It's just . . . if you'd join me . . ."

"I've no appetite for food." He rang the small silver bell in the center of the table. When Mrs. Shumway appeared in the doorway, he requested a bottle of wine.

She bobbed a curtsy and quickly fetched a bottle and a pair of crystal goblets, which she placed in front of him "Will there be anything else, Mr. Cabrera?"

"Thank you, no."

The cook bobbed a curtsy and left the room.

Roan filled his glass, then looked at Kathryn in question.

She nodded. Her appetite was gone, but perhaps a little wine would steady her nerves. She took a sip, and then another. She was no connoisseur, but she thought it quite good. But then, no doubt he could afford the best.

"You went exploring today," he remarked.

She stared at him over the rim of her glass, wondering how he knew, then decided Mrs. Shumway had likely mentioned it. "Are you angry with me?"

"Of course not. This is your home, for as long as you wish. Explore to your heart's content."

"Have you lived here very long?"

Lived, he thought, grinning inwardly. He didn't really *live* anywhere. "About twenty years."

"It's a lovely old place. Did you decorate it yourself?"

"No. All the furniture came with the house, save for the furnishings in the master suite."

"I've never seen a bed that big," she blurted, then

stared at him, stricken. Whatever had possessed her to say such a thing? What must he think of her?

"You're welcome to try it out if you like," he said with a roguish grin. "I'm sure you'd find it quite comfortable."

"I . . . I . . . no, thank you!" Pushing away from the table, she fled the room, her cheeks burning with embarrassment.

Laughing softly, he left the manor and headed for London. Wine shared with a beautiful woman was a pleasant diversion but did nothing to ease one's hunger.

As was his wont, Roan stopped in at the Hare and Hound after satisfying his hellacious thirst. He knew something was up as soon as he entered the tavern. The place was in an uproar, with everybody talking at the top of their lungs and gesturing wildly.

He threaded through the crowd and made his way downstairs, where he found his usual crowd—minus Arthur Dudley, who was mourning his niece—gathered around their usual table, their faces grim.

All eyes swung in his direction as he slid into a vacant chair. "What's going on?"

"Haven't you heard?" Westerbrook asked, his voice tight. "There's been another murder."

"Indeed."

Cormac nodded. "That pretty upstairs maid of the Hatton's was found dead in the herb garden earlier this evening."

"Drained of blood," Frank Lewiston added. "Just like Clara Beth."

"Sure, and the murderer seems to prefer young women," Mick Flaherty remarked.

Cormac snorted. "You've got five sons. I doubt you have anything to worry about."

"I've a pretty wife," Flaherty retorted. "And an unmarried sister."

"Any leads on who the murderer might be?" Roan asked. He looked up as Molly Lindstrom handed him a glass of red wine.

"I saw you pass through the tavern," she said, batting her lashes at him. "I thought you might be thirsty."

Roan nodded his thanks and tossed her a coin. Glancing over her shoulder, she gave him a smile and a wink before heading up the stairs.

". . . no leads, according to the latest word on the street," Lewiston was saying when Roan turned his attention back to the conversation at hand. "But it sounds like Eaton is no longer a suspect, since he was at supper at the Hatton's at the time of the murder."

The conversation continued in that vein for several minutes. Then Westerbrook leaned toward Roan. "I hear there's a rather pretty wench staying with you. Relative, is she?"

Cormac's eyes widened with interest. "Is that so?"

Roan nodded.

"She can't be a relative," Flaherty remarked. "I've never heard you mention any family."

Roan leaned back in his chair, arms crossed over his chest. "She's a runaway I've taken under my wing, so to speak."

The other men at the table exchanged knowing glances.

Westerbrook raised his eyebrows. "Under your wing, eh?"

"How young is she?" Lewiston asked with a leer. "My brother is looking for a wife."

"Your brother is old enough to be her father," Roan said dryly.

Cormac laughed. "Nothing like a young filly to make an old stallion sit up and take notice."

Roan grinned inwardly. Truer words had never been spoken, he mused as he pictured Kathryn in his mind.

Rising, he sketched a bow toward his cronies. "I don't know about the rest of you gents, but this old stallion is going home."

The sound of their amused laughter followed him up the stairs.

Chapter Eight

It was very late, the manor quiet, all the lamps out, when Roan returned home. He shrugged out of his coat and tossed it on a chair. He didn't really need a coat, but if he didn't wear one when it was cold and windy, people tended to look at him oddly. His gaze drifted toward the second floor, where Kathryn slept.

Moving to the library, he poured himself a glass of wine, then stared into the goblet. The Bordeaux, a rich, dark red, reminded him of his visit to the hospital, where he had looked in on one of the patients. Verna Jacobs was a plain woman, worn thin by poverty and grief. Her husband—her only family—had passed away recently, leaving her sick with consumption and no means of support. In her short life, she had borne three children and laid them all to rest while still infants. Life had not been kind to her, making it difficult for her to summon a single pleasant memory she wished to revisit. In the end, she had chosen her tenth birthday, the only happy time she could remember. Almost, he had felt guilty for preying on her, but he was what he was, and she would not miss the little he had taken. By tomorrow, her soul would be free to join her husband and children.

He drained the goblet, poured another drink, and sank into his favorite chair.

In his long, long existence, he had often pondered whether there was actually a heaven. He feared there was, because if there was a heaven after this life, then there was surely a hell. A place of endless burning. He shuddered.

Draining the glass, he left it on the desk. A thought took him to Kathryn's chamber.

She lay on her side, her cheek pillowed on her hand. Moonlight streamed through an open window, casting gold highlights in her hair. Her lashes lay like dark fans against her cheeks. Her lips, slightly parted, were pale pink and perfect.

Unable to resist, he combed his fingers through her hair, ran his knuckles down her cheek. Soft. So soft. His gaze slid down her neck and over her shoulder to the curve of her breast. An indrawn breath carried the lingering scent of lavender soap. And overall, the tempting scent of her life's blood.

He clenched his hands at his sides. Then, tempted beyond reason, he sat on the edge of the bed. He stared at her for a long time, listening to the soft sound of her breathing, the slow, steady beat of her heart. He fought his hunger, but in the end, need overpowered his guilt.

Murmuring "Forgive me," he bent his head to her neck and drank.

Kathryn woke with a start, her fingers flying to her throat, the remnants of her nightmare still fresh in her mind. Never, in all her life, had she experienced such a blatantly erotic dream, or one that seemed so real. She could still feel the monster's teeth at her throat, his hands moving over her, his body pressing down on hers. She had never known a man's touch. How could such images have penetrated her sleep?

She lifted her hands to her burning cheeks. How could she have enjoyed being ravished by a stranger?

"Not real," she murmured. "Not real."

She jumped when someone knocked at the door, then blew out a breath with the realization that it was just Nan.

"Morning, miss. I've brought your morning cocoa," the maid said with a cheerful smile. And then she frowned. "Are you feeling well? Your cheeks look flushed."

"No, I'm fine. Draw me a bath, will you, please?"

"Yes, miss."

Kathryn fell back on the pillows with relief when the maid left the room. "Just a dream," she whispered. And felt her cheeks grow hotter as she wondered whether the night might bring another. And even more curious to know whether the reality of being in Cabrera's arms, of feeling his lips on hers, would be as intoxicating as her dream.

Kathryn passed the afternoon sitting in the garden, sketching how she imagined the flower beds might look if the weeds were gone and the flowers weren't all dead. Would Cabrera object if she dug up the dried husks and planted roses? She glanced at the grass—mostly patches of brown with a scattering of weeds. A little water would do wonders.

She had hoped to see him sometime during the day, but he didn't show up—not for dinner, not for supper.

Now, she sat in front of the fireplace, gazing into the

flames, and wondering what the future held. She couldn't remain here indefinitely, but she lacked the funds to pay for a room. Perhaps Cabrera could help her find employment. Or maybe he would hire her . . . She shook the thought aside. He'd had no hired help until she came to stay and had only taken on help to look after her.

Out of ideas, she closed her eyes. His image immediately sprang to mind—long black hair, eyes the color of ebony, broad shoulders, and long, long legs. She had never known a man so self-possessed, so masculine, so enigmatic.

When she opened her eyes, he was standing in front of the hearth, staring down at her. "Oh!" she exclaimed. "I didn't hear you come in." She shivered when he didn't say anything, only continued to regard her through dark, hooded eyes. "Is something wrong?"

Hands clenching, his gaze slid to her throat.

"Sir? Are you ill?"

"No." It was a blatant lie, he thought. He *was* sick. Sick with wanting her. How many nights, both here and in the hospital, had he stood at her bedside, watching her sleep, thinking how easy it would be to steal her will and her blood, to make her want him beside her. He was making her uncomfortable. He heard the quickening of her heartbeat, scented the fear on her skin. It only served to arouse him more. "Go to bed, Kathryn. And lock your door."

He noted she had the good sense not to argue with him. Or run from his presence. Had she bolted from the room, he would have pursued her. But something—perhaps an inborn instinct for survival—prompted her to move sedately toward the staircase.

She didn't look back.

Only when he heard the sound of the door closing firmly behind her, the click of the lock as it slid into place, did he allow himself to sink down on the sofa. Cradling his head in his hands, he took several slow, deep breaths, praying he would never surrender to the insatiable hunger for her blood, or the lust for her sweet flesh that burned like hell's own fire within him.

Inside her room, the strength went out of Kathryn's legs and she sank to the floor. Heart pounding, she buried her head in her hands. She had to get away from here. Away from him and the look she'd seen in his eyes. It had terrified her as nothing else ever had.

She never saw him during the day. The word *vampire* whispered through the back of her mind. She told herself she was overreacting, that she hadn't been in any danger, but she didn't believe it. Tomorrow morning, first thing, she was leaving this place even though she had no place to go. But anywhere was better than here.

Because it had been death she had seen in Roan Cabrera's eyes.

Her death.

She woke with the dawn after a restless night. Rising, she washed her hands and face, brushed her hair, then bit down on her lower lip. It seemed wrong to take one of the dresses he had given her, but she had nothing else to wear. She eased her conscience by reminding herself that he *had* bought them for her. She put on the simplest frock, laced her shoes, and tiptoed out of her room.

She felt a twinge of regret as she descended the stairs. It was unlikely she would ever again find herself living in a place as grand as this. Or have servants at her beck and call. Or wear clothes as fine.

She paused at the bottom of the staircase. Maybe she had imagined that ominous look in his eyes . . . but no. It had been all too real.

Filled with new resolution, she hurried toward the front door and turned the lock. And nothing happened. The door remained securely closed. She tried again and when it still refused to open, she ran down to the kitchen and tried the door that led out to the gardens. But it, too, refused to open—as did all the windows she could reach.

Why had doors that opened yesterday refused to do so today?

Struggling to fight down her growing panic, she returned to her room and locked the door. The house she had thought of as a haven had become a prison. Why wouldn't he let her go? Were Nan and Mrs. Shumway also prisoners in his house? If so, they didn't seem at all upset about it.

She jumped when there was a knock at the door. Was it Cabrera? Had he somehow divined her intention to leave? That was impossible. How could he possibly know what she was thinking?

With a voice that trembled, she called, "Who's there?" when knuckles again rapped on the door.

"It's me, miss. Nan. I've brought your morning chocolate. And clean towels for your bath."

Kathryn pressed a hand to her heart. It wasn't him. Relief washed through her as she opened the door.

"Did you sleep well, miss?" Nan asked as she bustled about the room, making up the bed, opening the drapes.

"Yes, thank you." The morning was bright and beautiful. In the light of day, her fears seemed suddenly foolish. "Have you seen Mr. Cabrera today?"

"No, miss. He said to tell you the dressmaker will be here at noon."

"Oh? Whatever for?"

"He said you should have a new gown for the Pettibone's party on Saturday."

"Party?" Kathryn frowned. "Oh. The anniversary party. I don't think I want to go."

"I'm afraid Mr. Cabrera has already sent his acceptance."

Kathryn started to object, and quickly changed her mind. Perhaps a party was just what she needed. There was certain to be a crush of people. She could lose herself in the crowd and make her escape.

Roan emerged from his lair at sundown. He prowled the streets of a distant city for prey, drank quickly, and returned home, eager to see Kathryn.

He found her in the library. She sat in one of the overstuffed chairs in front of the fireplace, one leg folded beneath her, a copy of *Wuthering Heights* in her hands. Engrossed in her book, she didn't notice him standing in the doorway. He took a moment to study her. Something was wrong. Though she looked calm, her heartbeat was erratic. A slight sheen of perspiration marred her brow.

She looked up when he entered the room. He didn't miss the faint look of panic in her eyes.

He took the chair across from hers. "You tried to leave this morning. Why?"

"Why shouldn't I?"

"What are you afraid of?"

"Do I need to be afraid?"

"Are you going to continue answering my questions with questions?"

"I want to know why I can't leave here."

"And I want to know why you want to leave."

"Because of the look I saw in your eyes last night. I've seen that look in predators before."

Eyes narrowed, Roan leaned back in his chair as he pondered her words and his reply. The truth was out of the question. "You have nothing to fear from me," he said quietly. "I feel a strong attraction to you, and an even stronger need to protect you. I'm not sure what you think you saw in my eyes, but I mean you no harm." Smart girl, he thought. She didn't believe him. "If it will make you feel safer, I'll lodge in one of my other holdings as long as you're here."

"You would do that?"

"I said it."

"That's very kind of you. What do you want in return?"

"Your company at the Pettibone's on Saturday night."

She thought it over, then nodded.

"Did the dressmaker bring you something suitable?"

"Yes." Madame Fontaine had brought several gowns for Kathryn to choose from. No easy decision, as they had all been equally beautiful. "She speaks very highly of you."

"Indeed." He didn't miss the note of feminine curiosity in her tone. Rising, he reached for Kathryn's hand and kissed it ever so lightly.

The brief touch of his lips on her skin shot through her like lightning. Stunned by the sensation, Kathryn stared at him.

"Until Saturday night, then." Sketching a bow, he left the room.

Kathryn stared after him, then ran her fingertips over her hand. Her skin still tingled where he had touched her.

When she heard the sound of the front door closing behind him, she ran into the parlor and locked it behind him.

He was gone. The door was secure.

So why didn't she feel any safer than she had before?

Chapter Nine

Kathryn was a mass of nerves as Nan helped her dress for the Pettibone's anniversary party on Saturday night. True to his word, Cabrera had moved out of the house. She hadn't seen him since Wednesday night. Strange as it seemed, she had been keenly aware of his absence, even during the day, which puzzled her, since she had never seen him when the sun was up. She wondered where he'd gone. Not that she missed him, she assured herself. She was just curious.

"You look lovely," Nan remarked as she fastened the back of Kathryn's gown. "The green is the same shade as your eyes. Will you wear your hair up or down?"

"Up, I guess." She sat at her dressing table while Nan arranged her hair. What would Cabrera think when he saw her? And why did she care?

He arrived at eight o'clock. Attired in black, he looked handsome and formidable.

She flushed under his admiring gaze.

"Are you ready?"

She had forgotten how deep and rich his voice was, the way it seemed to caress her. Forgotten the sheer magnitude of his presence.

He took her wrap from Nan and draped it around her shoulders.

Kathryn shivered with pleasure as his fingers brushed her skin, felt a flutter of excitement in the pit of her stomach when he took her hand and escorted her down the stairs toward the waiting carriage.

The driver opened the door. Cabrera handed her into the conveyance, then climbed inside behind her. His presence, so close in the confined space, was overwhelming. He seemed larger than life. Ominous, somehow. Clad in ebony, he loomed over her like a dark cloud. A faint scent clung to him that she couldn't identify.

She grabbed the door handle as the coach lurched forward. *You can do this. You can do this.* Taking a deep breath, she looked out the carriage window. She *could* do this! They would arrive at the Pettibone's soon. Once there, she would wait until Cabrera was engaged with his friends and make her escape. By the time he realized she was gone, it would be too late.

The carriage hit a rut, throwing her against Cabrera's side. His arm snaked around her waist to steady her. Startled, she looked up at him. Time lost all meaning as she gazed into his eyes—eyes that were dark, fathomless. Filled with mystery. She felt as though she were drowning in their depths. Had the disconcerting feeling that he could see into the nethermost regions of her heart, the very recesses of her soul. As if he could ferret out her hidden thoughts and dreams, her deepest fears.

Her heart skipped a beat when he stroked her cheek, ever so tenderly, with his knuckles. What was he doing to her? Why did she suddenly feel breathless, weightless, as if a strong wind would blow her away?

When the carriage came to a halt, she felt as if she were coming out of a trance.

The door opened. Cabrera stepped out of the carriage, then offered her his hand.

She took it gingerly and let him lead her up the wide, flagstone path to the front door. Inside, a maid took her wrap.

Kathryn couldn't help staring as they entered the main ballroom. Never, in all her life, had she seen anything so grand, from the polished marble floor to the chandeliers to the mirrors that reflected the room's opulence. Everything seemed to sparkle, including the guests who milled about the edges of the dance floor or stood in small groups in the corners. Gentle laughter and conversation combined with the music to fill the air with a low hum. Numerous couples whirled around the floor, the dresses of the women like a living kaleidoscope of colors.

Kathryn looked up when Cabrera tugged on her hand. "Would you care to dance?"

Her gaze slid away from his as she confessed, "I . . . I don't know how." The confession made her cheeks grow warm.

"Shall I teach you?"

She was spared answering when Elsbeth Pettibone hurried toward them in a rustle of mauve taffeta. "Roan!" she exclaimed. "I've been looking for you. Come," she said, holding out her hands. "Waltz with me."

"It would be my pleasure. Excuse us, Kathryn."

She nodded, immensely relieved as she watched Elsbeth lead Cabrera away and disappear into the crowd on the dance floor. Now, she thought, now was her chance. Lifting her head, she marched out of the ballroom and hurried toward the front door as if she had every right to leave and knew exactly where she was going.

She was reaching for the latch when the butler appeared.

"Shall I summon your carriage, miss?"

She started to refuse but quickly changed her mind. It was likely to be a long walk to her destination, wherever she decided to go. "Yes, thank you."

When the carriage arrived, she instructed the driver to take her into Newberry. Where she would go from there, she had no idea, but she could surely sell her shoes and gown for enough money to buy food and lodging for several days while she decided what to do.

"We've not seen much of you these last few days," Elsbeth said, pouting. "Have you been ignoring me?"

Roan sighed as he prepared to play the game. "Why would anyone ignore a beauty such as you?"

"Do you think me beautiful?"

"Doesn't everyone?"

"I don't care what anyone else thinks." She batted her eyelashes at him as he twirled her around the floor.

"No?"

"No. Only you. Father has promised me a generous dowry, Roan, and a house in the country."

"I doubt if he would consider me a worthy match for his only daughter."

"Why not?"

"For one thing, I'm too old for you."

"Many women marry older men."

"I'm flattered, Elsbeth, but I'm not a marrying man."

As the music reached an end, she said, "I'd love some air."

Knowing exactly where this was headed—and dreading it—Roan led her out onto the balcony. It offered a clear view of the gardens and the fountain below. A young couple wrapped in each other's arms stood beneath a flowering tree. Other couples could be seen strolling along the winding garden paths.

Elsbeth threw her arms around Roan as soon as they were alone. Cursing inwardly, Roan put her away from him. "Here now, little girl, behave yourself."

"I am not a little girl! I'm a grown woman, and I know what I want. And I want you."

"No, you don't."

"I do!" She tapped his chest with her fan. "And I always get what I desire. I'll make you happy, Roan."

Looking over her head, he perused the ballroom, searching for Kathryn. She was nowhere to be seen.

"Roan, I . . ."

"Not now," he said, holding her at arm's length. "My charge seems to be missing."

Kathryn stared out the carriage window, suddenly overcome by doubts. What was she doing? She had no place to go except back home. Did she really want to put up with her stepfather's unwelcome advances again? Go back to the poverty and fear she had known day and night before Cabrera took her in?

She ran her hands over the smooth silk of her dress. Did she want to give up nice clothes and a decent place to live, not to mention three meals a day? She shook her head. As pleasant as it had been, she couldn't stay in Cabrera's house like a kept woman. Even though he had demanded nothing of her save her companionship, she was little better than the women who traded their bodies for the very things Cabrera provided.

Leaning back against the squabs, she closed her eyes. Better to be free and poor than to be at the mercy of Cabrera's generosity.

The lights of the township glowed ahead when the carriage came to a sudden halt in the middle of the road. Glancing out the window, she saw two shadowy figures. A third man flung open the carriage door.

Kathryn stared at the man. His wide-brimmed hat was pulled low. The bottom half of his face was covered by a black kerchief. Moonlight glinted off the barrel of the weapon in his hand.

"Get out of the coach," he demanded.

"I . . . I don't have anything of value."

"Oh, I'm sure you do," the highwayman said, leering at her.

She recoiled as his hand clamped on her forearm. A sharp tug yanked her out of the carriage. It was then she saw the driver sprawled facedown on the roadside. The hilt of a dagger protruded from the center of his back.

Kathryn struggled and kicked as her captor dragged her to where his two accomplices stood arguing over the dead man's meager belongings.

The taller of the two looked up at their approach. "Sure, and she'll fetch a pretty price."

"Aye. Maybe we should keep her for a few days," the second man said. "You know, break her in right."

"We'll talk about it later," the man holding her said curtly. "Let's get the bloody hell away from here."

She dug in her heels when he tried to lift her onto the back of a waiting horse. Kicked and scratched for all she was worth until his fist caught her on the chin. Her head snapped back, ears ringing from the force of the blow.

Her attacker was trying to lift her onto the back of a horse when a tall shape in a hooded black cloak materialized out of nowhere. Kathryn fell to her knees as the newcomer grabbed the highwayman by the shoulder. Spinning him around, he slit the man's throat with a knife pulled from the highwayman's belt, then tossed the blade aside.

Blood spurted from the ugly wound as he stumbled backward and spiraled to the ground.

Frozen in place, she watched the other two men. One of them, braver—or perhaps more foolish—rushed forward, a dagger in his hand. The stranger stood his ground, legs slightly spread, his arms at his sides. A gust of wind caused his cloak to billow behind him.

Kathryn held her breath as the highwayman raised his knife and drove it toward the stranger's chest. But the stranger was no longer there. As if by magic, he appeared behind the highwayman and with a quick twist, broke the man's neck and tossed the body aside.

The third man let out a strangled sob when the stranger turned toward him. For a moment, the two men faced each other, the highwayman visibly shaken, the stranger silent and unmoving. When he took a step forward, the third man turned on his heel and fled into the darkness.

Kathryn blinked as the stranger bent over the neck of the first man he had killed. What was he doing?

Unable to move, certain he intended to kill her, she watched him straighten and stride toward her.

"Kathryn, are you hurt? Kathryn!"

She stared up into Cabrera's dark eyes—eyes now tinged with an eerie red glow. Stared at the faint crimson smear around his mouth.

And fainted dead away.

Chapter Ten

Kathryn woke to find Mrs. Shumway bending over her, one hand shaking her shoulder, while Nan stood on the other side of the bed holding a candle and looking worried.

"What's wrong?" Kathryn asked, glancing anxiously from one to the other. "What happened?"

"Now, now, dearie, just rest," Mrs. Shumway said. "You were having a bad dream, you were. Screaming loud enough to wake the dead."

The dead. The events of the night flashed through Kathryn's mind. Running away from the party. Being dragged out of the carriage by an armed man. The dead coachman. Cabrera leaping to her defense, killing two of the highwaymen. And then . . .

Kathryn shook her head. She couldn't have seen what she thought she'd seen. She pulled the covers up to her chin as if that would protect her. "How did I get here?"

"Mr. Cabrera brought you home. You'd fainted dead away, you had. Not that we could blame you after what he told us. Poor lamb, those highwaymen might have killed you. Or worse," the cook added grimly. "Nan, why don't you go fetch Miss Kathryn a nice hot cup of tea? It will soothe her frazzled nerves, it will."

With a bob of her head, Nan set the candle in the holder on the bedside table and scurried out of the room.

"Where is he?" Kathryn asked, then recoiled as a tall, dark figure in a long black robe appeared in the doorway.

"I'll take over now, Mrs. Shumway," Roan said. "Tell Nan that Kathryn will ring for tea later."

"As you wish, sir." The cook gave Kathryn's shoulder a reassuring pat before hurrying out of the room.

"Are you all right?" Roan asked as he approached her bedside.

Kathryn stared at the man looming over her, her gaze searching his face, but there was no hint of red in his eyes, no blood staining his lips. Had she imagined it?

"Kathryn?"

"I saw what you did. You . . . you killed those men."

He nodded, his expression impassive. "What else did you see?"

Feeling like a rabbit trapped by a hungry lion, she sat up, her heart thundering in her ears. "Nothing." She shook her head vigorously. "Nothing."

His eyes narrowed. "You're lying."

Her mouth went dry. Everything that had happened earlier that evening replayed in her mind. The fear. The horror. The blood. Yet none of it was as frightening as this moment.

"Kathryn." His voice was no longer scary or threatening but achingly tender.

She flinched when he sat on the edge of the bed, sucked in a shaky breath when he took her hand in his.

"I know what you saw. I know you're frightened of me, but there's no need. I won't hurt you, I swear it." His thumb stroked the back of her hand. It was oddly comforting. "Do you believe me?"

"I want to."

"You know what I am, don't you?"

"There's no such thing as . . ." She couldn't bring herself to say the word.

"Vampires?" The word hung between them. Harsh. Unbelievable.

Oh, Lord, she thought, tugging her hand from his. It *is* true.

"Indeed it is."

She stared up at him. Had he just read her mind? But that was impossible. Or was it? Only moments ago, she hadn't believed in the existence of vampires, either. "What are you going to do with me?"

He arched one brow. "Do?"

She nodded, her hand going to her throat. Maybe he had already done it. How was she to know?

Roan smiled faintly. He had, indeed, already done it. Several times. "Kathryn, put your fears at rest. I'm not going to hurt you. I'm not going to drain you dry. I'm not going to turn you into a vampire."

"Why should I believe you?"

"Because I have no reason to lie."

"Why did you bring me here that first night?"

"Because you needed a place to stay. And because . . ." Hands clenched, he took a deep breath. "Because I was lonely and . . . drawn to you."

"Drawn to me?"

Roan smiled faintly. "You're an incredibly beautiful woman, Kathryn, with a soft heart and kind eyes. Any man would be attracted to you."

She blinked up at him. There was no denying that she found him attractive, too, or that she had often wondered what his kisses would be like. That seemed horribly wrong, now that she knew what he was. *Vampire.* She shuddered. *Undead. Monster. Drinker of blood. Killer of innocents.*

Kathryn shook her head. Maybe she was dreaming.

"I know this is difficult for you," he said quietly. "But please don't be afraid of me." He raked a hand through his hair, wondering how he could put her mind at ease, how he could gain her trust. "I know you must have questions. I'll be happy to answer them."

"If I wanted to leave here, would you stop me?"

He sighed. He could force her to stay. He could mesmerize her into believing she wanted to spend the rest of her life with him. But the thought of keeping her against her will held no appeal. Resigned to losing her, he shook his head. "Go, if you wish."

"Do you mean it?"

He nodded. "Pack your things and I'll drive you into town. Ring the bell when you're ready." He sent her a last glance and then left the room, quietly closing the door behind him.

Kathryn frowned. He was giving her freedom to leave, just like that? She didn't know what to think. First, he locked her in and now he was willing to let her go. What had changed? Was it because she knew what he was? That couldn't be it. Surely now that she knew, he would want to keep her here so she didn't tell anyone else. Wouldn't he?

It was all so confusing! He was lonely. Out of all the things he'd said, that stood out most of all. She might have doubted him if she hadn't heard the ring of truth behind his words. And then she frowned. She had seen the way Elsbeth Pettibone and the other women had looked at him at the party Saturday night. The blatant desire in their eyes. He was handsome. He had a beautiful old manor house and all the worldly goods wealth could buy. How could he possibly be lonely?

Swinging her legs over the side of the bed, she pulled on her robe, stepped into her slippers, and tiptoed down the stairs. She found Cabrera in the library, sitting in the dark in front of the fireplace. The flickering glow of the flames cast eerie shadows over the walls and ceiling.

"Are you ready to go?" He didn't turn to face her. How had he known she was there? She hadn't made a sound.

"Do you mind if I join you?"

He glanced over his shoulder, confusion in his dark eyes when he saw she was in her nightgown and robe. "You might want to put on something a little more suitable for the ride into town."

"I've decided to stay. That is, if you still want me to."

"I want you, Kathryn. Never doubt it for a minute." Rising, he walked around the chair to stand in front of her. "What changed your mind?"

She shrugged. "I really don't have anywhere else to go and it is very nice here and . . ." Her cheeks heated; her voice trailed off. He was so tall. So close. If she reached out, she could touch him. Why was that idea so tempting? He frightened her on so many levels and yet a part of her was certain that he would never hurt her. But what if she was wrong?

"Kathryn."

His voice washed over her, warm and filled with such longing it made her heart ache even as it sent a shiver of awareness down her spine. His gaze speared hers, so hot she thought she might melt. And then, moving ever so slowly, he reached for her.

She knew a moment of panic as he drew her body against his—panic that quickly turned to pleasure as his mouth moved lightly over hers. Her eyelids fluttered down, and she leaned into him.

He whispered her name as his arms closed around her. His tongue played over her lips—stroking back and forth, back and forth before dipping inside. The heat of his tongue sliding over hers sent unexpected ripples of delight coursing through her.

A sound of protest rose in her throat when he lifted his head. And then, feeling suddenly bold, she went up on her tiptoes, cupped his face in her hands, and kissed him.

Desire exploded through Roan, hotter than his hunger as her lips touched his. Afraid of what he might do if she kissed him again, he put her away from him, hands clenching at his sides as he fought his burgeoning lust.

"What's wrong?" Kathryn asked, bewildered. "Did I do something wrong?"

She was a virgin, he reminded himself. She likely had no idea how her nearness or her sweet kisses were tormenting him.

"No." He spoke between clenched teeth. "It's late. You should go back to bed."

She looked up at him. In the dark room, she saw again that faint red glow she had seen before. *Vampire.* She had been kissing a vampire. How could she have forgotten what he was?

Murmuring "Good night," she turned and walked sedately out of the room, rounded the corner, and ran up the stairs as fast as she could.

Roan stared after her, the taste of her still on his lips, her scent all around him. Would her decision to stay prove her undoing?

Or his?

Suddenly restless, he left the house. For a moment, he stood in the shadows. He was a part of the night, a part of the darkness. Only now, with the night seeping into his very being, did he feel whole, complete. With his preternatural senses, nothing was hidden from him. He was privy to sounds and sights and smells beyond mortal comprehension.

Leaving the manor behind, he made his way to the hospital. He passed by the nurses on duty unseen as he slipped into one of the rooms at the end of the corridor.

All the beds were empty, save one. The only patient was an old woman in a great deal of pain, yearning for the release only death could bring her.

And on this night, he was death.

On leaving the hospital, he headed toward a tavern in a part of town shunned by the gentry. He was nearing the place when the unmistakable scent of freshly spilled blood filled his nostrils.

He found the body lying in a ditch, face fish-belly white, eyes wide and unseeing. The two deep bites on the side of the man's neck gave little doubt as to what had killed him.

Roan uttered a short, pithy oath.

A rogue vampire was killing in territory he had claimed for his own.

Chapter Eleven

Elsbeth paced the floor of her bedroom. She paused now and then to study her reflection in the full-length mirror in the corner. Her hair was long and thick, her skin like porcelain, her figure flawless. Why didn't Roan want her? A half-dozen men had asked for her hand. Why not the one man she wanted?

She had been so certain she could charm him, yet he rebuffed her at every turn. Last night she had practically thrown herself at him and he had put her aside to go search for that common girl residing in his house. What did that woman, Kathryn, have that she did not? And how was she going to get Roan to give her the attention she deserved?

Hoping one of Cook's buttermilk muffins and a cup of tea would soothe her nerves, she went downstairs. Her father was already in the dining room, helping himself to eggs and sausage from the sideboard when she entered the room. He added two slices of toast to his plate, and a slab of cold roast beef.

He smiled when he saw her. "You're up early." He filled his cup with coffee and carried his meal to the table.

Elsbeth shrugged as she filled her own plate, then joined her father at the table.

"Your mother's sleeping late," he remarked.

"Too much dancing," Elsbeth muttered, adding milk to her tea.

"Not as young as she used to be," he said with a wink. "But, then, neither am I." He regarded her a moment. "What has you looking so glum this morning?"

"It's Roan."

A look of disapproval spread over her father's face. "Ah."

"I know you don't like him, Papa. But I love him."

Mr. Pettibone snorted. "Love! What do you know of love? You're just a child."

"I know what I want."

Pettibone shook his head. "There's something not right about the man, daughter. No one sees him during the day or knows anything of his background. He has no income that I'm aware of, yet he is never without funds. He always arrives late at dinner parties. He's an odd duck and not for you."

Huffing a sigh, Elsbeth pushed away from the table and ran out of the room. Roan would be hers, she vowed, fighting back her tears.

One way or the other.

Chapter Twelve

Kathryn spent all morning wandering through the house again, but this time with a purpose. If Cabrera was a vampire, and she had no reason to doubt it, then she wanted to know where he slept during the day. She had looked in his chambers. He wasn't there. The bed was neatly made and didn't look as if it had ever been slept in. Still, his clothes were in the wardrobe. A hairbrush and comb rested on top of the chest of drawers.

As for not sleeping in his room, he had said he would take lodging elsewhere. Still, she felt certain he was somewhere within the walls of the manor. Why she was so certain, she had no idea.

She started on the top floor, which housed only the servants' quarters. Moving to the second floor, she explored each bedroom and tower inch by inch, but there were no secret doors or hidden passages. At least none she could find.

After searching the first floor, she decided maybe she was wrong and he didn't sleep inside the house. But if not here, then where?

The cellar perhaps?

Mrs. Shumway cast a curious glance Kathryn's way when she asked for a candle.

"I want to . . . um, look in the cellar."

"It's powerful dirty down there. If it's wine you're wanting, I can send Nan to fetch it."

Kathryn shook her head as the cook lit a taper in a brass holder and passed it to her. "I'll go." Taking a deep breath, light held high, she crept down a narrow stairway into the bowels of the manor.

The cellar, every bit as dusty as the cook had warned, contained empty boxes and barrels and several wine racks, all of which were full. Standing in the center of the floor, she turned in a slow circle, but there was nothing else to see.

She was about to leave when she saw the iron door at the far end of the room. She stared at it, heart pounding. Did Roan take his rest in there? Did she dare look? What if he woke while she was snooping where she didn't belong?

Several minutes ticked into eternity before her curiosity got the best of her.

She flinched when the door opened with a screech loud enough to wake the dead.

Taking her courage in hand, she stepped into the room. No one had ever rested there. It wasn't a hidden bedroom, but some kind of dungeon. Barred cells lined the cold, damp walls. Dusty cobwebs dangled from every corner. The faint sound of running water underscored the silence. There were chains and manacles in every cell, tangled piles of them in the corners. Heaps of rags she guessed had once been used for bedding were scattered here and there. The air was foul with the stink of death and decay.

She jumped when a fat, brown rat scurried across her path. Turning on her heel, she hurried toward the cellar door. And that was when she saw it, a wooden coffin half-hidden behind the cellar staircase.

Had she found Roan's lair? Was he asleep inside?

Feeling like a sleepwalker, she moved toward the coffin.

Set the candle on an upturned barrel.

Took a deep breath.

Lifted the lid.

And screamed when a rat, even bigger than the last one, jumped out and darted across the floor.

Grabbing the candle, she bolted up the stairs.

"Merciful heavens!" Mrs. Shumway exclaimed when Kathryn burst into the kitchen. "Is the devil himself snapping at your heels?"

Stopping to catch her breath, Kathryn shook her head. "A rat!" she gasped. "I saw two of them. As big as cats!"

"Sure, and we get them from time to time," Mrs. Shumway said, looking apologetic. "I should have thought to warn you."

Nodding, Kathryn blew out the candle and left it on the counter.

In her room, she paced the floor until her heart no longer threatened to jump out of her chest, then sank into a chair.

She hadn't found what she was looking for, and now even more questions chased themselves through her mind.

How long had Cabrera been a vampire?

How had it happened?

Was there a way to undo it?

Were there other vampires in Newberry? And did they really live forever?

After dinner, she went into the library in hopes of finding a book that would answer her questions. His taste was certainly eclectic—*The Legend of Sleepy Hollow, Benjamin Franklin, Experiments and Observations on Electricity, The History of the Expedition Under the Command of Captains Lewis and Clark, Common Sense* by Thomas Paine, *The Private Life of the Late Benjamin Franklin,* as well as *Moby Dick, The Scarlet Letter,* and *Uncle Tom's Cabin.*

But nothing on vampires.

She was about to turn away when she spied a dusty volume high over her head. Dragging a chair closer to the bookcase, Kathryn plucked it from the shelf.

The words *Vampyre—Life, Legend, and Lore* were etched into the worn leather cover.

It was just what she was looking for.

Climbing down from the chair, she resumed her seat, and immediately lost herself in the text. Vampires were indeed real. They had been around for as long as mankind. Some sucked energy from their prey, some drank their blood. Some were born that way, some were made . . . Kathryn frowned. Had Cabrera been born a vampire?

It seemed vampires were notoriously hard to kill. Most could only be destroyed by a wooden stake in the heart, beheading, or being burned to ash. Silver was said to burn their flesh. Some were repelled by religious symbols, with crosses being used most often. They were "dead" from sunrise to sunset. Most took refuge from the sun in hidden vaults or crypts deep underground. No wonder she couldn't find him.

There were pages and pages of information, some accounts claiming to be based on fact, some said to be myths, although there was really no way to tell which ones were authentic. It was noted that animals shied away from the undead, especially domestic pets who instinctively recognized them as predators. She thought that tidbit at least sounded plausible.

Some of the other myths seemed outlandish. It was

purported that vampires were unable to cross running water. Was that true? And if so, why?

If you threw a bagful of nails on the ground, were they really compelled to stop chasing you and count them? That just seemed ridiculous.

Could they really turn into bats or wolves?

Were they truly able to fly? Scale walls and buildings? Read minds? Hypnotize mortals?

A cold chill ran down her spine. Had Cabrera hypnotized her? Was that why she didn't want to leave? But no, that couldn't be. He had offered to let her go. But she had decided against it.

Kathryn grudgingly spared a few minutes to eat supper, then returned to the library, eager to learn more about the mysterious world of vampires.

Roan found her there an hour later, so engrossed in the book she was unaware of his presence behind her.

He glanced over her shoulder, shook his head in disbelief when he saw what she was reading. She was living with a vampire and that wasn't enough? "Any questions I can answer?"

She jumped out of the chair as if she'd been shot from a cannon, the book in her lap tumbling toward the fireplace.

In a move almost too fast for human eyes to follow, Roan snatched the tome in midair mere seconds before it landed in the flames.

Kathryn stared at him, one hand pressed over her rapidly beating heart. "You scared me half to death."

"Sorry." He closed the book and set it on the table beside her chair. "Learn anything new?"

Not meeting his gaze, she nodded.

"Did you find what you were looking for?" he asked.

An image of the empty coffin flashed through her mind. What was it doing in the cellar? Was it his? If he didn't sleep in it, why did he have it? Did he know she'd been snooping around down there? So many questions she didn't dare ask.

"I wasn't looking for anything in particular. I was just . . . just curious." She glanced at the book on the table. Did he think she'd been perusing the pages, looking for ways to destroy him?

He gestured for her to sit down and when she did so, he took the other chair. "Why not just ask me what you want to know?"

"I didn't want to bother you."

"It's no bother. I've got nothing better to do at the moment, so fire away."

Where to start? "Can you fly?"

"Not exactly, but I can move extremely fast."

She nodded. Hadn't she just seen that with her own eyes? "Can you turn into a bat?"

He frowned. "Why on earth would I want to?"

"What about a wolf?"

"Yes."

Her eyes widened. "Truly?"

"Truly." It was an amazing sensation, running with the wild ones in wolf form, hunting with them.

She would have loved to see him change, but she didn't have the nerve to ask, nor was she sure she believed him. Maybe he was just teasing her, testing to see how gullible she was. "The book said you can't cross moving water or see yourself in a mirror."

He grunted softly. "The water thing is a fallacy."

"And the other?"

"Sadly true."

That explained why there were no mirrors anywhere in the house, she thought. And then she frowned. "But . . . I saw your reflection in the mirror in the Pettibone's ballroom."

"It was an illusion."

"An illusion? Like . . . like magic?"

"Of a sort."

"What does that mean?"

"I have a number of preternatural powers."

"Like what?" She leaned forward, curiosity shining in the depths of her eyes.

He made a vague gesture with his hand. "You seem awfully accepting of all this."

"What do you mean?"

"You're not afraid of me, of what I am?"

"Would it make you feel better if I ran screaming from your presence?"

"You would not be the first to do so," he muttered.

She sat back, hands clasped in her lap, her expression thoughtful. "I *am* afraid," she admitted. She didn't know if it was because she now knew what he was, or if he had been hiding his vampire abilities before, but she could feel the raw power emanating from him. It crawled over her skin, a silent warning of danger. "But also fascinated. I mean, how many people get to meet a vampire?"

"You should be asking yourself how many survive."

She blinked at him. Was she being naive, assuming that since he hadn't hurt her thus far, he meant her no harm? She was, after all, at his mercy. "Are you going to . . . to . . . ?"

"Of course not. Relax, Kathryn. I didn't mean to frighten you. You're perfectly safe with me." It was true, at least for the moment. "Anything else you wish to know?"

"How long have you been what you are?"

"Four hundred years, give or take a decade or two."

Four *hundred* years. She could scarcely wrap her mind about it. "So, vampires really do live forever."

"I suppose it's possible." The vampire who had turned him had existed a decade shy of nine hundred years.

"Are there more of your kind here, in our town?"

He debated whether or not to tell her the truth, then shook his head. "No."

"Do you have friends who are vampires?"

He barked a short laugh. "We are not social creatures by nature. Our instinct for survival compels us to destroy others of our kind."

"Why?"

"It's a territorial thing, a matter of defending one's . . ." He shook his head. Better not to go into the whole prey/hunting ground aspect.

Kathryn took a deep breath, then asked the question foremost in her mind. "Where do you spend the day?" She immediately wished she could call back the words.

His eyes narrowed, became darker, filled with suspicion as he glanced from her to the book and back again. "Why do you ask?"

"Never mind. It doesn't matter."

"Is that why you've been prowling around the manor?"

She swallowed hard, all too aware that they were alone and that she was helpless. "No." She forced the word through a throat gone suddenly dry.

"No?"

She was lying and he knew it. "All right, I . . . I'm sorry, but I was curious to know where you slept."

"Why?" His voice was rock-hard.

"Not for the reason I think you're thinking."

"And what reason might that be?"

"Please don't do this."

He cocked his head to the side. "Do what?"

"You're hurting me." She had felt his power earlier, but it was stronger now, weighing her down, making it difficult to breathe.

He frowned. Then, as comprehension dawned, he leaned back and closed his eyes.

Feeling weak and extremely vulnerable, Kathryn clenched her hands in her lap. She wanted to run away, to flee his presence, but she seemed unable to move. And then, to her astonishment, he simply vanished from sight.

She blew out a breath as all the tension in the room disappeared with him. He could have killed her. She knew it without a doubt. Killed her with no more than a thought.

It was the kind of knowledge that made for a poor night's sleep.

Roan fled the house, silently berating himself for his honesty. What foolishness had compelled him to answer her questions? He should have burned that blasted book centuries ago but who would have thought she'd go looking for information on his kind? Or search the house for his lair?

He cursed softly as he headed for his favorite hunting ground. Did he really think Kathryn was planning to drive a stake into his heart? And yet, he hadn't survived this long without being careful. He'd had several close calls over the years, made a few mistakes that could have been fatal, but none more dangerous than the error in judgment he had made with Livia.

He had been a young vampire back then, overconfident of his abilities, arrogant in his newfound powers, eager to seduce the women of the world with his charm. What a conceited ass he had been! Well did he remember the night he had met Livia. It had been in a tavern in late November. She had flirted shamelessly with him, her liquid brown eyes filled with the promise of pleasure beyond compare. He shook his head with the memory. He had thought he was seducing her when the opposite was true. She had lured him to her bed. And nearly destroyed him.

He vividly remembered rising over her, his nostrils filling with the scent of her lust and her blood, when pain unlike anything he had ever known exploded through his chest. Had she not been in such a hurry, she might have driven the stake through his heart. Luckily for him, she missed. It had not been so lucky for her. He had never again mistaken a hunter for a whore.

He paused on the street, nostrils flaring as he caught the scent of prey waiting just around the corner. Two women—a brunette and a redhead—stood talking to a sailor, who was trying to decide which harlot he preferred. Roan stayed out of sight, waiting while the man made his choice, finally settling on the brunette.

When the couple turned the corner, Roan approached the redhead. He mesmerized her with a thought, bent his head to her neck, and took what he needed, and all the while, he was wishing it was Kathryn in his embrace, willingly offering her sweet blood to satisfy his hellish thirst.

Chapter Thirteen

Kathryn woke feeling as if she hadn't slept at all. Not surprising, she supposed, since her dreams had not been dreams at all, but nightmares filled with grotesque scenes and bone-chilling images. Cabrera had played an integral part in all of them. Bigger than life, his eyes red as the fires of hell, his fangs extended and dripping blood as he drained the life from Mrs. Shumway and Nan before turning toward her. In one of her nightmares, she had plunged a wooden stake into his heart, watched in horror as his body disintegrated into a pile of ash and floated away on the wind.

Just dreams, she told herself. Nevertheless, she was relieved when Nan arrived—alive and well and bearing her morning chocolate.

Kathryn spent the morning in her room, her thoughts in turmoil. Yesterday, she had been certain staying here was what she wanted, but after last night . . . She shivered with the memory of Cabrera's power washing over her, the feral look in his eyes.

She had immersed herself in that book, trying to learn all she could about vampires, but nothing had prepared her for what she had experienced last night. It had been frightening beyond words. Imagine, having that much power at your fingertips! And then he had simply vanished from her sight. She didn't think it had anything to do with just moving fast. He had been there and then he wasn't. Where had he gone?

Where was he now?

After breakfast, she dressed and then, taking a deep breath, she went to the front door, put her hand on the latch, and wondered if it would open.

Surprisingly, it did, revealing a lowering sky with the scent of rain in the air. So, he now trusted her to leave? She thought it odd, given everything he had told her the night before. But then, if she ran screaming to the town about vampires, it was likely no one would believe her. Not that she would betray him. He had been kind to her. But, more than that, she didn't want to incur his wrath. She had felt his power once. It wasn't something she wanted to experience again.

Lost in thought, she went back inside and headed for the kitchen. Nan and Mrs. Shumway must go to town for supplies from time to time. Perhaps she could persuade Mrs. Shumway to take her this afternoon.

The cook looked at her askance. "Go into town? Child, how do you propose to get there?"

"I thought . . . how do you get supplies?"

"Mr. Cabrera has them delivered every week."

"Oh." So Nan and Mrs. Shumway were trapped here, as well.

"The lad who delivers the goods is due later this afternoon. Perhaps you could ride into town with him?"

"That's a wonderful idea! Please let me know when he gets here."

Kathryn couldn't stop smiling as she climbed up on the seat of the rickety wagon. She was going to town! She had no idea what she'd do there, since she had no money, and no idea how she would get back to the manor. But it was enough to get away from here, if only for a little while.

The delivery boy stared straight ahead, his cheeks reddening with embarrassment whenever the wagon hit a rut, causing their thighs to touch. He was so young, surely not more than ten and six. A man in some ways, she supposed, but not yet at ease with girls.

She thanked him profusely when he dropped her off in front of Hale's Bootery. Feeling free for the first time in days, Kathryn strolled down the crowded street, peering into shop windows, inhaling a multitude of scents and smells, not all of them pleasant.

Thanks to Roan's generosity, she was pleased to see that she was as well-dressed as the other ladies she passed. Most ignored her. A few smiled or bade her good day. And then, coming toward her, she spied Elsbeth Pettibone.

"Miss Winterbourne!" Elsbeth gushed. "How *very* nice to see you."

"Thank you."

"I was just on my way to Martha's Tea Shop. Would you care to join me?"

It was on the tip of Kathryn's tongue to refuse, but Elsbeth Pettibone was a friend of Roan's. Perhaps she might learn more about him by sharing tea with Elsbeth. "I'd be delighted," she said, before remembering that she had no way to pay her share. But it was too late to decline. Taking her by the arm, Elsbeth hurried her into the tea shop.

They were seated immediately. It was obvious Elsbeth went there often, since everyone knew her by name. Elsbeth ordered tea and cakes, then sat back in her chair, smiling, Kathryn thought, like the cat that had swallowed the canary. It suddenly occurred to her that Elsbeth had invited her to tea for the same reason she had accepted.

Elsbeth got right to the point. "How is Mr. Cabrera?"

"He was well, last I saw him."

"I haven't seen him since the night of my parents' anniversary party. I was hoping he might come calling." Elsbeth sat forward. "What is your relationship with Roan, exactly?"

"I needed a place to stay, and he was kind enough to take me in," Kathryn said, somewhat taken aback by the girl's bold question.

"Some might think it inappropriate, for you to be living in his house."

"I suppose it is improper," Kathryn agreed. "But I had nowhere else to go."

"So, you're friends?"

The question confirmed Kathryn's earlier suspicion. Elsbeth was fishing for information, wondering if Kathryn was a rival for Cabrera's affection. "I wouldn't say that."

"Are you staying with him much longer?"

There was no mistaking the jealousy in the other woman's voice, or the predatory gleam in her pretty blue eyes. "Miss Pettibone, I can assure you there's nothing going on between me and Mr. Cabrera. We're not friends. Barely more than acquaintances."

Elsbeth's whole demeanor changed in an instant. "I'm

sorry, I didn't mean to pry," she said contritely. "I just love him so much. And he doesn't seem to care for me at all."

Kathryn sipped her tea while she searched for something to say. She was tempted to ask if Elsbeth knew that Cabrera was a vampire, but it seemed obvious she did not. Tempting as it was to warn Elsbeth, Kathryn feared doing so might put both of them in danger.

Elsbeth reached across the table and placed her hand on Kathryn's. "Please don't tell him what I've said."

"Of course not."

"Do you know if he's planning to attend the theater Saturday night?"

"I'm sorry, I don't."

"Oh. I was so hoping to see him there. Perhaps you could ask him to escort the two of us?"

Kathryn hesitated. She had no desire to get caught in the middle, but the idea of going to the theater—something she had never done—was vastly appealing. "If I get a chance, I will."

"Wonderful!"

"I'll let you know," Kathryn said, suddenly eager to be gone. "If you'll excuse me, I really must go and find a ride back home."

"Please take my carriage," Elsbeth said. "It's parked just down the street, the white one with the gold trim. I won't need it for an hour or two."

"That's very kind of you."

Elsbeth shrugged. "If we're going to the theater, I simply must have something new to wear. Just tell my man to meet me in front of Vickery's Modiste Salon in two hours."

Kathryn bit down on her lip. "There's one more thing . . ." she said, her cheeks heating with embarrassment. "I'm afraid I can't pay . . ."

"Please, it's my treat," Elsbeth said with a dismissive wave of her hand. "And do try to talk Roan into going to the theater."

With a nod, Kathryn left the tea shop, unable to shake the feeling that Elsbeth Pettibone might seek her out whenever she wanted information about Cabrera, or just to make sure that Kathryn's feelings for him hadn't changed.

That evening, Roan was surprised to learn that Kathryn had taken afternoon tea with Elsbeth Pettibone. "What did the two of you talk about?"

"Nothing really. Just girl talk." Kathryn shifted in her seat. Roan had appeared shortly after supper. She had been sorely tempted to ask where he'd been, but decided she was better off not knowing. "She did ask if you would escort the two of us to the theater Saturday evening."

"Indeed?" The thought of spending the evening in Elsbeth's insipid company did not sit well.

Kathryn nodded.

"Do *you* want to go to the theater?"

"Yes, very much. I've never been."

He regarded her through narrowed eyes for several moments. "Very well. I'll make the necessary arrangements."

"Thank you." Though she had no desire to spend the evening watching Elsbeth flirt shamelessly with Cabrera, the idea of going to the theater filled Kathryn with excitement.

"What else did young Miss Pettibone have to say?"

"Nothing much. Our visit was very short."

He didn't say anything, just continued to look at her with that penetrating gaze.

"She's in love with you." Kathryn clapped a hand over her mouth. She hadn't meant to say that.

"Tell me something I don't know," he said dryly.

"You don't care for her, then?"

"Hardly. The chit doesn't have an ounce of common sense."

"Most men want beauty more than brains."

"I am not most men."

"Does she know what you are?"

"Of course not." His eyes narrowed ominously. "I trust you did not reveal my secret."

"No. No, I would never . . . honestly."

"You would likely regret it if you did."

His warning, mildly spoken, sent a shiver down her spine. As did his next words, but for an entirely different reason.

Rising from his chair, he held out his hand. "Would you take a walk in the gardens with me?"

In answer, she put her hand in his.

The night air was warm, the moon full and bright in the sky as they strolled along the winding garden paths. Kathryn was acutely aware of his nearness, of the cool press of his fingers against hers.

"I saw your sketches," Roan remarked. "You're quite good."

Her cheeks warmed at his praise.

He made a gesture with his hand that encompassed the grounds within the walls. "Is that how you envision this?"

"Yes."

"I give you leave to do with it as you will."

She smiled up at him, pleased. "Thank you!"

"I should like something in return."

She lifted a hand to her neck.

"Not that, Kathryn." His gaze moved to her lips. "I should like you to kiss me again."

Butterflies took wing in the pit of her stomach at the

mere thought of kissing him, of feeling his mouth moving seductively over hers. Even knowing what he was couldn't quell her anticipation. With hands that trembled, she cupped his face in her palms, went up on her tiptoes, and pressed her lips to his.

His arms went around her, pulling her closer, making her forget everything but the sense of wonder she felt each time he was near. How could she be afraid of him, of what he was, and still long to be in his arms? It made no sense at all, but for now, it didn't matter. Nothing mattered but his hands stroking up and down her back, delving into her hair.

Lost in his embrace, she let her hands wander over his back, his shoulders, his chest. The cloth of his coat was fine, the muscle beneath it hard and unyielding. An amazing contrast to his lips, which were cool and softer than they looked.

She moaned low in her throat when he lifted his head, gasped when she saw his eyes glinting red in the moonlight. She stumbled backward, watched in astonishment as he sprang effortlessly to the top of the garden wall and disappeared into the darkness beyond.

Roan landed lightly on the other side of the wall, his preternatural senses sifting through the myriad scents carried to him by the night breeze—earth and foliage, the lingering odors left behind by the passage of horses, carriages, and people, the faint stink of a decomposing dog in the underbrush across the way. He swore as the distinctive scent of vampire filled his nostrils. And then he frowned. It was troubling enough that there was another of his kind in the area, but even more disturbing to discover the vampire had been lurking on the outskirts of his property. To what end? If his intentions were peaceful, he would not have been skulking about. And if they weren't . . .

Hands clenched, Roan swore again. He had lived here for the last twenty years, with no one even suspecting his true nature. He never hunted close to home, though he wasn't adverse to taking a small drink from a dancing partner when the opportunity presented itself. He was well regarded by those he associated with; his eccentricities were accepted. For the first time in his life, he didn't feel completely estranged from humanity.

This rogue vampire put all that in jeopardy. He had already killed two women—women Roan had been acquainted with. He glanced at the peaked roof of his house, visible beyond the wall. Had the vampire come here sniffing after Kathryn? She was of the same age as Clara Beth and the Hattons' maid.

Did this vampire, whoever he was, intend for Kathryn to be his next victim? If so, he would be sorely disappointed. Roan had claimed her for his own, and as long as he lived, no one else—human or vampire—would have her.

Chapter Fourteen

Kathryn set to work in the gardens the next morning, digging up the old plants and raking the leaves into piles to be burned. One section of ground was thick with prickly weeds and briars. Maybe Cabrera would dig them up for her.

She took a break at noon and was about to go back outside when someone knocked on the door. Curious, she lingered in the living room while Nan went to see who'd come to visit.

"Miss Winterbourne," Nan called. "There's someone to see you."

Wondering who it could be, Kathryn went to the door. A young man with shaggy brown hair and pale blue eyes stood there, hat in hand. He was perhaps fourteen years old.

"Afternoon, miss," he said. "My name's Tim Blakely. Mr. Cabrera hired me to be your driver and do whatever else you need me to do. I'm to sleep in the shed."

Kathryn looked past him to the bay horse and brand-new buggy tied to a post near the front stairs. A driver. That meant she could go into town whenever she pleased. Even better, it meant she had someone to dig up the weeds and nettles choking the gardens. "Come in. I was just getting back to work."

Wide-eyed, he followed her through the house to the garden.

"I'd like you to dig up that bunch of briars," Kathryn said, pointing at one of the flower beds. "Can you do that?"

"Yes, miss."

"When you finish, please burn those leaves and weeds."

With a nod, he set to work.

Kathryn watched him a moment, then went back to preparing the flower beds. She referred to her sketches now and then, pleased as she visualized the end result.

She and Tim worked in the garden until late afternoon. "I'll see you tomorrow," she said, smiling. "You did a good job today."

"Thank you, miss."

"Are you going to be comfortable in that old shed?" There was nothing in there but a cot and a rickety table. Why hadn't Cabrera offered him a room in the house?

"Yes, miss. It's more than I'm used to."

She could believe that. His pants were torn, his shirt dirty and too large. He needed a haircut. And a bath. And new clothes. And shoes. His toes peeked through the pair he had.

Tomorrow, she thought. Tomorrow she would take him to town and buy him some new clothes.

"I see you've been working in the garden," Cabrera remarked when he joined her in the library that night.

"Yes. Tim's a good worker."

"Indeed?" He settled into the chair beside her. The heat

from the fire had no effect on him, but he found a similar warmth in being near Kathryn.

She nodded. "He worked hard today and never complained. But . . ."

"Go on."

"Does he have to eat and sleep out in that old shed? It's not fit for man nor beast."

"Until I know him better, yes."

"Oh."

"I found him on the streets late last night. Several older hoodlums were giving him a rather bad time. I offered him employment. He seemed very grateful."

"Doesn't he have any family?"

"He says not. If he proves himself to be trustworthy, I'll allow him to stay in the servants' quarters upstairs. In the meantime, he'll stay in the shed."

"He said it was more than he was used to."

"I'm sure it is."

Silence fell between them. Kathryn gazed into the flames, thinking how unreal it seemed that she could be living with a vampire. How quickly and completely her life had changed. From a room she had shared with seven other down-on-their-luck girls to living in a grand manor, eating regularly, wearing nice clothes.

She slid a glance at Cabrera. Had he really taken her in because he was lonely? Vampires were supposed to be mythical creatures, monsters who killed without mercy or regard for human life. Yet Cabrera was very real. He had saved her life. Why? What did he really want from her? She ran her fingertips over her lips, remembering the heat of his kisses, the thrill of being in his arms. Would the day come when he would expect more from her?

Roan smiled inwardly as he divined her thoughts. What

a remarkable woman she was, to have such thoughts, such
doubts, and not run screaming from his presence.

And yet, he had told her the truth. In spite of his friends
at the Hare and Hound and accepting occasional invita-
tions to soirees, he had been drowning in loneliness,
yearning for female companionship. And not the kind that
could be purchased on the streets. And then he had found
Kathryn, badly hurt, near death. Something about her—
something indefinable yet undeniable—had called to him.

As it called to him now.

He felt the change in her heartbeat when she looked up
and found him watching her.

"Kathryn."

What was it about the way he said her name that made
her feel as if she were melting inside? His eyes were dark,
filled with heat. It made her whole body tremble, not with
fear, but anticipation. He wanted her. Would he take her
by force if she refused?

Roan inhaled sharply, his nostrils filling with the scent
of her desire, her fear of the unknown. Well, he couldn't
blame her for being afraid of him. He was a powerful
being and she was at his mercy.

"Kathryn, how many times must I assure you that you
are safe here?"

Her eyes widened. "How do you know what I'm
thinking?"

"Isn't it obvious?"

"You can read my mind?" She shook her head. "That's
impossible. Isn't it?"

"Not for me."

She stared at him, her cheeks burning with embarrassment. If he could read her thoughts, then he knew . . .
everything. Every unmaidenly thought she had ever had

about him. She buried her face in her hands, wishing she could disappear.

She flinched when she felt his hand on her shoulder.

"Kathryn, look at me. You don't have anything to be embarrassed about."

She shook her head, refusing to meet his eyes, felt her heart skip a beat when he lifted her to her feet. Thinking she might faint, she looked up at him. His expression was so tender it made her heart ache.

"You wondered what I want from you? Just this. To hold you in my arms. To grant your every wish." He took a deep breath. "To have your love."

She blinked at him. He wanted her love? Even knowing what he was, she didn't think loving him would be too hard. Not when he looked at her like that. Not when his hands were stroking her back, caressing her nape, tunneling up into her hair. Not when he had been so kind, taking her in, providing her with food and shelter.

Lowering his head, he kissed her, ever so gently. "What do you desire, Kathryn? You have only to ask and if it's in my power to give, you shall have it."

"Are you trying to buy my affection?"

"I want only to make you happy. Is there nothing you want?"

She didn't even have to think about it. "I should like a horse of my own. A white mare."

"Do you ride?"

She shook her head. "But I've always wanted to."

"Then you shall have a horse. And someone to teach you to ride."

"You are too generous. Would it be all right if I took Tim into town and bought him a change of clothes? The ones he's wearing aren't fit for rags. Oh, and shoes."

"You have a kind heart, Kathryn Winterbourne. Buy the boy whatever you like. Tell the clerk to put it on my bill."

"Thank you."

"I want you to be happy here. Happy with me."

She smiled up at him. Vampires of myth and legend were vile, evil creatures who preyed on the helpless, turning them into monsters like themselves . . .

Her smile faded. Was that what he intended for her? To turn her into a vampire? Had that been his plan all along? Was he just biding his time, lulling her into a false sense of security, gaining her trust?

Roan shook his head. Did she really think he intended to bring her into the same kind of hell that he endured? He had never turned anyone, nor did he intend to. He had come to terms with what he was—a soulless monster. It was not a fate he would wish on his worst enemy, let alone on an innocent like Kathryn.

Drawing her into his arms, he murmured, "Put your mind at ease, love. I would never subject you to an existence like mine."

He was reading her mind again, she thought, laying her head against his shoulder. But this time she didn't care.

Chapter Fifteen

In the morning after breakfast, Kathryn went looking for Tim. She found him in the gardens, raking leaves. He bobbed his head when he saw her. "Mornin', miss."

"Good morning, Tim. Put the rake aside and hitch up the buggy. We're going into town."

She tried several times to engage the boy in conversation on the way, but he responded with nods or one-word answers. He was obviously uncomfortable at answering questions, which made her wonder if he was hiding something, or if he was just shy around women.

When they reached the store, she told him to pick out whatever he wanted, then, thinking her presence might make him uncomfortable, she waited for him near the entrance.

She smiled as she watched him move from rack to rack and shelf to shelf. Had he ever been inside a store before? He seemed reluctant to touch anything. She relaxed when a clerk went to assist him.

An hour later, Tim emerged from the dressing room wearing a pair of brown pants, a tan shirt, and a tweed vest.

"I cain't pay fer none of this," he said.

"It's part of your salary," Kathryn said. "Come along, we have one more stop to make."

New shoes came next. She insisted he buy a pair of shoes for everyday and a pair of work boots. She also bought him a wide-brimmed hat for working in the yard.

Kathryn and Tim spent the rest of the day working in the garden. By the end of the day, she decided it was time to think about buying new plants and maybe a fruit tree or two.

After supper, she went into the library, sketch pad in hand, to wait for Roan.

But he never came.

Kathryn had just finished dressing the next morning when Nan knocked on the door, then peeked inside to tell Kathryn she had a visitor waiting in the front parlor.

Wondering who would be calling so early, Kathryn followed the maid down the stairs.

A man attired in jodhpurs, a short leather jacket, and tall black boots stood before the hearth, his hat in one hand, a large package in the other. "Miz Winterbourne?"

"Yes."

"I am Conal Matheson, yer riding instructor."

"I'm pleased to meet you," she said, offering her hand. "But I have no horse."

"Ye do now." He handed her the package. "You'll find a riding habit and boots in there. I'll be waitin' for ye at the stables when ye're ready."

A half an hour later, attired in a smart black riding habit and her new boots, Kathryn hurried out to the stables. She found Conal inside, grooming the most beautiful animal she had ever seen. Cabrera had given her the horse of her dreams. Snow white in color, the mare had a luxurious mane, and a tail that almost touched the ground.

Unable to believe what she was seeing, she moved forward, letting the mare smell her hand before she reached out to stroke the satiny coat. "Is she really mine?"

"Yes, miss. And a fine animal she is."

"What's her name?"

"Her former owner called her Bianca, though I expect ye can change it if ye've a mind to."

"Bianca. No, it's perfect."

Matheson set the dandy brush aside and quickly saddled the horse. "She has an easy gait and a soft mouth, perfect for a lady such as yerself." After leading the mare out of the stall, he helped Kathryn mount, then led her into the small corral behind the stable.

Kathryn spent the next hour feeling like she'd died and gone to heaven. Riding was everything she had hoped for and more.

"Ye have a natural seat," Conal remarked as Bianca trotted around the corral. "Are ye sure ye've never ridden before?"

"Never. But I intend to do so every chance I get from now on."

Kathryn spent the afternoon supervising Tim in the gardens. Just after dusk, she went into the stable to spend a few minutes with Bianca. The mare whickered a soft greeting when Kathryn stepped inside, poked her nose over the stall door when she smelled the apple in Kathryn's hand.

"You are such a beauty," Kathryn murmured. "I can't believe you're mine. How shall I ever repay Cabrera?"

"I can think of a way."

She turned at the sound of his voice. As always, he was clad in black. It suited him, she thought. A shiver of awareness went through Kathryn when he came up beside her.

"You're pleased with the mare?"

"Oh, yes! Thank you so much." Impulsively, she went up on her tiptoes and kissed him. She had intended it to be a brief token of thanks, but it quickly turned into something more intense when he gathered her into his arms, his mouth moving seductively over hers. She returned his kiss fervently, every other thought forgotten but the joy of being in his embrace. The longing to stay there forever.

Lifting his head, he smiled down at her. "That's what I call a thank-you," he murmured. Then, bending down, he kissed her again, longer, deeper, until she was breathless and aching with need.

Clamping down on his burgeoning desire, he released her and shoved his hands into his pants' pockets to keep from reaching for her again. One day he would make her his, but not here, in the stable, as if she were no more than a trollop. Clearing his throat, he took a step back and said, somewhat gruffly, "Mrs. Shumway sent me to tell you supper is ready."

Still caught up in the heat of his kisses, Kathryn stared up at him, his words meaningless.

"Kathryn?"

She blinked at him. "What?"

"Your supper is ready."

"Oh." How could she think of food when all she wanted

was for him to kiss her again? Licking her lips, she thought, *Read my mind.*

He lifted one brow. And then his arm circled her waist, drawing her body against his.

She went willingly into his embrace, her eyelids fluttering down as his tongue traced her lower lip, then slid inside. Heat shot straight to the core of her being. She moaned low in her throat as he kissed her again and again, his hands slowly caressing her back, sliding down to cup her bottom.

She was on fire for him, afraid of the longing he stirred within her, eager to explore all the new feelings he aroused.

She didn't know what would have happened next if Tim hadn't entered the stable.

Seeing them, the boy let out a gasp of surprise, muttered an incoherent apology, and quickly backed out the door.

"We should go," Cabrera suggested. "Your food's getting cold."

Kathryn nodded. She didn't know about her supper, but she was so hot inside, she didn't think she would ever feel cold again.

Kathryn was still thinking about the kisses in the stable while she dressed for the theater that night. Her gown was sea green. Her high-heeled shoes matched her dress, as did the ribbons Nan had woven into her hair.

Cabrera was waiting for her as she descended the stairs, her wrap over his arm. "You are a vision," he murmured, draping the silk shawl over her shoulders.

There were no mirrors in the house, but the admiration in his eyes told her everything she wanted to know.

Cabrera had rented a carriage for the evening. The driver waited outside. He held the door as Roan handed Kathryn into the conveyance, then climbed in beside her. The interior was lovely, with butter-soft leather squabs and a footrest. Curtains the same shade of dark green as the carriage itself hung at the windows. Carpet of the same color covered the floor.

Cabrera had made previous arrangements to pick up Elsbeth on the way to the theater. Kathryn felt a twinge of jealousy as he went to the door to collect her. She liked Elsbeth well enough but had secretly hoped something would prevent her from joining them. But Elsbeth emerged from her home smiling and all aflutter as Cabrera escorted her down the walk to the carriage and handed her inside.

Elsbeth smiled as she settled herself across from Kathryn. "Isn't it a lovely night!" she exclaimed.

But Kathryn couldn't help noticing that Elsbeth was looking at Cabrera as she spoke.

Elsbeth had eyes only for Cabrera as he climbed into the carriage, but her smile quickly faded when Roan chose to sit beside Kathryn.

Kathryn tried not to stare as they entered the theater, but it was difficult. The theater itself was elegant, with plush carpets and draperies, but the decorations paled when compared to the men and women milling in the lobby. They were like colorful butterflies as they fluttered from one group to another, their lighthearted laughter filling the air until it was time to take their seats.

Elsbeth managed to arrange it so that she sat between Kathryn and Roan.

Kathryn fumed silently while waiting for the curtain to

go up. The play was even more wonderful than she had imagined. The costumes were lavish and beautiful, the music mesmerizing, the acting so convincing she almost forgot it was all just make-believe. She quickly lost herself in the story unfolding on the stage, Elsbeth and Cabrera nearly forgotten until she glanced their way. Elsbeth would have had to sit in Cabrera's lap to be any closer to him. Her hand, in its delicate lace glove, rested boldly on his knee.

Things only got worse at the intermission. Elsbeth stayed glued so tightly to Cabrera's side, it was as if they were joined at the hip. Surprisingly, he didn't seem to mind.

Roan introduced her and Elsbeth to a Mr. Lewiston. "We play cards on occasion," Cabrera said as they made their way back to their seats. Once again, Elsbeth managed to squeeze in between Kathryn and Cabrera.

With a shake of her head, Kathryn focused her attention on the stage and kept it there until the play was over.

Elsbeth prattled on about the production as they waited for their carriage. On the way home, she took the seat beside Kathryn, thus assuring that Roan couldn't sit beside her. When the all-too-obvious Miss Pettibone suggested stopping at the Rosemont for scones and cocoa, Kathryn held her breath, then sighed with relief when Cabrera politely declined. Kathryn didn't know about him, but she'd had her fill of Elsbeth Pettibone.

Elsbeth accepted his decision with apparent good grace, but Kathryn didn't miss the petulant set of her lips.

At the Pettibone house, Cabrera walked Elsbeth to her door, bowed over her hand, and bid her good night.

He blew out a sigh when he returned to the coach.

"Let's *not* do that again." Closing the door, he settled in beside her.

"I'm sorry you didn't have a good time," Kathryn remarked, all too aware of his hard-muscled thigh brushing hers.

"Did you?"

"Oh, yes! I loved the play, the music. Everything!"

"That's because you weren't fighting off the estimable Miss Pettibone's not-so-subtle advances all evening."

Kathryn bit down on her lower lip to keep from laughing.

"You find it humorous? Her hands were all over me."

"You didn't seem to mind," she muttered, and instantly wished she could recall her words. She sounded like she cared. Which she most definitely didn't. Well, not very much.

"Had we not been in the theater, surrounded by people, I assure you I would have taken her over my knee and spanked her like the spoiled child she is."

"You can't blame her," Kathryn said, feeling suddenly sorry for Elsbeth. "You know she's in love with you."

"I can't do anything about that." His arm slid around Kathryn's shoulders. "Enough about her."

His nearness sent a shiver of awareness down her spine.

"I think I deserve a reward for spending the evening in her company," he said.

"Do you?" She hated the tremor in her voice. "What kind of reward would you like?"

"Can't you guess?"

Her breath caught in her throat when his gaze moved over her face, soft as a lover's caress. He lowered his head slowly, giving her all the time in the world to pull away.

But the thought never crossed her mind. She closed her eyes as his mouth covered hers. Who would ever have thought that something as simple as a kiss could be so intoxicating?

They reached home all too soon.

Cabrera walked her to the door. "Good night, Kathryn."

"Thank you again for this evening."

"You're more than welcome."

She shifted from one foot to another, wishing he would kiss her again. Instead, he reached past her to open the front door. "Sweet dreams."

Feeling like a child being dismissed by her father, she could do nothing but go inside.

Roan stared after her, noting the sway of her hips as she climbed the stairs, the way the candlelight turned her hair to gold. He had seen the yearning in her eyes as he bade her good night. He had almost followed her inside. But his hunger refused to be denied any longer.

There would be other nights, he thought as he dismissed the fancy carriage he had hired for the evening.

For now, he needed to feed.

A short time later, his thirst assuaged, Roan stopped in at the Hare and Hound. He found Henry Westerbrook and Mick Flaherty sitting at their customary table on the main floor, a bottle of bourbon between them.

Westerbrook gestured for Roan to join them.

"So, how was the theater?" Flaherty asked.

Roan shook his head. "Not one of my favorite ways to spend an evening, as you both know."

Westerbrook leered at him. "I ran into Lewiston earlier. He said you were with two beautiful women."

"One for each arm, eh?" Flaherty said.

"Indeed," Roan said, signaling the barmaid. "I don't recommend it."

"Does old man Pettibone know his pretty young daughter was one of them?" Westerbrook asked. "He has plans for Elsbeth that I'll wager don't include you."

"And for that small mercy I am thankfully and eternally grateful."

Roan left the Hare and Hound an hour later. He paused when he caught the unmistakable scent of vampire. The same vampire who had been lurking on the far side of the wall surrounding his lair.

Curious, he followed the scent to the Mothers of Mercy Hospital.

Ghosting past the night nurse, he followed the vampire's trail down the dingy, poorly lit corridor into the last room on the right. The stink of death hung heavy in the air. He didn't have to look at the patient to know he was dead, drained of blood.

Hands balled into tight fists, Roan stalked out of the room. This was *his* territory. *His* hunting ground. He had staked it out twenty years ago and he intended to keep it.

He went from room to room, but there was no trace of the other vampire. No more bodies drained to the point of death.

Leaving the hospital, he followed the vampire's scent until it disappeared.

Roan frowned. First the other vampire had been lurking outside his home. Now he was encroaching on his hunting grounds. There was little doubt that this was the same vampire who had killed Clara Beth and the Hattons' maid.

A memory from long ago struggled for recognition.

Returning to the hospital, Roan stood in the middle of the dead man's room and let the vampire's scent engulf him . . .

Memories surfaced slowly.

A dusty city in Spain almost four hundred years ago.

The alcalde's daughter, Varinia. The first woman he had loved after being turned. She had been brutally attacked and drained of blood by a vampire.

The same vampire whose scent was all around him.

"Pascual." The name hissed past Roan's lips. "What mischief are you up to this time, my old friend?"

Roan had been a fledgling back then, drunk on blood and the preternatural power that flowed through his veins. Vampires rarely made friends, but he and Pascual had teamed up, hunting and whoring to their hearts' content.

He had been with Pascual in the marketplace one night when Varinia happened by. Roan had wanted her the moment he'd seen her, knew he would not rest until she was his. Not surprisingly, Pascual had also set his sights on her.

For several weeks, they both called on Varinia, each hoping for a chance to get her alone, to taste her sweetness.

And then one night, she agreed to meet Roan alone. He had intended to drink from her, but looking into her guileless brown eyes, sensing her innocence, her goodness, his lust for her blood had vanished.

In the days that followed, the attraction between them had grown deeper. They met secretly for weeks, their mutual attraction turning to affection, affection into something that might have lasted forever if Pascual—furious because Varinia had chosen Roan over him—hadn't killed her in an uncontrollable fit of jealous rage. Killed her and fled Spain like some coward, something Roan had never understood. Pascual was older, stronger. Had there been a fight, Pascual would likely have won. Yet he had fled the country.

At the time, Pascual's reasons for running away hadn't mattered. Engulfed with fury and grief, Roan had searched the world over looking for Varinia's killer, but to no avail. It was as if Pascual had vanished from the face of the earth.

And now, centuries later, Pascual was here.

Chapter Sixteen

Attired in her favorite robe and slippers, Elsbeth paced her bedroom floor. She had been so excited at the prospect of spending time at the theater with Roan. She had been certain having Kathryn along wouldn't matter, that Roan would have eyes only for her. She had worn a new gown and he hadn't even noticed. How could she have been so wrong? He had paid scant attention to her all night, the cad, seemingly charmed by everything Kathryn said. Kathryn, who had assured Elsbeth she had no interest in Roan. *Ha!*

Tomorrow night, she would do the unthinkable and call on Mr. Cabrera without a chaperone. When her father found out—and she would make sure that he did—he would insist that Roan Cabrera do the right thing.

Chapter Seventeen

Kathryn frittered the afternoon away—riding for an hour, working with Tim in the gardens for an hour, reading for an hour. She pulled out her pad and pen and sketched Bianca. And all the while she was wondering where Cabrera spent the day. Days ago, she had explored the house from top to bottom and found nothing but that creepy, old empty coffin. So, where *did* he spend his days?

Putting her sketch pad aside, she went down into the kitchens where Mrs. Shumway was making bread.

The cook looked up from kneading a large lump of bread dough. "Is there something you need, child?"

"No. I was just . . ." Kathryn made a vague gesture with her hand. "Just bored. Would you mind if I stayed here for a while?"

"Of course not, ducky. I'd welcome the company. Nan's upstairs doing the floors." Mrs. Shumway put the dough aside and covered it. "I was about to make some custard tarts. Would you like to help?"

Kathryn nodded. The next thing she knew, she was wearing a crisp white apron and learning how to make pasty. "Have you always cooked for other people?"

"No, 'tis a recent thing."

"Oh?"

Mrs. Shumway nodded. "I had to take on a position when my dear Nate passed on."

"Your husband?" Kathryn asked as they stood side by side rolling the crust out on a table dusted with flour.

"Aye."

"I'm sorry."

The cook nodded. "A wonderful, sweet man he was! A soldier when first we met. Tall and handsome, and he'd led a grand life. I loved to hear of his exploits in India. Why, he even taught me to shoot his weapon. I was quite a good shot, if I do say so myself. A few years after we wed, he was wounded in battle. After that, we had a few adventures of our own, we did. He passed away last year and I buried him beside our daughter, bless her soul. Our sons were grown and gone by then. Sure, and it was a blessing when Mr. Cabrera hired me. Speaking of his lordship, did you have a good time at the theater last night?"

"Oh, yes! It was all so wonderful! The music, the costumes." It would have been a perfect night, she thought, if only Elsbeth hadn't been there.

"If you don't mind my asking, did Mr. Cabrera enjoy himself?"

Kathryn bit back a grin as she remembered his reaction to Elsbeth's unwanted advances. "I believe he did. Why do you ask?"

"Forgive me. I was out of line."

"There's nothing to forgive, Mrs. Shumway. Is there something about Mr. Cabrera that troubles you?"

The cook glanced around the kitchen, as if she were afraid of being overheard. Then, lowering her voice, she said, "He appears most unhappy. Always so quiet and withdrawn. Why, I don't believe I've ever seen the poor man smile or heard him laugh."

His smiles *were* rare, Kathryn mused. But all the more welcome because of it.

By the time the tarts were out of the oven, her hands and skirts were liberally spotted with flour.

"Thank you for the lesson," Kathryn said, removing her apron and hanging it on a hook by the door. "It was fun. Maybe we could do it again sometime."

"Sure, and your company is always welcome," Mrs. Shumway said cheerfully. "But ye must run along now, child. I need to scrub the counters and mop the floor and start thinking about what to prepare for supper."

Nan had just started clearing the supper dishes when there was a knock at the door.

"I'll get it." Kathryn tossed her napkin on the table and hurried down the hallway, hoping to find Cabrera on the front steps. To her complete disappointment, it was Elsbeth Pettibone, dressed to the nines.

"Oh, it's you," Elsbeth said, not bothering to hide her disappointment. "I've come to see Mr. Cabrera."

"I'm sorry. He's not here just now."

Elsbeth peeked around Kathryn, as if to see for herself that Kathryn was telling the truth. "Will he be back soon?"

"I really couldn't say."

Elsbeth worried her lower lip a moment, then glanced over her shoulder, as if afraid someone might see her.

"Would you like to come inside and wait for him?" Kathryn asked, though entertaining Elsbeth was the last thing she wanted to do. Elsbeth had beauty and breeding and an air of self-confidence that Kathryn lacked. But it was more than that. Kathryn was jealous of Elsbeth and she didn't like feeling that way. But she just couldn't help it.

"No, thank you." Elsbeth glanced over her shoulder again. What was she doing here? She had hoped to see Roan alone and perhaps force a proposal from him. But that wouldn't happen as long as Kathryn was there to chaperone. "Don't tell him I was here," she said, gathering her skirts. "Don't tell anyone!"

And with that, she turned and hurried down the path.

With a shake of her head, Kathryn closed the door.

Roan turned onto the long, narrow road that led to the manor's front door, only to pause as the scent of blood and death and vampire was borne to him on the breeze.

Cursing under his breath, he hurried forward, swore again when he saw Elsbeth Pettibone sprawled at the bottom of the stairs, her face waxy pale, her expression one of terror, her eyes empty of life.

The thin trail of blood seeping down the side of her neck into the collar of her coat looked black in the faint light of the moon.

"Pascual." Roan spat the name into the night as he knelt beside the girl's body, even though he knew he was too late to save her. She had annoyed him with her constant flirting, amused him with her single-mindedness. Young and innocent, she'd probably never had a serious thought in her head.

Rising, he stared into the distance, his senses probing the darkness, but Pascual was gone. He stood there a moment, trying to decide what to do. He couldn't have it known that she had been killed at his home. Couldn't afford to raise anyone's suspicions. He never hunted where he lived, hadn't killed anyone in decades except to save his own life. Or Kathryn's. He didn't want the authorities snooping around his house, nor did he want them questioning him about where he had spent the evening.

Damn. Elsbeth hadn't deserved to die, not like this.

As gently as he could, he picked up the body. After making sure there was no trace of blood on the stairs or the walkway, he willed himself to the Pettibone estate. Standing in the shadows, he expanded his senses. Elsbeth's father was not in residence. Her mother was in the back parlor. The maids had retired for the night.

A thought took him to the second floor where the bedrooms were located. He had no difficulty finding Elsbeth's. Painted pale pink, with frilly white curtains and a fluffy white rug, it had to be hers.

He lowered her carefully onto a bed covered with a ruffled, white spread, folded her hands over her breasts, tugged her skirt down over her legs.

She was dead and it was his fault. Had she not known him, she would still be alive. Filled with remorse, he stood there a moment, his guilt swiftly turning to anger. How dare Pascual invade his territory and commit murder!

At the sound of heavy footsteps in the hallway, he dissolved into mist and returned home.

He found Kathryn sitting in front of the fire in the library, a book in her lap. Looking up, she smiled when she saw him.

He nodded in her direction, then settled into the chair beside hers. "How was your day?"

She shrugged. "The same as always. Oh! I learned to

make custard tarts," she exclaimed. "Too bad you can't have one. Sorry."

"No need to apologize. So, nothing out of the ordinary happened?"

"No." She bit down on her lower lip, then blurted, "Elsbeth Pettibone came to call earlier tonight."

"Indeed." But perhaps it was a good thing Kathryn had spoken to Elsbeth earlier in the evening. If anyone asked, Kathryn could confirm that he hadn't been home at the time of her death. "Did she say what she wanted?"

Kathryn shook her head. "She asked me not to tell you she'd been here, but I thought you should know."

He nodded. "Are you still happy with the mare?"

"Oh, yes. She's wonderful," Kathryn said, wondering at the sudden change of topic. "I wish you could come riding with me."

"I'm sure that could be arranged, if you don't mind riding at such a late hour." Spending time with Kathryn would solidify his alibi should anyone try to accuse him of Elsbeth's murder.

"I don't mind at all, as long as you're with me."

"All right. Go up and change your clothes and I'll meet you at the stables in twenty minutes."

Tim had just finished saddling Bianca when Cabrera rode up on a big chestnut gelding.

Kathryn could only stare at him. Dressed all in black, with his cloak billowing behind him, she thought he looked like the angel of death. And then she grinned, thinking the description fit him perfectly.

"Is that animal yours?" she asked.

"I borrowed him from Flaherty." Roan leaned forward

to stroke the gelding's neck. "But I'm thinking I might buy him so we can ride together more often. Would you like that?"

"You know I would."

"Ready to go?" he asked.

Nodding, she put her foot in the stirrup and swung into the saddle. "Where are we going?"

"A deer trail runs behind the manor. After a mile or so, it winds around a small pond."

"Oh, that sounds wonderful. Let's go."

The trail was just wide enough for two horses. Riding side by side, Kathryn kept stealing glances at Cabrera. She had never believed vampires were real. Even though she knew what he was, it was still difficult to believe. But there was no denying it. She could sense his power, even now. It surprised her that she had accepted the reality of it so quickly, that she wasn't afraid of him.

She wondered what Elsbeth would think if she knew the truth about Cabrera. Would she still pursue him like a rabbit after a fox? Or run away in fear for her life?

Kathryn glanced at Cabrera again. He rode easy in the saddle, his hands light on the reins. They made a beautiful picture, man and beast, both handsome and powerful. The book she'd read mentioned that animals instinctively shied away from vampires. Had Cabrera worked some kind of magic on the horse?

Riding on, Kathryn frowned, thinking Roan seemed far away. Preoccupied, as if something was troubling him. She was about to ask what was bothering him when the pond came into view.

Kathryn gasped, stunned by how beautiful it was. The full moon was reflected on its surface. Slender trees surrounded the calm water. They swayed gracefully in the slight breeze, as if dancing to music only they could hear.

A night bird screeched in the distance. The sound sent a shiver down her spine. Was it the victory cry of a predator or the death cry of prey?

"It's just an owl," Roan said. "Nothing to be afraid of."

She peered into the darkness. "An owl? Are you sure?"

Roan nodded. Should he tell her about Pascual? He didn't want to frighten her, yet he couldn't forget about Elsbeth.

Or Clara Beth. Or the Hattons' maid.

Or Varinia.

All dead by Pascual's hand.

His jaw tightened with the memory. Pascual had never been one to bridle his hunger or his lust. Was he hunting in Roan's territory because he knew Roan was here and he wanted to cause trouble for him? Or was it just coincidence?

Feeling Kathryn's perusal, he forced himself to put his old enemy out of his mind. "Would you like to stop for a while?" he asked. "There's a wooden bench in a small clearing up ahead."

"That would be nice."

He reined the chestnut to a halt. Dismounting, he lifted Kathryn from the saddle. His gaze burned into hers as her body slid against his. When her feet touched the ground, his arm snaked around her waist, pulling her close. He growled low in his throat as his lips claimed hers in a kiss that sent fire skittering along her nerves and stole the strength from her legs.

"Kathryn." He moaned her name against her lips as she swayed against him. "Tell me to stop before it's too late."

Stop? The word had no meaning, not when he was raining kisses along the side of her neck. Not when his hands were stroking up and down her back, sending shivers of pleasure rippling through her. Not when her body was screaming for his touch.

She almost fell when he released her, frowned when his arm crushed her close to his side. Before she could ask what was going on, a dark form separated itself from the shadows.

Like Cabrera, the stranger was dressed all in black, but the resemblance ended there. This man was short and slender. His hair, a dark brown, carried a slash of white on one side. His eyes were pale—blue or gray, she couldn't tell.

Roan's arm tightened around her. "Pascual."

"Cabrera."

"Get the hell out of my territory."

Pascual snorted. "When I'm ready." His pale gaze flicked over Kathryn before returning to Roan. "Did you find the gift I left for you?"

"There was no reason to kill her."

Pascual shrugged. "I've never needed a reason."

"What are you trying to prove?"

"Nothing." Pascual's predatory gaze raked over Kathryn again. "You always managed to find the prettiest women. Is she as tasty as she looks?"

"You'll never know."

Pascual threw back his head and laughed. And then, in the blink of an eye, he disappeared from sight.

"Who . . . who . . . ?"

"His name is Pascual."

"He's . . . he's a . . ."

"Yes, a vampire. Very old. Very dangerous."

"He said he left you a gift. What did he mean?"

"I'll tell you later. Let's go home."

He lifted Kathryn onto the chestnut's back, then vaulted

up behind her, one arm circling her waist. He clucked to the chestnut and the horse moved out. The mare followed.

Kathryn leaned back against Cabrera, mind reeling, body trembling from head to foot. She wasn't afraid of Roan, but Pascual terrified her. Roan might be dangerous, but Pascual was evil. She had sensed the malevolence emanating from him like some foul stench when she looked into his soulless eyes.

She was still shivering when they reached home.

After ordering Tim to stable the horses, Roan lifted Kathryn into his arms and started for the house.

Wrapping her arms around his neck, she said, "I can walk, you know."

"I know." But he didn't put her down.

And she didn't argue. Instead, she rested her head on his shoulder as he carried her into the house and up the stairs to her room. He turned his back while she changed into her nightgown, then tucked her into bed.

"You're safe here," he murmured, nudging a wisp of hair from her brow. "He can't enter my home without my permission, and that's something he will never have. Go to sleep now." He kissed her cheek, then turned to go, only to stop when her hand grasped his arm.

"Don't leave me. I don't want to be alone."

He hesitated, then nodded. But when he headed for the chair in the corner, she caught his arm again. "Stay beside me."

He groaned low in his throat. "Kathryn, you don't know what you're asking."

"Please."

With a sigh of resignation, he shrugged off his cloak, peeled off his shirt, removed his boots and stretched out on top of the covers beside her.

Edging closer, she rested her head on his shoulder and closed her eyes.

Roan felt the tension drain out of him as she drifted off to sleep. She really was an innocent, he mused, asking a man—and a vampire at that—to share her bed. Had she no idea of the sexual urges that rode a man with whip and spurs when he was lying next to a beautiful woman? A woman he desired?

Swearing softly, he eased out of her bed. Lost in thought, he wandered over to the window and stared out into the darkness.

And there, lurking in the shadows beyond the side wall, he glimpsed Pascual staring back at him.

Chapter Eighteen

Kathryn thought the day would never end. Time and again, she found herself wondering what kind of "gift" Pascual had left for Cabrera. They didn't really seem to be friends, so why would the other vampire be giving Roan a present?

She replayed the exchange in her mind.

Did you find the gift I left for you?

There was no reason to kill her.

Had Pascual killed someone? If so, who? And why? She shuddered. Was *that* the gift? A dead girl?

It was the first thing she asked Cabrera when she saw him that night. "You never told me what kind of present Pascual gave you."

"It was not a gift. It was a message."

"What kind of message?"

A muscle twitched in Roan's jaw. He paced the floor for several moments, then dropped into the chair across from the sofa. "He killed Elsbeth last night and left her body on the walkway where I'd be sure to find it."

"Elsbeth is dead?" Kathryn felt the blood drain from her face. "Why would he do such a dreadful thing?"

"We have an old score to settle, he and I. It was his

way of telling me he hasn't forgotten. Pascual is a vicious creature. There is no mercy in him, no hint of humanity. He kills indiscriminately and takes pleasure in it."

Feeling suddenly nauseous, she wrapped her arms around her middle. Did she really want to hear this? She should have insisted Elsbeth come inside and wait, but how could she have known that that creature was lurking in the shadows? Her stomach churned with the realization that it might just as easily have been her body that Cabrera had found.

Roan blew out a breath. He wanted to comfort Kathryn, though he wasn't sure she would welcome his touch.

But when she reached out blindly, he moved to the sofa and took her in his arms. Sobbing quietly, she collapsed against him. Her trust pleased him on many levels.

He stroked her back. "You must not go outside alone after dark. Not for any reason. Do you understand? He can't come inside the house and you mustn't invite him, or anyone else."

She looked up, her eyes red and swollen and filled with confusion. "Not anyone?"

"Vampires have the power to hypnotize people to do their bidding. He can't come inside, but someone else could drag you outside."

Sniffling, she asked, "You can do that, hypnotize someone?"

He hesitated, then nodded.

A faint hint of suspicion shadowed her eyes. "Have *you* hypnotized *me*?"

"No." He brushed a wisp of hair from her cheek. "I will keep you safe, Kathryn. I swear it."

* * *

Roan stayed with Kathryn until she went to bed. Then, curious to hear what was being said about Elsbeth's untimely death, he transported himself to the Hare and Hound.

He heard whispers and rumors in the main room as he made his way downstairs. The usual crowd sat around their usual table. An unopened deck of cards waited in front of Flaherty.

Cormac nodded in Roan's direction as he took the single vacant seat. "Have you heard the latest news?"

Roan shook his head, though he was fairly certain he knew what that news might be.

"Elsbeth Pettibone was found dead in her room last night."

"What happened?"

"No one knows for sure," Lewiston said. "Old man Pettibone found her on her bed, fully dressed—hat, shoes and gloves."

"There's some speculation she was strangled," Flaherty remarked, "but that doesn't explain the puncture wounds on the side of her neck."

"Or how the murderer got into her room, unseen," Cormac added. "The butler said she left the house about eight that night. No one else saw her leave or heard her come home. Her father found her when he went to check on her later. Stone-cold dead."

"It's obvious there's a killer in the neighborhood," Westerbrook said, refilling his wineglass. "I've warned my womenfolk and the maids not to go out after dark."

Nods from the other men suggested they had done the same.

Lewiston leaned back in his chair, arms folded across his chest. "So, Cabrera, what do you think?"

Roan shrugged. "Isn't it obvious? We've got a maniac on our hands."

Sated on the blood of his last victim, Juan Pascual strolled through one of the town's back alleys. He had spent the last two hundred and fifty years searching for Roan Cabrera and had, at long last, found him.

Cabrera seemed to have prospered since he'd known him centuries ago. He lived in an old manor house with a lovely young woman. He had friends at the local pub. By all accounts, he had everything he desired.

They had been friends once, then rivals for the fair Varinia. Even now, centuries later, his gut twisted when he remembered how she had chosen Cabrera over him. No woman had ever refused him. He had been surprised by the depths of his anger, his rage. His jealousy. But then, he had never wanted a woman the way he wanted Varinia. He had lusted for her blood, her flesh, her very soul. But for Cabrera, he would have made her his forever.

He remembered all too well how he had fled the country after killing Varinia. No doubt Cabrera thought it had been cowardice, but he'd been driven by guilt and regret. And when, at last, he had learned to live with his act, his hatred for the man who had stolen the woman he loved surfaced again. Cabrera had taken his woman. It was time to get even.

Once he destroyed Cabrera, he would take his rival's woman. She was a pretty thing. He had intended to drain her dry, but after seeing her up close, he'd had second thoughts. Perhaps he would give her the Dark Gift, thereby keeping her forever as young and beautiful as she was now.

He could always dispose of her once he tired of her . . .

His steps faltered. What would be the fun of taking the woman after Cabrera was dead? Sure, he could tell his old friend what he intended to do before he ripped his heart out, but how much more satisfying to leave Cabrera alive, knowing that his worst enemy had turned the woman under his protection? And that she was his enemy's slave, helpless to resist the commands of the vampire who had turned her, compelled to obey his every wish? He smiled as he contemplated the pain he could inflict on her, the shame and misery she would feel, the hatred for Cabrera that would fester in her heart because he had been unable to save her.

Ah, yes, that was a far more satisfying and lasting means of vengeance.

The front-page story in Monday's *Newberry Beacon* was all about the mysterious death of Elsbeth Pettibone. According to the family butler, she had gone out at eight that night. No one had seen her return. When her father went up later to check on her, he found Elsbeth on the bed, still fully clothed. The local magistrate had no clues, no witnesses to the crime, and no suspects. A small notation at the bottom of the story stated that the funeral would be held privately for the family and a few close friends.

Kathryn's heart went out to the girl's parents. How awful, to find your daughter dead in her room, with no idea of who had murdered her or why. Cabrera could have told them the truth of it, she thought. Perhaps he should have done so, but to what end? No one really believed in vampires anymore. The police would likely think him mad, and if, by some chance, people believed him, it would likely cause a panic in the town, which would benefit no one.

She tossed the paper aside, then sat there, staring into space. As much as she liked living here, how much longer could she go on accepting Cabrera's charity? Decent women didn't live with a man unless he was a blood relative. It was hard to believe Roan was looking after her out of the kindness of his heart, or that he merely wanted her company. And yet, he had asked nothing of her. If she left, where would she go?

If she left . . . She thought about that horrid vampire, Pascual. He had killed Elsbeth Pettibone for no reason that made any sense. What had he said? *I've never needed a reason.* Cabrera had told her that Pascual was a vicious creature, totally lacking in mercy and humanity. If she'd ever had any doubts, she had every reason to believe it now.

Lost in her own morbid thoughts, Kathryn barely tasted the dinner Mrs. Shumway prepared. Pushing her chair away from the table, she went into the library in search of a book.

She picked one off the shelf and sank into a chair, only to sit there, gazing into the cold ashes in the hearth, her mind thankfully numb.

When Nan called her to supper hours later, Kathryn couldn't believe she had spent the whole afternoon staring into space.

She had little appetite.

"Are you ill, child?" Mrs. Shumway asked. "You've hardly eaten a thing."

"I'm sorry, I just don't seem to be very hungry this evening."

"Sure, and you're troubled by that story in the *Beacon,* aren't you? 'Twas a terrible thing, that poor girl being killed. None of us will rest easy in our beds until her murderer is found."

Kathryn nodded.

"Mr. Cabrera has warned us not to go out after dark. And not to answer the door to strangers." The cook shivered. "The way he said it . . . it was almost like he knew the murderer would come here." She smiled self-consciously. "Pay me no mind. My mother always said my thoughts tended to be wild and a little morose."

In this case, the wilder, the better, Kathryn mused, and almost smiled as she imagined telling Mrs. Shumway the truth. "I think I'll just go up and have a long soak."

"Good idea, lamb. I'll have Nan fill the tub."

From his lair deep beneath the dungeon, Roan listened to Kathryn and Nan moving around Kathryn's bedroom. He had moved the tub from his room into hers. Now, he heard the splash of water as the maid filled the tub, the whisper of cloth sliding over flesh as Kathryn disrobed.

Rising, he listened to her step into the tub as he slid into the shallow pool in a corner of his lair. Resting in the warm water, he imagined sharing a bath with Kathryn, feeling her wet, soapy skin against his, running his hands over her smooth, bare flesh. Making love to her there, in the tub, savoring the sweetness of her blood . . .

Cursing under his breath, he left the pool. He dried off, then willed himself to the master bedroom upstairs. Though he didn't take his rest there, he kept his clothing and personal items in the wardrobe for appearances' sake. He dressed quickly. Combed his hair. A thought took him to her bedroom door.

He knocked once, then stepped inside.

Kathryn glanced over her shoulder, hairbrush in hand, when he entered the room.

"Am I intruding?" he asked. She wore a long blue robe over her nightgown. Her feet were bare.

Kathryn shook her head, glad that he hadn't arrived ten minutes earlier, when she was reclining in the tub. As always, she couldn't stop looking at him. He was tall and dark and forbidding, yet undeniably attractive and sensual, making her think of things no unmarried woman should be thinking.

"I thought you might like to go out."

"Out?" She glanced at her robe. "Now?"

"It's early yet."

"Is it safe?"

"You'll be with me."

"I don't know." She felt a twinge of guilt for wanting to go, for wanting to be with him. Elsbeth had loved Roan. If she hadn't come here that night, she might still be alive.

"Kathryn?"

"It seems wrong somehow, going out so soon after what happened to Elsbeth."

"This will sound harsh, but she's past caring. It will do us both good to have a change of scenery, don't you think?"

She nodded.

"I'll wait for you downstairs." He paused at the door and glanced over his shoulder. "Dress warmly. It's raining."

Kathryn joined him in the front parlor twenty minutes later, startled when he slid his arm around her waist.

"Relax. I'm taking you to town."

She glanced at the door, then back at him, a question in her eyes.

"Take a deep breath. I'm going to show you a bit of vampire magic."

"Magic?" Her eyes mirrored the doubt in her voice.

"You'll see."

Kathryn gasped as the world as she knew it vanished and she was swallowed in a whirlwind of darkness. Eyes closed, she clung to Cabrera's arm, certain that destruction awaited her.

But when she opened her eyes, they were standing in front of a small eatery that sold tea and cakes and fine wine. "How did you do that?" she asked, breathlessly.

"As I said, a little vampire magic. Are you all right?"

"I don't know. I've never felt anything like that before. It was . . . I don't know. Like flying, I guess."

He smiled down at her, then opened the door and bowed her inside.

It was a quaint café—small, round tables covered with exquisite linen, delicate gold paper on the walls, flickering candles in wrought-iron wall sconces.

A waitress ushered them to a table in the back. Kathryn ordered a cup of souchong and a lemon-cheese tart. Roan ordered a glass of red wine.

Glancing around, she noticed that all the tables were occupied by couples, mostly young, with eyes only for each other.

"This place is known as a rendezvous for young lovers," Roan remarked, following her gaze.

She looked up at him, a faint blush warming her cheeks. "We aren't lovers."

He raised one brow. "We could be."

Her cheeks grew hotter. Did he know how often she

thought about that? Dreamed about it? But he was a vampire and that thought chilled her desire every time. Yes, he was kind to her. Yes, he was handsome and rich. Yes, she cared for him more than she should. But to surrender her virtue to such a man? A man who was not really a man? How could she?

Roan watched the play of emotions chase themselves across her face. He didn't have to read her mind to know what she was thinking. Her desire scented her skin. The rapid beat of her heart spoke of her trepidation.

"How does it work, that . . . magic of yours?" she asked after the waitress brought their order.

"I'm not sure. I just think about where I'd like to be and I'm there."

"What other tricks can you do?"

"Tricks? I'm not a magician, Kathryn, or a circus pony."

"I didn't mean that." She nibbled on her tart, took a sip of her tea. "I'd love to see you turn into a wolf."

"Now?"

"Of course not." She giggled, imagining the looks on the faces of the other patrons if Cabrera suddenly transformed himself into a big bad wolf. And then she frowned. "Why would you want to be a wolf?"

He leaned back in his chair, swirling the wine in his glass. "There are times when changing form comes in handy," he said slowly. "If I'm wounded and a hunter gets too close, turning into a wolf has a certain shock value, giving me time to escape." Sometimes, when the loneliness of being a vampire had overwhelmed him, he had run with a pack of wild wolves. It had been freeing, exhilarating. In his wolf form, he could endure the sun's light, revel in the hunt with his canine brothers, throw his head back and howl at the moon. But he decided not to mention it to Kathryn for fear she wouldn't understand.

"Anything else?" she asked.

Her curiosity was insatiable, he thought, amused. "I can dissolve into mist."

Her eyes widened. "No."

He nodded. "A handy talent."

"I don't believe you."

"Maybe I'll show you later." It has been frightening, the first time he had accomplished it.

She finished her tea, brushed the last of the crumbs from her fingertips. "Could we go for a walk in the rain?"

"If you wish."

"I've always loved the rain. The way it washes everything clean."

He dropped a few coins on the table, then took her arm. Outside, the rain had turned to a light drizzle.

"Do it now," Kathryn said.

"It?"

"Turn into a wolf." She had wanted to see him change ever since they had first talked about it, but she hadn't had the nerve to ask until now.

"Very well." He glanced up and down the street, then pulled her into an opening between two buildings.

Kathryn's eyes went wide as the air shimmered around Roan and a large black wolf took his place. She stared at him. She hadn't really believed he could do it, but the proof was there in front of her. He was beautiful, his coat like ebony.

There was another shift in the air and the wolf disappeared and a hazy gray mist, barely discernable from the drizzle, hovered in the air. It moved around her, not quite touching her.

And then, between one heartbeat and the next, Roan stood before her again.

Kathryn shook her head. "If I hadn't seen it with my own eyes, I never would have believed it."

Stepping out from between the buildings, they strolled down the street. "It must be amazing, to be able to do that. But . . . where do your clothes go when you're the wolf? And that misty thing? And how do you get them back?"

"I don't know," Roan said, chuckling. "It's as much a mystery to me as it is to you."

"Have you ever tried . . . ?" Her words trailed off when she saw a woman wearing a hat and a ragged shawl walking in their direction. "Mama? Mama!"

The woman looked up, her eyes widening in disbelief. "Kathryn? Is that you?"

Closing the distance between them, Kathryn threw her arms around her mother. "I'm so glad to see you!"

"And I you."

Roan watched the two embrace. Kathryn looked like a younger, healthier version of her mother. Both had the same fine blond hair, the same green eyes, though, at the moment, one of her mother's eyes was black and blue. It matched the bruise on her cheek.

At length, the two separated. Kathryn gasped as a shaft of moonlight filtered through a break in the clouds. "He hit you again, didn't he?"

Ducking her head, Victoria lifted a hand to her cheek. "He didn't mean it," she mumbled.

"Didn't he? You're cold. Here," Kathryn said, removing her coat and draping it over her mother's shoulders. "Take mine."

"I couldn't."

"Of course you can. And you're coming home with us."

"No. No, I can't. He'll only find me. Kat, I have to go. If I'm not back soon with his . . . his medicine . . . he'll . . ." Tears welled in her eyes. "I have to go."

Kathryn looked at Cabrera. "Make her come home with us."

He shook his head. "I have a better idea."

Chapter Nineteen

Kathryn stared at Cabrera. "*This* is your better idea? Bringing her back here?" They were standing outside the broken fence that surrounded the dilapidated farmhouse Kathryn had once called home.

"Mrs. Darlington, do you love your husband?"

She shook her head. "I . . . I never did. I only married him because I thought Kat needed a father."

"Does he beat you often?"

She looked away, her eyes filled with shame.

"He'll never touch you again," Roan said. "I swear it on my life. Come along. Oh, Mrs. Darlington, do I have your permission to enter your home?"

She frowned at the odd question but nodded.

Roan smiled at her, then led the way to the front door. He didn't bother to knock, simply lifted the latch and stepped inside.

"It's about time you got back, woman. What's this?" he exclaimed when Roan stepped into the parlor. "Who the hell are you?"

"Ladies," Roan said, "please go into another room and close the door."

"Here, now," Basil Darlington growled as Kathryn and

her mother hurried down the hall. "What's the meaning of this?"

"You're leaving town tonight," Roan said. "And you will never come back. You will never try to contact Kathryn or her mother. Do you understand?"

Darlington snorted disdainfully. He was a big man, thick through the neck and shoulders and as tall as Roan. "This is my house. Victoria's my wife, the girl's my daughter, and I'll bloody well do as I please. So you can just go to hell."

"After you."

Shifting from one foot to the other, Darlington balled his fists, but whatever action he had planned never happened. An outpouring of preternatural power held him immobile.

"I'm going to say this just one more time." Roan let his eyes go red, then bared his fangs. "If I ever see you again, you won't like what happens next." Eyes narrowed, he increased the power holding Darlington.

Suddenly unable to breathe, Darlington gagged, his face slowly turning purple, his eyes bulging.

"Do you understand?" Roan released his hold, waiting for an answer.

Darlington rubbed his throat. "What are you?"

"Your worst nightmare. Remember what I said. Now, get out of here and don't come back."

Darlington moved across the floor with as much dignity as he could muster, then bolted out the door.

"All right, Kathryn," Roan called. "You can come out now."

She peered around the corner, her worried gaze sweeping the room. Victoria stood behind her.

"He's gone," Roan said. "He won't be back. We

should . . ." Darting forward, he caught Kathryn's mother before she hit the floor.

"Mama!" Kathryn glanced at Roan, her eyes wide with alarm. "What's wrong with her?"

"I'm not sure." Lifting the woman into his arms, he carried her to the worn sofa and lowered her gently onto the cushions. Her face had gone pale, her pulse was slow, her heartbeat irregular.

Kathryn fell to her knees beside the sofa and took her mother's hand in hers. "Mama?"

Victoria's eyelids fluttered open. "Kat?"

"I'm here. Don't worry, I won't leave you."

Roan ran his hands over the woman's arms and legs. She flinched every time he touched her. He didn't have to see the bruises to know they were there. He should have killed Darlington, he thought as he stepped away from the sofa.

During the next hour, Kathryn fixed her mother tea and toast, helped her out of her clothes and into a nightgown, brushed her hair, and tucked her into bed.

Leaving her mother's room, she closed the door and went into the parlor. "I think she'll be all right now."

Roan nodded, then frowned. "What is it?"

"I'm staying here."

He'd seen that coming. Still, it affected him strangely, as if he was losing a part of himself.

"It's not that I haven't appreciated all you've done for me," she said, her voice quivering, "but I can't leave her here alone."

"And you can't stay here with no one to protect you from Pascual."

How could she have forgotten about that horrible creature?

Roan blew out a sigh. There was only one thing to be

done. Beckoning for Kathryn to follow him, he returned to the bedroom. Lifting Victoria, he held her close to his chest with one arm, put his other arm around Kathryn's shoulders, and willed the three of them to the guest room in Cabrera Manor.

Needing solace and someone to talk to after his frightening encounter, Basil Darlington headed straight to the local pub. Seated on a stool at the end of the bar, hunched over his second pint, he muttered under his breath about the treachery of women and the impossibility of what he thought he'd seen.

"Trouble at home?"

Darlington slid a glance at the man standing at his elbow. For a moment, he thought it was the creature he'd seen with Kat. Both had been dressed in black. But the resemblance ended there. This man had brown hair. And his eyes were gray, not black. "What's it to ya?"

"Let me buy you another drink and we can talk about it."

"Never been one to turn down a free pint or two."

His new friend signaled for another round. "Now, why don't you tell me what has you so upset? Perhaps I can help."

Darlington shook his head "You wouldn't believe me if I told you."

"You'd be surprised at what I believe."

Darlington snickered. "Yeah? Well, I bet you've never seen a man with eyes as red as the devil's own and fangs like a bleedin' snake."

"Actually, I've not only seen a few, but I've taken their heads as well."

"Taken their heads?" Darlington exclaimed, suddenly sober. "Who the bloody hell are you?"

"A vampire's worst nightmare."

Roan prowled through the house. He had lived alone for centuries. Now, suddenly, he was surrounded by women.

Mrs. Shumway and Nan shared a room in the servants' quarters on the third floor. Kathryn slept in one of the bedrooms on the second floor. Her mother tossed and turned in the room at the end of the hall. He shook his head. Victoria Darlington was a complication he hadn't counted on and didn't want.

Four women of varying ages, he mused. The very air he breathed carried the scent of their hair and skin. The essence of their sex.

The inviting scent of their blood.

As a matter of course, he had tasted the blood of both the cook and the maid. Having many enemies, it was a precaution he took that enabled him to find Nan and Mrs. Shumway, wherever they might be. He had also taken Tim's blood for the same reason.

He ran his tongue over his fangs as his hunger stirred to life. He had taken Kathryn's blood from time to time, while she slept. Not enough to do her harm. Not enough to satisfy his hunger. But having tasted her once, he couldn't resist doing it again. And again. It was like a drug, an addiction he didn't want to break.

Going to the front window, he stared out into the darkness—and frowned as a faint movement caught his eye. When it came a second time, he opened the front door and stepped outside. He swept the area with his preternatural senses. He had expected it to be Pascual, but the scent carried to him was that of a stranger.

A stranger with blood on his hands.

Roan swore a vile oath. There was no mistaking the lingering smell of death that clung to a hunter.

He swore again. He had lived in this place for the last twenty years, had chosen the location because it was a small town, far away from the bigger cities. His property was warded against vampires, but the wards would not keep out other enemies. So far, Newberry had been free of hunters. Nothing much had happened here. But all that had changed. First Pascual showed up, leaving bodies in his wake.

And now a hunter had wandered into town. Had he followed Pascual?

Or was he hoping to claim the bounty on Roan's head?

Chapter Twenty

Kathryn woke abruptly. Last night, she had fallen asleep in a chair at her mother's bedside. What was she doing back in her own room? Had something dreadful happened in the night?

Flinging the covers aside, she hurried down the corridor to the room at the end of the hall. She breathed a sigh of relief when she opened the door and saw her mother sitting up in bed.

Nan stood beside her, pouring a cup of tea. "Can I get you anything else, Miss Victoria?" the maid asked.

"Not right now," Victoria said with a smile. "Thank you, Nan."

Dropping a curtsy, the maid left the room.

"How are you feeling, Mama?"

"Much better, dear." Victoria held out her hand. "Come, sit with me."

Kathryn perched on the edge of the mattress. The bruise on her mother's face looked even worse today. The hand holding hers was cold. "Is there anything I can do?"

"Kat, I know I told you to leave home. Perhaps I was foolish to suggest it. I never intended for you to . . . to . . ." She glanced around the room. "This is a luxurious place and it must be wonderful to have servants and nice clothes, but Kathryn . . ."

"Mama! It's not what you think! Cabrera isn't my lover."

"No? What is he to you, then? More importantly, what are *you* to him?"

"He's asked nothing of me. Only my company."

"Child . . ."

"It's true!"

"It may be. But he's a man and you're a lovely young woman. Sooner or later, he's going to expect something in return for his hospitality. Something you may not wish to give. What will you do then?"

Kathryn bit down on her lower lip. What would she do? Yes, Cabrera was a vampire. Yes, he was dangerous. But somehow, at this moment, none of that really mattered. He wanted her. She knew that, but he had never tried to force himself on her, never done or said anything to make her feel obligated or uncomfortable. But, more than that, she wanted him.

And, truth be told, she could think of worse things than giving herself to him.

Of course, she didn't dare admit that to anyone, especially her mother!

"We need to go home, Kat. Now that Basil's gone, we'll be all right. We can take in laundry. I can take up dress-making again. We'll get by."

"Mama . . ."

"We'll talk more later," Victoria said, smothering a yawn. "I feel so . . . so . . ."

To Kathryn's astonishment, her mother went limp in midsentence.

Kathryn grabbed the cup just in time to prevent it from spilling down the front of her mother's nightgown.

After setting the cup aside, she laid her hand on her mother's brow. It felt warm. Too warm. There were dark shadows under her eyes and she looked pale. So pale. Had Basil hurt her worse than they thought? Her breathing was shallow and erratic.

Frightened, Kathryn called for Nan and Mrs. Shumway. But it was Cabrera she wanted. Where was he when she needed him?

Deep in his lair in the bowels of the manor, Roan fought his way out of the Dark Sleep, awakened by Kathryn's distress. It was like fighting his way through layers of thick, black fog. He had roused himself during the day only a handful of times in his long existence as a vampire, and each time it had been a matter of survival.

But he couldn't deny the need to help Kathryn.

Rising, he pulled on his trousers and a shirt, ran a hand through his hair, then willed himself to the corridor outside the guest room. He stood there a moment before opening the door and stepping inside.

Nan and the cook stood near the bed, wringing their hands.

"Cabrera!" Kathryn's voice was thick with relief when she saw him.

He didn't have to ask what was wrong. Her mother was unconscious.

"Do something!" Kathryn cried. "I think she's dying!"

After sending Nan and Mrs. Shumway out of the room, Cabrera examined Victoria. He wasn't a doctor, but he had lived a long time, seen sickness and death in all its forms. "I think she's bleeding internally."

Kathryn stared at him.

"There are faint bruises on her back and stomach. I think your stepfather beat her regularly. This last time he must have hit her with more force than usual."

"Can you do anything?"

"I can try. Why don't you wait outside?"

"Why? What are you going to do?"

"I'm going to give her a little of my blood."

Kathryn's eyes widened in horror. "Your *blood?* I don't want you to make her a vampire!"

"Do you remember when I visited you in the hospital?"

"Yes."

"You were dying. I gave you some of my blood."

"How?"

"I compelled you to drink it."

All the color drained from her face as she sank into the chair beside the bed. "I . . . I drank from you? Am I . . . ?"

"Kathryn, trust me. You are not going to become what I am. When I compelled you to drink, I didn't know if it would help you recover or not. All I knew was that you were dying." He scrubbed a hand over his jaw. "I figured if my blood didn't make you stronger, it wasn't likely to hurt you." He had gambled with her life and won.

She nibbled on her thumbnail as she digested what he'd said.

He knew it was only a matter of time before she asked the obvious question. He wasn't surprised when it came, only surprised she hadn't asked it sooner.

"Did you drink from me?"

The truth? Or a lie?

"Did you?" she demanded, her voice rising.

"Yes."

"More than once?"

Again, he debated whether to go with the truth or a

lie. "Yes." Thus far, he had only taken a little each time, although the temptation to take it all was ever present.

Victoria moaned softly, drawing Kathryn's attention. Gaining her feet, she took her mother's hand in hers. "I'm here, Mama," she murmured. "Please, don't leave me."

Kathryn bowed her head, wishing she knew what to do. In the end, there was only one choice. She couldn't let her mother die, not if there was any way, however morbid, to prevent it. Keeping her back to Cabrera, she said, "Help her, please."

"You should go. It will only take a moment."

Kathryn shook her head.

"Very well."

Moving to the other side of the bed, Roan bit into his left wrist.

Kathryn gasped as he gently pried her mother's mouth open and let his blood—so dark a red it was almost black—drip onto her tongue. She pressed a hand to her stomach, repulsed by the idea that he had done the same to her. And yet, she should be grateful. He had saved her life, after all.

Roan ran his tongue over the wound in his wrist. The bleeding stopped immediately. "Give her a little wine and keep her warm."

"All right. How long until we know if it worked?"

"Perhaps by tonight. Certainly by the morning."

"Thank you. Whether it works or not, thank you for trying." Rounding the end of the bed, she went up on her tiptoes and kissed him.

It was meant to be a gesture of gratitude, but it quickly turned into something far more intimate than anything they had shared before. He wrapped his arm around her waist, drawing her body close to his. His lips were firm and cool. She shivered as his free hand slid up her back to delve into the hair at her nape. Lightning shot through her when his tongue caressed hers.

And then, as he had on other occasions, he put her away from him. "I'll see you tonight."

She looked up at him, confused by the myriad sensations he had aroused in her. "Where are you going?"

"I need to go," he said, fighting the urge to carry her down to his lair and keep her at his side while he rested. "The sun is up."

She frowned as it occurred to her that this was the first time she had seen him during the day. "You're awake. How?"

"You needed me," he said, his voice thick. "And now I really must rest." He brushed a kiss across her cheek, then vanished from the room.

Kathryn stared at the place where he had been standing. How amazing, to be able to just disappear like that. What did it feel like? How did he do it? And how kind he was, to rouse himself from his bed—if he slept in a bed—simply because she had needed him.

Sometimes his being able to read her thoughts was a good thing.

Kathryn sat at her mother's bedside all that day. Nan and Mrs. Shumway looked in on her from time to time, bringing her meals or a cup of tea, or merely staying for a few moments to keep her company and offer what encouragement they could.

It was, Kathryn thought as the clock downstairs struck four, the longest day of her life. Pushing up from the chair, she walked around the room, then paused beside the bed to lay a hand on her mother's brow. Was it just wishful thinking, or was the color returning to her cheeks?

The temperature of her skin felt normal. Her breathing was easier.

For the first time, she believed her mother might get better.

It was just before dark when Nan poked her head into the room. "Miss Kathryn, there's a man waiting on the porch to see you."

"A man? Who is it?"

"He didn't say, miss."

"Did he ask for me?"

"Not exactly. He just asked for the lady of the house."

Kathryn glanced at her mother. She was still asleep. "Will you stay with her until I return?"

"Of course, miss."

Curious about who the visitor could be, Kathryn made her way slowly down the corridor to the stairs. She had no friends in town, and certainly no male acquaintances. Likely it was one of Cabrera's friends, perhaps one of the men he played cards with. But why would the man ask for her?

It was not yet dark, so she had no fear that it might be Pascual. Taking a deep breath, she opened the door to find a middle-aged man waiting on the porch. He had short, brown hair, brown eyes, and a wicked scar down the left side of his face.

After removing his hat, he said, "I'm sorry to bother you, *mademoiselle*. I'm looking for Roan Cabrera. I was told he's unavailable."

"And you are?"

"Gilen Leblanc."

"Mr. Cabrera isn't here at the moment. Might I ask why you wish to see him?"

"It's a private matter. Do you know when he'll be back?"

There was something about him, she thought, something that roused her distrust. "I'm sorry, I have no idea."

His gaze pierced hers.

He knows I'm lying, she thought, and stiffened her spine. "If I see Mr. Cabrera, I'll tell him you're looking for him."

"Please do. One word of caution. If I were you, I would leave this house and never return."

A chill ran down Kathryn's spine, and with it the certain knowledge that he knew Cabrera was a vampire. "Good day, sir."

He swept her a bow, settled his hat on his head, and left the house.

Going to the window beside the front door, Kathryn watched him descend the stairs. When he reached the driveway, he paused to glance over his shoulder, his gaze sweeping the house before he climbed into the waiting carriage.

When she entered the parlor, she was surprised to find Roan waiting for her in front of the fireplace.

"Who was here?"

"Someone looking for you. He said his name was Gilen Leblanc. Is he a friend of yours?"

Roan shook his head. "Never heard of him. Did he say what he wanted?"

"No. He told me I should leave here and never come back."

"It's probably good advice."

Kathryn frowned. "What's going on?"

Lifting his head, Roan took a deep breath. Leblanc's scent lingered in the air. Like all hunters, he carried the smell of death with him. It had been strong enough to rouse him from the Dark Sleep. "He was likely here for my head or the bounty on it. Or both."

"There's a reward for your head? Why?" Good Lord, was he a wanted criminal *and* a vampire?

"There are hunters who are dedicated to destroying my kind, and others who only hunt vampires with a price on their heads. I've no way of knowing which category Leblanc falls in. But I'll give him this—he's a brave man to come looking for me in my home." Had Katherine not been home, Roan had no doubt Leblanc would have searched the manor from top to bottom in hopes of finding his lair.

"What would have happened if you'd been the one to answer the door?"

Roan shrugged. "One of us would be dead."

Kathryn thought about what Cabrera had said as she made her way back to her mother's room. *One of us would be dead*. He'd said it so calmly, so matter-of-factly, as if there was no doubt in his mind as to the outcome.

She was reaching for the latch when the door flew open. "Oh, miss, I was just coming to find you. Your mother's awake!"

Kathryn hurried toward the bed, a wave of relief sweeping through her when she saw Victoria sitting up.

"Mama, how do you feel?"

Victoria smiled. "Better than I have in months, dear. It's like a miracle."

A miracle, indeed, Kathryn thought. And his name was Roan Cabrera.

* * *

Roan grunted softly when he heard the good news about Kathryn's mother. Perhaps he should bottle his blood and sell it to hospitals.

He quickly dismissed the idea, his thoughts turning toward Gilen Leblanc. At first, the hunter's name hadn't rung a bell. Thinking about it as he left the house, he knew he had heard the name before, perhaps thirty years ago, in France.

Vampires had been numerous in Paris back then, indiscriminate in their choice of prey. When a fledgling killed the daughter of a prominent member of society, the French government had offered a handsome bounty on vampires.

Tempted by the generous reward, men—and a few adventurous women—had become hunters overnight. They had swarmed into Paris from all parts of the country. Leblanc and his younger brother, Farrin, had quickly become two of the most notorious, with more kills to their credit than anyone else. Just their names had been enough to strike terror into the hearts of vampires, young and old alike.

Roan frowned. Leblanc's presence now had to be a coincidence.

Or was it?

Chapter Twenty-One

Kathryn was in the parlor, sitting on the floor in front of the fireplace, when Roan entered the room.

Sitting cross-legged beside her, he asked, "How's your mother?"

"Better, thanks to you. So much better, she insists on going home."

"You know that's not a good idea."

"I tried to talk her out of it, but she's determined to go and take me with her. She thinks . . ." Kathryn clamped her lips shut.

"What does she think?"

"She's convinced that you want . . . that you're going to . . ." Her cheeks turned pink as her voice trailed off.

"Ah. I think I understand."

Kathryn nodded. "So, she wants to leave. And since I can't tell her *why* we need to stay, I don't know what to do."

"I see your problem. I have a solution, though you may not like it."

She lifted an inquiring brow.

"If I burn your house down, you'll have little choice but to stay here."

"What!"

"Your mother won't know who did it, and with nowhere else to go . . ." He shrugged.

"But . . ." She bit down on her lower lip. "There must be another way." How could she agree to such a thing? What if her mother ever found out Roan had burned down their home with her blessing?

"It's an old building," he remarked. "It won't take much to burn it to the ground. I'll build you a new house. One with no bad memories."

"There's nothing in it worth saving," Kathryn said, thinking aloud. "My stepfather sold everything my mother had that was of any value long ago."

"Is there anything in it that you want?"

"No."

"So, you're all right with my solution?"

Kathryn nodded slowly. Truth be told, she would be more than happy to see the place that held so many un-happy memories go up in smoke.

Late that night, after satisfying his hunger, Roan set the Darlington's farm house on fire.

In the morning, over breakfast, Kathryn told her mother about the fire.

"The house is no great loss," Victoria said with a sigh. "But it leaves us with no place to go. We might be able to go and stay with my old friend Agnes."

"I have some good news," Kathryn said. "Mr. Cabrera has offered to rebuild the house for us."

"No." Victoria shook her head emphatically. "That will only put us deeper in his debt."

"Mama, I don't want to go stay with Agnes and her six children. They only have three small bedrooms. We'd have to sleep on the floor. And they barely have enough food for themselves. I don't think we should refuse Cabrera's offer. He's never here during the day and he has more than enough room."

Victoria spread a generous amount of strawberry jam on her biscuit, her expression pensive as she glanced around the dining room, taking in the striped paper, the heavy sideboard, the bountiful breakfast spread before them. "I suppose we can stay," she decided, "since I'll be here to chaperone you."

That afternoon, to Victoria's chagrin, Kathryn insisted they go shopping in town.

"We have no money," Victoria said with a woeful shake of her head. "And no credit."

"Mama, Cabrera said we could charge our purchases on his account. It's only a loan, until I find a job, or you do. You can't wear that old dress you had on when he brought you home. It's torn and stained beyond repair. Anyway, I told Nan to burn it. We're starting a new life and you need new clothes."

Victoria's lips tightened as she looked at the frock Mrs. Shumway had lent her. She wanted to argue with Kat, but the promise of a new dress, something she hadn't had in years, was too tempting. She would keep track of how much they spent and, one way or another, she would repay Mr. Cabrera.

Gilen Leblanc knocked on the door of Cabrera's house. Earlier, he had seen the lovely young woman he had talked to before get into a carriage with an older woman and drive away from the manor.

It was the moment he had been waiting for.

When there was no answer, he knocked again, harder this time.

From within, a voice asked, "Who's there?"

"I'm here to see Mr. Cabrera," Gilen replied, keeping his voice light and friendly. One gentleman paying an afternoon visit to another.

"I'm sorry, the master's not here."

"Roan will want to see me. It's a matter of urgent business regarding Miss Kathryn."

Nan hesitated. What should she do?

The man knocked again. "I'm only in town today," he called.

Nan opened the door just a crack. The man on the porch was dressed like a fine gentleman. Did she dare disobey Roan's orders and let the man inside? Best not to, she decided.

She was easing the door closed when the man pushed his way into the house and strode into the parlor as if he had every right to be there. "I'll just wait."

Nan followed him uncertainly. "I think you should leave, sir. I don't know when the master will return."

"I'm in no hurry," Gilen assured her. "Just go about your duties. Don't worry about me."

Nan stared at him, her fingers worrying the hem of her apron. "Would you like some refreshment?"

"No, thank you." Taking a seat on the sofa, he smiled at her.

Biting down on her lower lip, Nan went upstairs to finish changing the linens in the bedroom. Mr. Cabrera never had company. She wasn't quite sure what was expected of her when someone came to call. She wished

Mrs. Shumway was here, but it was her day off and she had gone to visit her granddaughter.

Gilen waited five minutes before going in search of Cabrera's lair. In his experience, vampires preferred to rest below stairs or below ground. With that thought in mind, he moved silently from room to room, looking for the door that led to the cellar.

He found it in a small nook off the kitchen. Excitement quickened his breathing as he reached into his coat pocket for the stub of a candle and a match. After lighting the candle, he tossed the spent match aside and pulled a stout wooden stake from inside his coat, then opened the door.

Candlelight flickered on the gray stone walls as he slowly descended the narrow staircase. He wrinkled his nose against the stench as he passed several cells. Rows of wine racks stood in the center of the floor. Frowning, he paused and did a slow turn.

And that was when he saw it—a simple wooden coffin half-hidden below the staircase.

This was it!

Swallowing hard, he spilled a little wax on the floor and set the candle in it. Then, holding the stake tight, he lifted the heavy lid.

"Looking for me?"

The lid of the casket slammed down as Leblanc whirled around, his heart hammering like thunder in his ears when he saw a shadowy figure separate itself from the darkness of the room. An oath erupted from his lips. "Cabrera."

"It isn't polite to enter a gentleman's chamber without an invitation."

Leblanc stared at Cabrera in shock. The sun was up. Why hadn't the vampire been resting in his coffin? But there was no time to ponder that now. He licked his lips as he weighed his chances of driving the stake into the vampire's heart before Cabrera ripped out his throat.

Roan smiled, revealing his fangs.

"Are you going to kill me?"

"It seems only fair, don't you think, since that's what you were going to do to me."

Leblanc blinked the sweat from his eyes. Determined not to go down without a fight, he squared his shoulders, took a wider stance, and tightened his grip on the stake.

Only, the fight never came. He gasped as Cabrera darted forward in a blur of motion, plucked the stake from his hand, and broke it into tiny pieces. "What are you going to do now?"

"Just get it over with!" Leblanc snarled.

Roan flashed his fangs again. "Get the hell out of my house. If you show your face around here again, you won't get a second chance to walk away."

Fighting the urge to run—and constantly glancing over his shoulder—Leblanc hurried up the stairs and out of the house, the sound of Cabrera's amused laughter echoing in his ears.

Kathryn frowned in the act of stepping out of the carriage as a man ran by and jumped on the back of a horse tethered near the gate. Was that Gilen Leblanc? The bounty hunter? What on earth was he doing here?

Relieved that they had cut their outing short, and filled with a sudden dread, she hopped to the ground and ran up the path to the front door. She flew by Nan and then came to an abrupt halt. She had no idea where to find Cabrera. He had told her he would take his rest elsewhere, but on more than one occasion, she had been certain he was somewhere in the house, though she had no idea why she felt that way. She knew he didn't sleep in any of the bedrooms.

"Kathryn, what's wrong?" Coming up behind her, Victoria dropped down on the sofa, one hand pressed to her heart. "You ran in here like you were being pursued by devils."

"It was nothing. Nan, was that Mr. Leblanc who just ran out of here?"

The maid glanced around the parlor. "I expect so, miss, since I don't see him now."

"What did he want?"

"He was lookin' for Mr. Cabrera. I told him the master wasn't home, but he said he'd wait. I wasn't here in the parlor when he left, but no one else has come calling."

"He left in a powerful hurry," Victoria remarked. "Perhaps he was called away."

"Yes, ma'am. Miss Kathryn, would you and your mother care for tea?"

"None for me," Victoria said. "I'm going upstairs to rest for a while."

"None for me either, Nan," Kathryn said. "I think I'll go riding. I've neglected Bianca these past few days."

Wishing it was safe to ride the trails outside the walls, Kathryn saddled the mare and led her into the fenced enclosure behind the stable. She rode for almost an hour, her thoughts in turmoil. Where was Cabrera? Was he all right? What had Gilen Leblanc been doing here? A foolish question, she mused, reining the mare to a walk. Leblanc was a vampire hunter. Cabrera was a vampire.

She shook her head. Strange as it seemed, she sometimes forgot that.

And what about that other vampire? Pascual? He was still out there, somewhere.

But, thanks to the wards Roan had told her about, she was safe behind the high walls that surrounded the manor.

Victoria decided to take her evening meal in her room.

"Are you feeling all right, Mama?" Kathryn asked.

"Yes, child. I just have some thinking to do." Sitting on the edge of the bed, she removed her shoes. "I'll see you in the morning."

Concerned, Kathryn kissed her mother's cheek, then slowly made her way downstairs, where she picked at her own supper.

She was lingering over a second cup of tea when Cabrera slid into the chair across from hers.

"You look troubled," he said. "Is something wrong?"

"What was Leblanc doing here?"

"Looking for me, of course."

She started to ask why, but the answer was obvious. Leblanc was a hunter, Roan was a vampire. She was surprised, and relieved, that there had been no blood shed on either side.

"Is anything else bothering you, Kathryn?"

"I don't know. My mother seems . . . distant. She spent most of the day in her room, and then took supper there."

"I imagine being here upsets her. She's worried about her future, and yours. She's lost her husband and her home. Am I forgetting anything?"

"No." Kathryn smiled in spite of herself. "I guess I can't blame her for being worried."

"I've arranged for the rebuilding of your house to start tomorrow. I've instructed the builder, Alan Hastings, to set men to the task day and night. Will two bedrooms be sufficient or do you require another?"

"Two should be enough," she said, then frowned. "It might be nice to have an extra, in case one of Mama's friends comes to visit." Taking his hands in hers, she said, "You know we can never repay you for all you've done for us. For all you're doing."

"Have I asked for anything other than your company?"

"No, but . . ."

"Victoria thinks I'm luring you into a false sense of security."

"Are you?"

"No, Kat. It pleases me to have you here." A smile teased his lips. "If you feel the need to thank me, a kiss will do."

Her heart jumped into her throat when he stood and rounded the table. Taking her hand, he pulled her gently to her feet and into his arms.

A thought carried them to the sofa before the fireplace. Sitting, he cradled her on his lap, his arm at her waist, his hand lightly stroking her back as he lowered his head and pressed his lips to hers. Heat suffused her. Heat that had nothing to do with the flames that sprang to life as if by magic in the hearth and everything to do with being so close to him. His mouth moved over hers, teasing, tasting, testing. She clung to him, her arms around his neck, wanting to be closer. To be a part of him. To have him be a part of her.

"Kathryn." He whispered her name against her lips. "Do you know how much I want you? How easy it would be for me to take you?"

"Then do it."

He drew back, his eyes burning into hers. "Be careful, Kathryn. You're treading on dangerous ground."

His warning sent a sudden chill down her spine, a stark reminder that Roan Cabrera was no ordinary man.

But she made no move to get up.

"Kathryn, you're playing with fire."

"You won't hurt me."

"Won't I?"

She shook her head, her fingertips caressing his nape. "I trust you."

"Foolish little girl."

"I'm not a little girl."

He groaned low in his throat. She most definitely wasn't a little girl. The warmth of her breasts penetrated his shirt. Her kisses were more tempting than the blood he craved, her touch more welcome and inviting than that of any other woman he had ever known. And he had known many.

"Kathryn, do you know what you're asking?"

"For you to love me."

"I do love you. But if I *make* love to you, that will change everything."

Lifting her from his lap, he lowered her onto the sofa. Rising, he gazed down at her. "Think about it tomorrow, about what it will mean, sharing your life with a vampire. The secrets you'll have to keep, the lies you'll have to tell."

Bending down, he kissed her lightly. "I'll see you tomorrow night."

"Where are you going?"

"I have some thinking to do, too. And I need to feed."

Kathryn watched, as, with a wave of his hand, Roan vanished from her sight.

Vampire.

Leaning back, she stared at the flames.

Think about what it will mean, sharing your life with a vampire.

I need to feed.

Without his arms around her, she began to have second thoughts. He was hundreds of years older than she was, yet he looked no more than thirty.

He would never grow old.

He lived by night.

She didn't know where he rested during the day. Perhaps he would never trust her enough to tell her.

A part of his life would always be closed to her, a mystery she might never unravel. Perhaps a mystery best kept that way.

Getting to her feet, she paced the floor. He had been nothing but kind to her. He had saved her life, perhaps for his own selfish reasons, but she was grateful nonetheless. He had been kind to her, shown her a life she had only dreamed of. He had freed her mother from Darlington's cruelty, and then saved her life.

Kathryn sighed. He intrigued her. Sometimes he frightened her.

And yet, in spite of what he was, she wanted him desperately.

And he could be hers, if she only had the courage to take what she wanted.

Roan prowled the dark streets. Kathryn's scent lingered on his clothing, on his hands. He could taste her on his tongue. She was so young, so innocent. So damn tempting. He could have taken her at any time since he'd brought her to his home and then erased the memory from her mind. He could have compelled her to come to him willingly, to do whatever he asked. But he had never done anything like that before and the thought of turning Kathryn into little more than a mindless creature was loathsome. He liked his women warm and willing, and she was that and more.

In her innocence, she wanted him. But she had never been with a man, didn't really know what she wanted, only that she yearned for his touch, for more than his kisses.

But he was an old vampire, and an old-fashioned one, as well. He would not take her unless she was his wife. Perhaps he should have made that clear.

He couldn't imagine her wanting to spend the rest of her life with him. She couldn't know how difficult it would be, nor could he imagine how she would feel when she grew old and he did not.

You could bring her across. The words drifted through the back of his mind. He smiled as he pictured her as a vampire—her youthful beauty subtly enhanced by the Dark Gift, his forever.

He paused in the shadows. What was he thinking? Did he want to take that rare flower and condemn her to a life in darkness?

It was a question he refused to answer.

Chapter Twenty-Two

"You're very quiet this morning," Victoria remarked, adding a spoonful of honey to her tea.

Kathryn sipped her breakfast cocoa, then set the cup aside. "I've got a lot on my mind."

"Care to share what's troubling you?"

"Cabrera asked me about the house, about whether two bedrooms were enough. I said maybe three would be better. You know, in case we have guests sometime." It was a poor lie but the only one she could think of.

"That's what has you looking so distracted this lovely morning? Bedrooms?"

"Mama . . ."

Victoria reached across the table and took Kathryn's hand in hers. "Whatever it is, you can tell me."

Kathryn nodded. She longed to tell her mother everything, but she couldn't. Cabrera's voice whispered through her mind again. *Think about what it will mean, sharing your life with a vampire. The secrets you'll have to keep. The lies you'll have to tell.*

"Kathryn, I can't help you if you won't confide in me."

How was she going to explain her decision to stay with Cabrera, to be his mistress? He had said once they made love, he wouldn't let her go. She hoped he'd meant marriage, but he hadn't mentioned that.

Taking a deep breath, Kathryn blurted, "He's asked me to stay with him indefinitely, to . . ." She couldn't say the words, but she was sure the heat rising in her cheeks told her mother everything she needed to know.

"I don't understand. You're already living here, at least temporarily What else . . . ?" Victoria shook her head as she took in Kathryn's meaning. "I told you, didn't I? I told you he wanted something from you, something you can only give once."

"I love him, Mama. I want to be with him in every way."

"If he cared for you, he would not ask such a thing."

"He does care. The choice is mine."

"Kathryn, you hardly know this man. You don't know anything about him."

"I know that he saved my life. *And* yours." She paused to take a deep breath. "And that I love him."

"Oh, Kat. I hope you're not mistaking . . . that you're not thinking—" Victoria's cheeks turned bright pink as she said in a rush, "That your attraction to a rather handsome man is anything more than that."

"It is more. Much more! He . . . he needs me."

Victoria looked vaguely amused. "Believe me, that man doesn't need anyone."

"You're making assumptions, aren't you, Mama? You've only known him a few days."

"And you've only known him a few weeks."

"I'm sorry you don't approve," Kathryn said resolutely. "But my mind is made up."

Roan woke from the Dark Sleep with a sense of dread. He shouldn't have said anything. No woman was going to want to share his life, at least not his whole life. Without intending to, he had given Kathryn something of an ultimatum—my way or no way.

Going upstairs to his room, he washed his hands and face, dressed, ran a comb through his hair. Opening his senses, he tracked the people living in his house. Nan and Mrs. Shumway were in the kitchen, cleaning up after supper. Victoria was in the library, reading.

Kathryn was strolling through the gardens, headed toward the stables. He caught the smell of the apple in her hand, heard the creak of the barn door as she stepped inside.

He was deciding whether to spend a few minutes with her before he went hunting when her horrified cry pierced the night.

A thought took him to her side. She sat on the ground beside Tim, stroking his hair. The boy lay sprawled on his back, his head in her lap, his pale gray eyes wide and staring. Thin rivers of bright red blood leaked from the punctures in the side of his neck, turning her skirt from pale pink to crimson.

He took it all in at a glance—the open gate in the back fence, the churned-up earth left by the boy as he crawled back through the gate, the smattering of blood drops from the gate toward the barn.

Pascual's scent—still fresh—was all over the boy's body.

Kathryn looked up at him, her eyes wide with horror. "Is he . . ."

"Yes."

"Can you . . . can you save him, the way you saved me?"

"No. He's gone."

"What was he doing outside the gate?" she asked, her voice thick with unshed tears.

"I don't know. Pascual must have lured him out there

somehow." Vampires were notorious for being able to mimic other voices, even animals. It would have been easy for Pascual to imitate a wounded animal and draw the boy from the safety of the yard.

Reaching down, he lifted Kathryn to her feet. Had she come outside a few minutes earlier, it might have been she lying there with her life's blood watering the ground. "Come on," he said, urging her toward the back door. "There's nothing you can do for him."

"Why?" she asked sorrowfully. "Why kill him? He was just a boy."

"It's what vampires do."

She looked up at him, her face pale, her eyes filled with unshed tears. "You don't do that, do you? Kill innocent children? Tell me you don't."

"No," he said, his voice flat. "But I will surely kill Pascual if I ever get my hands on him."

She glanced down at Tim's body, silent tears tracking her cheeks. "We can't just leave him lying there!"

"Don't worry, I'll look after him. Come along now, love."

Victoria, Nan, and Mrs. Shumway were gathered at the back door when Roan and Kathryn returned to the house.

"Mercy, what's happened?" Victoria exclaimed, seeing the blood on Kathryn's dress. "Is that her blood? Is she hurt?"

"No." Roan led Kathryn into the parlor and settled her on the sofa. "I don't want any of you going outside. There's been an accident in the yard."

"What kind of accident?" Victoria asked, hovering over her daughter.

"Not now," he said curtly. "Mrs. Shumway, please get

Kathryn a glass of wine. Nan, would you get her a blanket? Victoria, come sit beside her. I'll be back shortly."

He went out the back door to the stable. After wrapping the boy's body in a horse blanket, he grabbed a shovel, then willed himself to the potter's field outside of town, where he quickly dug a grave and laid the still-warm body inside. It took only moments to fill the hole. When it was done, he stood there, hands tightly clenched, his gut churning with anger.

Leaving the cemetery, he scoured the city from one end to the other. He caught faint traces of Pascual's presence, but the vampire was nowhere to be found.

When Roan returned to the house, he found Victoria waiting for him in the parlor, hands folded in her lap.

"I'd like to speak to you for a moment," she said.

"As you wish."

"Kathryn tells me she wants to stay here, with you."

He nodded.

"You know it's not seemly for an unmarried young woman to live in a man's house."

He nodded again.

"I want you to send her away before her reputation is completely ruined."

"She isn't safe anywhere else."

"What does that mean?"

"It means an old enemy of mine is in town. He's a madman. He's already killed several women. He killed Tim, the young man who worked in my stables."

Her face paled. "You said it was an accident."

"I didn't want to alarm you or the household staff with the truth."

"And you think this man means to do Kathryn harm?"

"I'm sure of it. As for Kathryn's reputation . . ." He smiled faintly. "Your presence here should keep idle tongues from wagging."

Victoria nodded slowly. "Yes. Yes, that's true." She pursed her lips, then said, in a rush, "Please don't take advantage of my daughter. She's so young, and she knows so little of men, or their base desires."

"Rest assured, madam, I have no intention of defiling Kathryn."

"I'd very much like to believe you, but I've seen the way you look at her," Victoria said candidly. "The way she looks at you."

"The attraction between us is quite real," he admitted. "And very strong. I'm afraid there's nothing I can do about that. But I'm not some callow youth who can't control his—how did you put it? Base desires."

Victoria pressed her hands to her suddenly heated cheeks. Rising, she mumbled a hurried "good night" and fled the room.

Roan stared after her, wondering if he would be able to do as he'd said and keep a tight rein on his hunger for the fair Kathryn, who was even now lurking in the hallway. "You can come out now," he called softly.

Looking slightly abashed, she came around the corner.

He noticed she had changed her clothes and washed her face, though her eyes were still haunted. "Taken to eavesdropping, have you?"

"I didn't mean to, but . . ." She made a vague gesture with her hand. "Eavesdroppers often hear highly interesting things."

"Indeed. And what did *you* hear?"

"Nothing I didn't already know. My mother is worried about me. About my reputation."

"What else?"

"That you're attracted to me."

A faint smile curved his lips. "I'm sure that comes as no surprise. What else did you hear?"

"Never mind."

He laughed softly as he drew her into his arms. "I know a way to soothe your mother's fears about your good name."

Head tilted back, she gazed up at him. "Do you?"

He nodded. "You could marry me."

Speechless, lips slightly parted in surprise, she stared up at him, everything else forgotten. A moment passed. Then another. "Marry you?"

"Judging from your expression, it doesn't appear to be one of my better ideas."

"But you . . . you're . . ."

"Not human?"

"I wasn't going to say that. But . . . married? I didn't know vampires even got married. I mean . . . they can't have children, so . . ." Her voice trailed off.

"So, what's the point?"

She'd hurt his feelings, she thought, hearing the edge in his tone.

He took a step away from her. "You should go to bed now."

"Cabrera . . . Roan . . ."

"Get out of here."

She didn't argue. Feeling hurt and confused, she ran up the stairs to her room and locked the door behind her.

Roan stared after her. Cursing himself for being a complete and utter fool to think she would ever be his, he stormed out of the house, his anger spurring his hunger.

Pity the poor mortal who crossed his path this night, he thought darkly. Their odds of survival were slim.

Kathryn paced the floor of her room, her thoughts in turmoil. He had proposed marriage, and tonight of all nights. An image of Tim, lying dead in her lap, swam to the surface of her mind and she shook it away.

Roan had proposed to her. Try as she might, she couldn't wrap her mind around the thought of being his wife. Why would anyone want to wed a vampire? True, she was attracted to him. She loved his kisses and the way it felt to be in his arms, but . . . marriage? She wanted a man who could share her whole life, a father for her children. Someone to grow old with. She dreamed of seeing her sons and daughters grow up and have children of their own.

But did she want to share another man's bed? Bear another man's children?

Life with Roan would be far different from the life she had once imagined. He couldn't give her children. He would never grow old. They would never share a meal, laugh at the antics of their grandchildren, walk hand in hand in the sun, go to church at Easter and Christmas. Did he ever miss doing the ordinary things mortals took for granted? Did he regret that he would never father a child? Or did becoming a vampire make one forget about the mundane things?

Tears stung her eyes. She hadn't meant to hurt him. He had saved her life, saved her mother's life, given her a home. But marriage . . . Wailing softly, she threw herself on the bed and let her tears flow.

She cried for her own misery. She cried for Tim, who

had been killed by a monster for no reason other than as vengeance again Roan.

That thought brought her up short. They were all in danger, she thought. Her mother. Mrs. Shumway and Nan. Herself. She had known that before, of course, but Tim's death made it more real. More frightening.

Drowning in misery, she cried herself to sleep.

Chapter Twenty-Three

Roan prowled the dark streets, preying on any and all who crossed his path. He had lived alone for centuries, needing no one, taking who and what he wanted with little regard for the consequences. He had never thought of himself as cruel, though he had been undoubtedly self-centered. Still, he had never taken a life without cause once he learned to control his hunger. He had never killed a child. Never ravaged a maiden. Never forced or compelled anyone to his bed.

Never loved anyone since Varinia.

Until now.

He had been a fool to propose marriage to Kathryn. It had been an impulse, born out of fear of losing her. *Like must marry like,* his mother had always said. She had been right about that, just as she had been right about everything else she had ever taught him all those centuries ago.

He unleashed a string of vile oaths as he cut across the street. The pain of Kathryn's rejection cut deep, more agonizing than the splash of holy water on preternatural flesh.

How could he have been such a fool? She cared for him; he knew that. She wanted him in the most primal way. But not enough to give herself to him. But then, it would take a very brave woman indeed to tie her life to his. He had no illusions about what he was. He was a monster in human form, a creature that survived on the blood of others.

In the days when he had first been turned, he had killed without a qualm, driven by the need for blood, terrified by that incessant craving. In those days, he had been willing to do anything to appease that awful thirst and the pain that accompanied it if he went too long without feeding.

He wondered fleetingly if the vampire who had turned him still existed. He had met Gyorgy when a band of Gypsies passed through their village. He had been fascinated by their colorful costumes, their carefree lifestyle. The women were exotic, with their dark flashing eyes and swirling skirts, the men handsome and exuberant, filled with the zest of life. When he'd been young, Roan's mother had often teased that he was a Gypsy, which only increased Roan's curiosity. The camp was filled with acrobats, jugglers, snake charmers, fortune-tellers, and ventriloquists. Decent people warned their children to stay away from them. They wandered where they would, subject to no one.

Roan had been lingering on the outskirts of their camp when Gyorgy spied him. *Come,* Gyorgy had said, slapping him on the back. *Join us for an evening of singing and dancing.* It had been a night unlike any Roan had known. Wine had flowed like water. High on Gypsy wine, he danced and sang as if he was, indeed, one of them. The women, both old and young, cast their eyes in his direction, flirting shamelessly, and he reveled in it.

Gyorgy was gregarious and charming, with a voice like an angel and the heart of a demon. Only later had Roan discovered there was a monster beneath the Gypsy's carefree demeanor.

To this day, Roan had no idea why Gyorgy had decided to turn him instead of drinking him dry. But turn him he had, draining Roan almost to the point of death. The following night, Gyorgy had told Roan what he had become and what he must do to survive. He had warned him to stay out of the sun and to beware of hunters, stated in lurid detail the ways he could be destroyed, then wished him well. When Roan woke the following night, the Gypsies had gone.

He was still amazed that he had survived that first, nightmare year, when all he could think of was satisfying his hellish thirst. He had never known anything like it—a brutal, insatiable hunger. He had fed on humans and animals alike, anything to ease the pain that engulfed him if he went too long without feeding. It had taken decades to learn to control the beast within, to learn that it was possible to satisfy his voracious hunger without killing his prey.

His kind had been hunted relentlessly in those dark days, when fear and superstition ruled the world. Things weren't so desperate now, but there were still hunters out there, men willing to risk their lives to destroy the undead. Men like Gilen Leblanc and his brother, Farrin.

Acceptance of what he was had come slowly but in time he had learned to fit into society again, to hide what he was, to feed often enough to keep the desire to kill at bay.

Tonight, with Kathryn's refusal still fresh in his mind, he realized he had been kidding himself for years. He was a vampire, a monster, and all the trappings of a fine gentleman would never change that fact.

It was near dawn when he returned home. He gazed up at the dark house for a long time before going inside.

The women of his household were asleep.

Going down to his lair, he stuffed a small fortune into a sack, wrote a note of farewell to Kathryn, and left both on her bedside table, where she would find them in the morning.

He gazed at her for several moments, memorizing the color of her hair, the curve of her cheek, the warm, sweet, womanly scent of her skin. Bending, he kissed her brow, then willed himself out of the house.

He was tempted to leave the country, but he couldn't do that, not while Juan Pascual still roamed the streets.

Not when Kathryn's life was in danger.

Chapter Twenty-Four

Kathryn woke late, her eyes swollen from the tears she had shed, her throat raw. Her dreams had been filled with dark images of chasing a tall man clad in a hooded black cloak through a thick mist, begging him to come back. Time and again she had awakened to find herself crying bitter tears of sorrow and regret.

Hours until nightfall. Hours until she would see Roan again. Hours until she could tell him she had made a dreadful mistake, that it didn't matter what he was, she loved him. Surely he would understand her initial trepidation and forgive her. His proposal had come as such an unexpected surprise. They scarcely knew each other and yet, sometimes she felt as if she had known him all her life.

She sat up, about to ring for Nan, when she saw the folded sheet of paper lying beside a small brown sack on the bedside table. Frowning, she picked up the letter.

My dearest Kathryn ~ I have decided to leave the city. Please make my home yours for as long as you wish. I hope you will stay here, where you will be safe from Pascual. I have warded the grounds so that he cannot enter. When I have dispatched

*him, I will send you word so that you no longer
need to be in fear for your life.*

  *Regarding the rebuilding of your home, I have
paid the builder in advance, though I would not
advise you to take possession while Pascual
still lives.*

  *There is enough money in the sack to cover the
cost of running the house and provide for your
immediate needs. I have also opened an account
for you, so that you need never worry about being
able to provide for yourself and your mother.*

                        Your humble servant,
                        R. Cabrera

She read it again, and yet again, unable to believe he
had left her without saying good-bye. But then, she knew
why he had gone and that it was all her fault.

"Oh, Roan," she murmured, pressing his letter to her
heart, "what have I done?"

"It's for the best," Victoria remarked when Kathryn explained what had happened over breakfast. "There was
something about that man, something . . ." She shook her
head. "I can't explain it, but I was never comfortable
around him. He carries an air of . . . of . . ." She frowned,
searching for the right words. "Of darkness. Yes, that's it.
Didn't you feel it?"

Kathryn shook her head. "No."

"I can understand your infatuation, daughter," Victoria
said with a sigh. "But he's too old for you. Too worldly-
wise. You'll soon get over it."

Kathryn stared at her mother. "No, I won't. I'm not a

foolish child. I know the difference between infatuation and love. Sadly, I didn't realize how much I loved him until it was too late." Pushing her untouched plate aside, she went down to the kitchen.

"Is there something you need?" the cook asked, wiping her hands on her apron.

"Yes. Do you know how to get in touch with Mr. Cabrera?"

Mrs. Shumway shook her head. "I'm afraid not. Is something amiss?"

"He's left," Kathryn said, her voice thick with unshed tears. "And I need to get in touch with him right away."

"Now, now, not to worry. I'm sure he'll be back by dark, like always."

"You don't understand! He hasn't gone for the day. He's gone for good."

"Are you sure?" Mrs. Shumway asked, her brow furrowing.

"Yes."

The cook was silent for several moments. "Will you be closing the house, then?"

"No. He's given us leave to stay as long as we wish. And enough money to pay your salary and Nan's for a good long time." More money than Kathryn had ever seen in her life, or hoped to see. Enough to live in comfort for as long as she lived. He loved her, she thought. No man would provide for a woman in such a way if he didn't. She fought back her tears. How could she have been so foolish as to let him go?

Leaving the house, Kathryn glanced nervously from side to side as she made her way toward the stable to feed Bianca, a chore Tim had previously taken care of. Poor Tim. Dead before he had ever really lived. She felt a sharp twinge of guilt. If she hadn't come to the manor, Roan would never have hired Tim and the boy would be alive today.

Bianca whinnied softly as Kathryn entered the barn. She mucked the stall, forked the mare some hay, filled the water bucket.

She stood outside the stall for several minutes, absently stroking the horse's neck. Where was Roan? Was he missing her as much as she missed him? Why was it that it was only after he had gone that she realized how deeply she cared for him?

If only she knew where he was, she would run to him and beg him to give her another chance. Please, she thought, please don't let it end like this.

Roan stalked the streets again; only, it wasn't his hunger that drove him this night but the need for vengeance. He searched every pub and bar, every house in the red light district, the dark alleys and abandoned buildings. He found no sign of Pascual and yet the vampire's scent was everywhere.

Frustrated by his inability to find his quarry, he dropped in at the Hare and Hound.

Molly approached him as soon as he stepped through the door. "We haven't seen you here in a while," she said, a pretty pout teasing her lips.

"I'm here now."

She smiled up at him, her brown eyes shining. "What would you like, milord Cabrera?"

"The usual. Are the gents downstairs?"

"Aye. Talking about the latest murder."

"Another one?"

She nodded. "Haven't ye heard? Some poor old scrub-woman was found dead out on Smythe Road." She lowered her voice. "They said she didn't have a drop of blood left in her body. Rumor has it there's a vampire afoot."

Roan grunted softly. "Be a good girl and bring me a glass of wine."

"Aye, milord," she said, bobbing a curtsy.

Head cocked, Roan watched her sashay toward the bar. She was a comely wench, eager to share his bed. He'd not bedded a woman in quite a while, he mused as he made his way downstairs. Perhaps she was just what he needed.

"There you are," Hampton remarked as Roan slid into an empty chair. "We've not seen much of you of late."

"Busy with that pretty young lass you've taken under your wing?" Westerbrook asked with a leer.

"A man can't spend all his time at the gaming tables."

Cormac shuffled the cards but didn't deal them out. "I take it you've heard about the latest murder?"

"Molly told me when I came in."

"There's a lot of talk about a vampire being responsible for these deaths," Lewiston said. "The police dismissed the notion at first, but this last body was drained of blood."

"Had two punctures in her neck, she did," Flaherty said. "They're taking it seriously now."

Westerbrook looked at Roan, his expression grim. "Dudley thinks it might be you."

"Indeed?"

Westerbrook nodded.

"And what makes him think that?"

"Some of us paid him a call the other night, to see how he's doing, you know, since Clara Beth was killed. I don't recall how the subject came up, but he remarked that he'd never seen you out and about in the afternoon."

"And that makes me a vampire?"

Lewiston cleared his throat. "Once we started thinking about it, we realized that none of us can remember ever seeing you during the day."

Sitting back, Roan folded his arms over his chest. "I can only assume you're joking, since if you really believed I was a vampire, none of you would be foolish enough to mention it to my face."

Flaherty burst out laughing. "I told you he'd see through your silly joke."

The other men at the table joined in the merriment. Until Westerbrook said, "Just where *do* you spend your days?"

"I have my own affairs to attend to," Roan replied easily. "Much like the rest of you. Are we playing cards or not?"

Cormac dealt a round and the conversation turned to the upcoming soiree to be held in honor of the engagement of Lewiston's eldest daughter.

An hour later, Roan took his leave.

Molly was waiting for him at the top of the stairs, one hand on her hip, a provocative smile curving her pretty pink lips. "Tonight, milord?"

His gaze moved over her. She had a slim but voluptuous figure, skin the color of fresh cream, and a promise in her lovely brown eyes.

Cupping her nape in his hand, he lowered his head and kissed her. "Tonight."

He couldn't take her home, so he took her to the Lion's Head Inn. He had fully intended to make love to her, to take what she had been offering for so long, but when she lay pliant in his embrace, he could think only of Kathryn, of how she had enriched his existence, of her sweet smile, her gentle laughter, the way she felt in his arms, the scent of her skin. When Molly reached for him, he trapped her gaze with his and mesmerized her with a look. After satisfying his hunger, he erased everything that had happened since they'd left the Hare and Hound and sent her on her way.

He left the inn shortly after she did.

Lost in thoughts of Kathryn, he paid little heed to the sound of footsteps behind him. He turned as they drew closer. Three of them. They looked harmless. Only when he started walking again did he realize he had misjudged them.

With a cry, they launched themselves toward him.

He cursed as one sprayed him with holy water while the other two drove silver-bladed knives into his chest and back, barely missing his heart.

With a roar, he flung the first man aside.

It was then a fourth man materialized out of the shadows.

It was Gilen Leblanc. Lifting a crossbow, the hunter fired a wooden stake into Roan's chest.

Roan fell back, gasping with pain as the wood, which had been dipped in holy water, buried itself deep in his chest scant inches from his heart.

Feeling himself weakening from the loss of blood and the burning agony of the wounds inflicted by the silver, he summoned the last of his rapidly waning strength to yank the stake from his flesh and then willed himself home.

Kathryn let out a cry of surprise when Roan suddenly materialized in the parlor. She stared at him in horror. The entire front of his shirt and coat were soaked with blood.

Jumping up from the sofa, she took a step toward him, only to pause when she saw the red in his eyes. "What's happened?"

Before he could answer, Victoria stepped into the room, followed by Mrs. Shumway and Nan.

"Merciful heavens!" Victoria exclaimed as Roan dropped to his knees. Dark red blood leaked onto the carpet with no evidence of stopping.

Mrs. Shumway dropped the tea tray she was holding, sending cups, saucers, and a teapot rolling across the floor.

Nan took one look at all the blood and fainted dead away.

"Roan!" Kathryn hurried toward him, alarmed by the way he knelt there, unmoving, his face as white as parchment, his cheeks sunken. "Roan, say something."

"Blood," he gasped. "I need . . . blood."

"What's he talking about?" Victoria asked.

"Not now, Mama!" Kathryn said sharply. "Mrs. Shumway, get Nan out of here. Mama, go to bed." She bit down on her lower lip as Roan toppled over onto his side. "Roan, tell me what to do!"

"Give me . . . your arm."

Kathryn stared at him, her stomach lurching when she realized what he wanted. Kneeling beside him, she rolled up the sleeve of her robe, only vaguely aware that her mother and Mrs. Shumway were carrying Nan out of the room.

Murmuring, "Forgive me," Roan took hold of her arm, closed his eyes, and sank his fangs into her wrist.

Kathryn tensed, but there was no pain. Sighing, she brushed a lock of his hair from his face. He had taken her blood before, she knew, but only a little, and never like this, when she was conscious and it was a matter of life and death. For the first time, she felt like prey.

"What is going on here?"

Kathryn glanced over her shoulder to see her mother standing in the doorway, one hand pressed to her heart, her eyes wide with horror and disbelief. "Mama, please go."

"What are you doing? What is *he* doing?"

"He's drinking my blood. Now, please, just go away."

"Stop it this instant!" Victoria took a step forward, fully intending to drag her daughter away. A look from Kathryn stopped her.

Victoria stood there another minute, then, looking as if she was going to be sick at any moment, she dashed out of the room.

Kathryn looked back at Roan, relieved to see he appeared to be much better. There was a faint tinge of color in his cheeks, his breathing seemed easier, the lines of pain that had bracketed his mouth were gone.

She was feeling light-headed when he released her arm.

"Are you all right?" he asked. "Kat?"

She nodded. "Just a little woozy."

"Stay here."

Before she could argue, he rose in a single fluid motion and left the room.

He returned moments later carrying a large goblet of wine. "Drink this," he said, handing her the glass. "All of it."

She did as he asked and immediately felt better. "What happened to you?"

"Leblanc and three of his cronies caught me off guard."

She glanced at the rips in his shirt, at the blood drying on his clothing. "You could have been killed." She paused before asking, "What happened to them?"

A muscle throbbed in his jaw. "Nothing."

Kathryn set the glass on a nearby table. "I didn't think anyone could sneak up on you."

He grunted softly. Offering her his hand, he pulled her to her feet.

"What aren't you telling me, Roan?"

He didn't miss the fact that she had called him by his first name again. "I need to go and get cleaned up."

"Tell me."

"If you must know, I was thinking about you."

She stared up at him. "This happened . . . because of me?"

"So it would seem."

He took her hand in his and kissed her palm. The gesture sent tingles of awareness skittering through her.

"Thank you, Kathryn, for . . . you know."

She nodded, thinking he looked embarrassed by what he'd done. "What am I going to tell my mother? It won't take her long to put two and two together and get *vampire*."

"I was going to wipe the memory from her mind."

"Oh."

"You don't approve?"

"It seems wrong."

"Can she keep a secret?"

Kathryn shrugged. "Usually. But I don't know if she can keep this one."

"I'm going to get washed up and then I'll go have a talk with her."

"You won't hurt her?"

"No." He hesitated briefly, then bent down and kissed her brow. "I love you, Kathryn," he murmured fervently, and then he was gone.

Victoria looked up, startled, when Roan opened her bedroom door. Scrambling off the bed, she backed into a corner when he crossed the threshold and shut the door. "Go away!"

"Victoria, relax, I am not going to hurt you."

"I saw what you did to Kathryn."

"I needed her help."

"You drank her blood!"

"Yes." He stayed by the door, his hands in his pockets. "You know what I am?"

She nodded, her face drawn and tight.

"I need your promise that you won't tell anyone. Not just for my sake, but for yours and Kathryn's as well."

"And if I refuse?"

"Don't."

"Are you going to make my daughter what you are?"

"No. I would never do that. Not to her. Not to you." His gaze held hers. "Promise me, Victoria. Promise me you'll never breathe a word of this to anyone."

"I promise," she said quickly.

Too quickly. He didn't believe her for a moment. Capturing her gaze with his, he said, "Promise me, Victoria."

She looked at him, unblinking, as his mind took hold of hers. "I promise."

"Thank you." Opening the door, he backed out of the room. "And good night."

When he returned to the parlor, Kathryn was perched on the edge of the sofa, her expression apprehensive.

"Do you always heal so quickly?" she asked.

He nodded as he sank down on the sofa beside her. "It's one of the good things about being what I am."

"What did my mother say?"

"She won't tell anyone."

Katherine looked doubtful. "You're sure?"

"Yes." He hadn't wiped the memory from Victoria's mind, only made it impossible for her to tell anyone what he was. Should she try, she would stutter and stammer, unable to find the words.

"You said you were thinking about me when you were attacked. What were you thinking, exactly?"

"How much I missed you. And now I should go."

She placed her hand on his arm. "No, wait, please."

"I can't stay here with you, Kathryn," he said, gently removing her hand from his arm. "I can't see you every night and not hold you, touch you. I want you more than you can imagine. All of you. In every way a man can possess a woman."

"You must know that I want you, too."

"Do you? Enough to tie your life to mine?"

"Enough to be your wife, if you still want me."

He regarded her through narrowed eyes, not daring to believe. "What's changed?"

"When I read your letter, when I knew you were gone and that I'd never see you again . . . I realized I didn't want to live without you."

"Kathryn!" He swept her into his arms and held her close. "Ah, Kathryn. I will love and cherish you all the days of your life."

She rested her cheek against his chest, his words echoing in her mind—*all the days of your life . . . your life . . . your life.*

It was a stark reminder that while her days were numbered, his were not.

Chapter Twenty-Five

Gilen Leblanc paced the narrow confines of his room while Gregory and Claude treated Paul's injury. The boy had suffered a severe head wound when Cabrera hurled him into a brick wall. It was doubtful that Paul would recover, and if he did, unlikely that he would ever be fit to be a hunter again.

If Farrin had been with them tonight, it might easily have been his brother lying there, babbling nonsense.

Leblanc swore under his breath. Farrin had been urging him to quit the hunt for the last year. For months now, his brother had refused to accompany him. Time and again, Gilen had promised Farrin he would quit, but they had no other skills to fall back on. And bounty hunting was a lucrative trade for those who had the stomach for it.

Damn Cabrera. He was as elusive as smoke in the wind. Leblanc had been certain of victory tonight, but the wily vampire continued to elude his grasp.

As did the other vampire, Pascual.

But it was Cabrera's head he wanted.

And the generous bounty on it.

* * *

Pascual stood outside the hunter's room, listening to the low hum of conversation within. Leblanc wasn't having any better luck bringing Cabrera down than was he. Perhaps the two of them working together would have more success.

Pascual scrubbed a hand across his jaw. He had little doubt that if he convinced Leblanc to work with him to destroy Cabrera, the hunter would turn on him as soon as the job was done. But he would worry about that later. Leblanc could be out and about when he could not. In times past, Pascual had mesmerized ordinary humans to do his bidding, but in this case, he needed someone with experience.

He needed a hunter. And Leblanc was one of the best.

Their best hope of taking Cabrera was to abduct his woman, or perhaps all the women in his household.

Cabrera had a streak of honor unheard of among vampires. It was a weakness easily exploited.

His decision made, Pascual knocked on the door.

Chapter Twenty-Six

Roan paced the floor of his lair as he listened to the hum of conversation between Nan and Kathryn. He had erased the memory of what had happened the night before from the maid's mind. He had considered doing the same to Mrs. Shumway, but he had long suspected she already knew what he was.

Nan made no mention of what had happened the night before, assuring him that he had successfully wiped it from her mind. Instead, she and Kathryn were in the parlor discussing the manor—how large it was, how bare the walls, lacking art and other decorations as they were—wondering why the rooms were bare of bric-a-brac or other personal touches. Nan opined it was because he was unmarried and remarked that it was usually the wife who filled the house with the figurines and fripperies that turned a house into a home.

He grunted softly, thinking Nan had the right of it. What use had he for soft pillows or paintings or porcelain sculptures? Or any of the other mundane objects that cluttered the houses of the men he associated with.

Of course, all that would likely change when Kathryn became his wife. No doubt the rooms in the manor would soon be filled with all manner of feminine clutter.

"I used to have a music box," he heard Kathryn say, somewhat wistfully. "My father gave it to me one year for Christmas. It was such a pretty thing. It had the figure of a woman playing the piano on the lid. She had black hair and wore a bright yellow dress. And when you wound it up, it played the most beautiful song."

"It does sound lovely," the maid agreed.

Roan paused in his restless pacing. "A music box," he muttered.

And then he smiled. He knew right where to find one just like it.

Kathryn listened to the chiming of the clock as she reclined on the sofa in the parlor. The hour was growing late. The fire had burned down to embers. Her mother had gone up to bed some time ago after failing, once again, to persuade Kathryn to leave Cabrera's house.

Kathryn was wondering if she would see Roan before she went to bed, when he stepped into the room carrying a gaily wrapped package.

"For you," he said, handing her the box.

"For me? Why?"

He shrugged. "I saw it in a store window and thought you might like it."

Kathryn ran her fingers over the brightly colored ribbon. Until she met Roan, she had received few gifts in her life. The ones she had received had been for special occasions.

"Aren't you going to open it?"

Smiling with anticipation, she carefully untied the ribbon, peeled back the paper, and lifted the lid. And gasped, unable to believe her eyes.

"Do you like it?"

Blinking back tears of joy, she nodded as she lifted

the music box from the wrappings. "Wherever did you find it?"

"A little shop I know."

"Oh, Roan, I don't know what to say. It's exactly like the one my father gave me." She wound the mechanism. "It even plays the same song!"

"You like it then?"

"Oh, yes!" Setting it carefully on the table beside the sofa, she stood and threw her arms around him. "Thank you!"

It had, he thought, been well worth the cost to see the look of happiness in her eyes. "Consider it an engagement gift. Have you told your mother we plan to wed?"

"Not yet. But I will, when the right moment comes."

"Maybe it's time I taught you to waltz," he said, drawing her into his arms. "So we can dance at our wedding."

Kathryn's heart skipped a beat as he drew her closer. He was so tall, she had to tilt her head back to see his face. He was watching her, his eyes dark with an emotion she didn't comprehend.

"Just follow my lead."

That shouldn't be hard, she thought, breathless. Not when he was holding her so tightly. His hand at her waist felt strong, confident. He moved with effortless grace as he guided her around the floor.

He smiled down at her. "You're a quick study, Kat," he murmured, and lowering his head, he covered her mouth with his.

She was lost. Lost in a world of sensation as his mouth ravished hers. But for his arm tight around her, she might have slid to the floor in a boneless puddle. His tongue traced her bottom lip, then crept inside to duel with hers. His kiss sent a shaft of heat straight to her very center, then exploded outward, until every fiber of her being was on fire for him, yearning for something she knew little about.

His lips caressed her while his hand slid up and down her spine, eliciting shivers of delight. Unbidden came the memory of the erotic dream that had so shocked her, a dream she suddenly wished he would fulfill.

He was kissing her again, his lips leaving trails of fire along the side of her neck.

She froze in his arms, every other thought forgotten in the realization that his teeth—his fangs!—were brushing against her skin.

"A taste," he said, his voice guttural with need. "Just one taste, love."

She swallowed hard. If she was going to stay with him, she would have to get used to his . . . needs. "You won't hurt me?"

"No." His voice was gruff, barely recognizable.

Heart pounding, mouth suddenly too dry to speak, she could only nod her consent.

His arm tightened around her waist as his fangs pierced her flesh. She had expected it to hurt. Instead, a sudden lassitude swept through her, making her legs go weak. A little sigh escaped her lips as she closed her eyes, not caring if he took a little or if he took it all, if only he would never stop.

Roan cursed himself with every foul epithet he knew as he carried Kathryn to the sofa. Her face was as white as his shirt, her breathing shallow. What had he done?

He filled a glass with wine and added a few drops of his blood, then held it to her lips and demanded she drink.

She did so sluggishly, but by the time she had emptied the goblet, the color had returned to her cheeks, her breathing become more regular.

So much for his vaunted self-control. He could have killed her.

"Kathryn?" He took her hand in his and patted it. "Kathryn, can you hear me?"

Her eyelids fluttered open and she stared at him, her eyes slightly unfocused. "Roan?"

He blew out a sigh of relief. "Are you all right?"

"I feel a little dizzy. What happened?"

"Something that must never happen again." Closing his eyes, he sent a silent prayer of thanks toward heaven, although he doubted if there was anyone there who would give heed to one such as he.

It was noon the next day when Kathryn woke in her own bed with no memory of how she'd gotten there. Or who had undressed her and put her into her sleeping gown.

Sitting up, she lifted a hand to her head. She had never overindulged in strong spirits, never experienced a hangover, but she felt sort of woozy, as if she'd had too much wine.

"Miss Winterbourne? Are you awake yet?"

"Yes. Come in, Nan."

The maid opened the door and peeked inside, her brow furrowed.

"Is something wrong?"

"What? Oh, no. I just wanted to make sure you were alone . . ." Cheeks flushed, Nan glanced away. "Shall I tell Cook you're ready for breakfast?"

Kathryn nodded. "Just tea and toast this morning, please."

"Yes, miss." Dropping a curtsy, Nan closed the door.

"That was odd," Kathryn muttered, swinging her legs over the side of the bed. And then, in a rush, she realized Nan hadn't expected to find her alone in her bed.

Kathryn pressed a hand to her heart. What had she done last night?

Nan and Mrs. Shumway were both uncharacteristically silent when Kathryn came down to breakfast. She didn't miss the unspoken questions in their eyes when she entered the dining room. What did they think had gone on between herself and Roan the night before?

What *had* she done?

She recalled Cabrera teaching her to dance . . . asking if he could drink from her . . . Everything was hazy after that.

She was still trying to remember the night's events when her mother swept into the dining room. "Good heavens, Kat, what's wrong with you?"

"Nothing. Why?"

Victoria moved to her daughter's side. "I'm not sure. You look . . . different."

Kathryn's stomach lurched. Had Cabrera turned her into a vampire last night? But no, that was impossible. If he had turned her, she wouldn't be awake now. "Different how?"

"I'm not sure." Victoria ran her fingertips over her daughter's cheek. "There's a kind of glow to your skin, a brightness in your eyes. Have you a fever?"

"I don't think so." Kathryn lifted a hand to her brow, then shook her head. "Maybe I'm just hungry." As soon as she said the words, she realized she was famished.

By the time breakfast was over, she'd eaten three eggs, four slices of bacon, two muffins smothered in butter and honey, and washed it all down with two cups of cocoa.

Victoria shook her head as Kathryn pushed her plate away. "Well, whatever else is going on, daughter, it hasn't affected your appetite . . ." She paused, her eyes widening. "Stars above! That glow, your appetite . . . Good Lord, you're not . . . ?"

"Not what?"

"In the family way?"

Shocked at the very idea, Kathryn could only stare at her mother.

"Tell me you haven't . . . that he didn't . . . ?"

"No, Mama! How can you even think such a thing?" But even if she had been indiscreet, vampires couldn't reproduce, so there would be no child born out of wedlock to tarnish the family name.

Slumping in her chair, Victoria blew out a sigh, then smiled with relief. "Of course, you didn't."

"Would you like to go out and look at the new place?" Kathryn asked. Her mother still wasn't comfortable with the idea of Roan rebuilding their house, but Victoria Winterbourne was nothing if not realistic. She had two choices—let Roan pay for their new accommodations or live with him in his house indefinitely. She had chosen the lesser evil. "Oh, wait. We can't go. We don't have a driver."

Victoria made a tsking sound. "As if I needed one."

Suddenly uncertain, Kathryn bit down on the corner of her lip. Maybe going out to the house wasn't such a good idea. Her mother was well able to drive the buggy, but was it safe for them to leave the protection of the manor? She glanced out the window. The sun was up, the sky was clear. They should be safe enough as long as they were back home before dark.

And it might be the perfect time to tell her mother she was getting married—and ask for her blessing, as unlikely as that might be.

* * *

Kathryn sat beside her mother in the buggy. Too nervous to sit still, she found herself constantly glancing left and right, fidgeting with the folds of her skirt. She told herself again there was nothing to worry about. It was daylight. There were a number of people in sight, couples dining at an outdoor café, townsfolk talking and laughing as they strolled along. Several other carriages lumbered past.

Sighing, she worried the ribbons of her bonnet. It was a beautiful day, but she was too nervous to enjoy it. Somehow she had to find the nerve to tell her mother that she had decided to marry Roan.

"What's wrong with you?" Victoria asked as they left the town behind. "You're as fidgety as an old woman."

"Nothing. Nothing at all. I'm fine."

"Fine, indeed. Tell me what's bothering you."

"Roan and I are . . ."

"Are what?" Victoria asked sharply.

"Engaged to be married." Dead silence followed her announcement. "I know you don't approve, but I would love your blessing."

"I cannot believe you would ask for it, let alone expect to have it."

Kathryn's shoulders slumped. She hadn't really expected her mother to be happy about her announcement.

"You know he's . . . that he's not one of us. He's . . ." A sound of frustration rose in Victoria's throat. "I have to tell you that . . ."

"Tell me what?"

"I can't say the words!" Victoria stamped her foot in frustration. "What has he done to me?"

Kathryn frowned. Had Roan worked some kind of vampire magic on her mother? Something that prevented her from telling people what he was? That had to be it, she decided. "I know, Mama."

"You know?" Victoria's hands tightened on the reins. "You know what he is and you're *still* going to marry him?"

"I don't care what he is," Kathryn said quietly. "I love him. And he loves me."

An unladylike grunt of contempt rose in Victoria's throat. "Things like that . . . that *creature* are incapable of love."

"Do I need to remind you *again* that if it wasn't for Roan we would both be dead now? That he has provided us with shelter? Clothed and fed us? Not only that, he's replacing our old house with a far better one than we've ever had!" Kathryn shook her head. "How can you be so ungrateful?"

Victoria dismissed her words with an angry wave of her hand. "You're mistaking gratitude for love."

"I am going to marry him, Mama. Nothing you can say or do will change my mind."

Kathryn frowned when her mother muttered something under her breath. Something that sounded ominously like "We'll just see about that."

The taut silence between Kathryn and her mother lasted until they reached their destination. Kathryn was surprised to see that the outer walls and the chimney were finished. Half a dozen men were hard at work on the inside. They must have been laboring night and day, she thought, peeking through a window. When complete, the house would be at least twice the size of their old one. And ten times as nice.

Walking around to the back of the building, Kathryn

smiled when she saw the barn taking shape. How like Roan to think of it. She would have suggested it herself, but she had no plans to live here.

Returning to the front of the house, Victoria remarked, "I think we'll be comfortable here."

"*You* will be," Kathryn said curtly.

Victoria's mouth thinned into a tight line.

"We should go," Kathryn said as a workman dodged out of her path. "We're in the way here."

Victoria didn't reply, merely resumed her seat in the buggy and took up the reins.

"Mrs. Shumway asked me to stop and pick up some fish for dinner," Kathryn said, her voice cool.

With a stiff nod, Victoria turned the horse toward town.

It was market day and there was no place to park the buggy near the food stalls, so Victoria elected to wait a short distance away while Kathryn shopped.

Which suited Kathryn just fine. While waiting for Mr. Alston to wrap several cod, she wondered if it might be a good idea for her mother to stay elsewhere until the house was habitable. The tension between them made her uncomfortable and she feared her mother would continue to voice her disapproval right up to the day of the wedding, whenever that might be.

She smiled as she imagined herself in a long white gown, walking down the aisle toward Roan. She knew a moment of regret that her father wouldn't be there to give her away, that her mother thought she was making a mistake. And if it turned out to be a mistake, well, so be it. It was hers to make.

She paid for the fish, tucked the bundle under her arm, and strolled along the street toward where her mother waited, pausing now and then to peruse the goods offered at one stall or another—fresh fruits and vegetables, bolts of cloth, spools of ribbon, rugs and blankets from faraway places.

When she reached the buggy, it was empty.

Kathryn glanced around, expecting to see her mother near one of the booths. But there was no sign of Victoria.

Alarmed, she dumped the fish on the seat, then hurried back in the direction she had come, her gaze darting left and right as she fought her way through the crowded street, up one side and down the other, her panic rising with every step.

Breathless, she returned to the buggy, hoping to find her mother waiting, foot tapping angrily at having cooled her heels for so long.

But Victoria wasn't there.

"Not there?" Mrs. Shumway said, frowning. "Where did she go?"

"I don't know." Kathryn paced the parlor floor. "We had a bit of a spat. But she wouldn't just go off and leave the horse and buggy. Or me. No matter how upset she was." Getting home had been a bit of an ordeal, she thought, since she had never driven a horse and buggy before.

"Of course she wouldn't," the cook said. "Perhaps she met a friend and they went for tea."

"Perhaps," Kathryn murmured. But she wasn't convinced.

Kathryn grew more and more worried as the day wore on. She came up with a half-dozen reasons why her mother might have gone off without so much as a word, but none of them eased her anxiety. Something was very wrong. She knew it.

By the time Roan joined her in the parlor that night, she was a nervous wreck.

Roan listened patiently while Kathryn related the conversation between herself and her mother, then went down to the stable to examine the buggy. Opening his preternatural senses, he walked around the buggy. The scent of fish was unmistakable. He recognized Victoria's scent, as well as Kathryn's. Leblanc's scent overlaid that of the women. Roan also caught the sweet-smelling odor of chloroform, something he recognized from his frequent visits to the Mothers of Mercy Hospital.

But even more troubling was the barely discernable scent of the vampire, Pascual.

Roan stared into the distance, hands clenched at his sides.

Like it or not, it seemed his enemies had joined forces and kidnapped Kathryn's mother.

Chapter Twenty-Seven

"We've got to find her!" Kathryn exclaimed, her voice rising in anguish. "What if she's hurt? Or worse?"

"I don't think they'll hurt her," Roan said. "They'll want her alive. She's no good to them dead." Which was true, to a point. He was reasonably certain that once Victoria's usefulness was over, Pascual would kill her out of hand as he had killed so many others.

"They?" Kathryn blinked at him, her mind whirling.

"Pascual and Leblanc. It seems they're working together."

Kathryn's face paled. "And my mother is the bait, isn't she? To draw you out?"

Roan nodded.

"Can you find her?"

He nodded again. He wished fleetingly that he had taken Victoria's blood. It would have made finding her that much easier. Instead, he would have to track Pascual or Leblanc. No simple task. Both were expert in covering their tracks, though they had been negligent this time.

Frowning, Kathryn asked, "Isn't it unusual for a hunter and a vampire to work together?"

"Unheard of." Roan dragged a hand over his jaw. "I

would love to know what kind of devil's bargain they made. And what makes either one of them think the other will keep it."

Seeing the crestfallen look on Kathryn's face, he drew her into his arms. "Don't worry, Kat. I'll find her. I promise."

She nodded. She had to trust him. Had to believe he could find her mother because she couldn't bear to think that the angry exchange between herself and her mother had really been their last words.

Victoria woke in a dark place with no idea of where she was and no memory of how she'd gotten there. The last thing she remembered was arguing with Kathryn about her decision to marry a vampire . . .

Where was she? She couldn't see a thing. Gaining her feet, she held her hands out in front of her and walked slowly forward. She grunted when she hit a cold, stone wall. So, she was in a cellar, or a dungeon, she thought, or something like that.

With nothing better to do, she continued her exploration. There was no furniture in the room, no windows as far as she could tell, only four bare walls and a hard-packed dirt floor. The door was locked, but that came as no surprise.

Who had locked her in here? And how was she going to get out?

Sinking down on the floor, she closed her eyes and searched her memory. A man, a stranger, had approached the buggy and tried to sell her a rather shabby-looking bonnet. While she was trying to convince him that she didn't have any money, someone had come up behind her and slapped a foul-smelling rag over her nose and mouth.

The realization that she had been drugged and kidnapped sent an icy shiver down her spine. Wrapping her arms around her middle, she began to sing her favorite hymn in hopes of fighting off the panic that now threatened to engulf her.

She told herself that Kathryn would send Cabrera to look for her, tried not to think about what her fate might be if they couldn't find her.

Leaving the house later that night, Roan went to the place where Kathryn had told him she'd left Victoria waiting in the carriage.

Leblanc's scent was faint here. Victoria's was stronger, no doubt due to the perfume and powder she wore.

Roan followed the fading aroma of perfume away from the fish market, out past the end of the town, toward an abandoned tanner's. He circled the building twice, his senses detecting a single human heartbeat from somewhere inside.

The iron door made a hideous grinding sound as he ripped it off the hinges and tossed it aside.

He paused, his senses sweeping the interior before he crossed the threshold. There were three sets of footprints in the dusty floor. He followed them to a locked, iron-strapped wooden door in the rear that he guessed led down to what had likely been an underground storeroom.

Leblanc had been here and gone, but Victoria was in the cellar. The scent of the fear emanating from her permeated the air. The frightened beat of her heart was like thunder in his ears.

He was about to break down the door when he heard footsteps moving stealthily behind him.

A glance over his shoulder showed Leblanc and four other men advancing toward him. All were armed with long, wooden stakes and wicked-looking, silver-bladed knives.

Roan huffed a sigh of exasperation. He was getting damned tired of this. "Again?"

Leblanc made a dismissive gesture with his hand. "This will be the last time."

"On that we can agree."

Tension hummed through the air as four of the men fanned out, trapping him in the middle of a tightening circle as they slowly advanced toward him.

Roan let them come. He didn't like killing but sometimes it was the only answer.

He noticed that Leblanc hung back a little while the other four made their move.

Roan held his ground until they were at arm's length. One man, braver or more foolish than the others, shouted, "Death to all vampires!" and darted forward.

Moving faster than human eyes could follow, Roan broke the fool's neck. The other three closed in like dogs fighting over a bone. He grabbed one by the neck and tossed him against the wall. The force of his head hitting the stone killed him instantly.

He ripped the heart from the third man, broke the neck of the fourth.

And then he crooked a finger at Leblanc. "What are you waiting for?"

Leblanc stood a few feet away, unmoving, his face mottled with rage as he stared at his four dead companions. Glowering at Roan, he cried, "Well, come on, bloodsucker, what are you waiting for? Get it over with."

"I thought I'd let you make the first move."

Leblanc snorted. "And if I don't? Are you going to let me walk away?"

"I don't think so. I'm tired of watching my back."

The hunter slid his hands into his pants pockets. "What if I swear not to come after you again?"

"What if I don't believe you?" The man was lying. It was evident in the quickening of his pulse, the pounding of his heart, as he gathered the courage to make his move.

"Do what you want," Leblanc said, turning toward the door. "I'm leaving."

Roan braced himself for the attack he knew was coming, but it wasn't a stake the hunter pulled from his pocket but a bottle of holy water. In one swift motion, Leblanc pulled the cork and flung the contents into Roan's face.

Roan swore as the liquid seared his skin, but he was ready for Leblanc when the hunter darted toward him, chin tucked in, knife raised to strike.

Roan's arm snaked out, one hand closing around Leblanc's throat while his other hand snatched the knife from the hunter's grasp.

"You should have left when I gave you the chance," Roan muttered, and sank his fangs deep into the hunter's neck.

Leblanc let out a shriek of protest, arms and legs thrashing wildly, as Roan drained the life from his body, then dropped the empty husk to the floor.

After wiping his mouth with the back of his hand, Roan knocked on the cellar door. "Victoria?"

"Cabrera? Is that you?"

"Yes. Stand away from the door." He listened for the sound of her footsteps backing away. A single kick broke the lock and the door creaked open. "Let's go home."

She scrambled up the stairs, only to come to an abrupt halt when she saw the bodies sprawled on the floor beyond.

Her gaze darted to the dead men and then back to Roan. Her relief at seeing him was as palpable as her horror at what he had done.

He made no move toward her. "Are you coming?" he asked, his voice gruff.

With a curt nod, Victoria followed him out of the building. She glanced around. There was no carriage waiting. No horses. "How are we going to get home?"

"It's hard to explain."

She flinched when he reached for her. "What are you doing?"

"I'm taking you home." He knew a brief flare of anger. It didn't matter that he had saved her life once before—and had in all likelihood just saved it again—she would always think of him as a bloodsucking monster.

Roan put his arm around her, felt her stiffen in his grasp. "Just close your eyes. You'll be with Kathryn before you know it."

Victoria reclined on the sofa, huddled under a blanket, while Kathryn poured her a cup of tea. Roan had brought her mother home half an hour ago, assured her that Victoria hadn't been hurt, and taken his leave. She hadn't seen him since.

"Five men," Victoria said, her voice flat. "He killed them all."

"Mama, don't think about it. You're safe now."

"I can't stop thinking about it. I know I should be grateful for what he did. And I am." She lifted her cup, but her hand was trembling so badly, she put it back down. "But that doesn't change what he is."

Kathryn sighed. She had hoped that her mother would

come to accept the fact that Roan was a vampire, but she was beginning to think it was impossible.

Long after her mother had gone to bed, Kathryn sat in the parlor in front of the fireplace, gazing at the flames while she waited for Roan. As the hour grew late, she wondered if he would come to her tonight. Or if he thought she would rather be alone.

Closing her eyes, she whispered his name. When she opened them, he was beside her on the sofa. Cupping his face in her hands, she kissed him lightly. "After everything that happened earlier tonight, I was afraid you'd stay away."

"I wasn't sure you'd want to see me. I imagine your mother gave you a detailed account of what happened."

Kathryn nodded.

"She's never going to accept me, Kat. Or us. You know that, don't you?"

"I know." She stroked his cheek with her fingertips, loving the way he leaned into her touch. "But I don't care. I love you, no matter what."

He pulled her gently into his arms, his fears of rejection vanishing in the love he saw shining in her eyes. He could think of no other woman who would accept him so wholeheartedly. She had seen him at his worst, and still she loved him.

"We could elope," Kathryn suggested, snuggling against him. "I don't need a big wedding. Just the two of us."

"Are you sure?" In his rather limited experience, he'd found that most women favored a wedding that put all other weddings to shame.

"Very. I don't need anyone but you."

"Ah, Kathryn," he murmured, his voice husky with desire, "you make me weak."

"And you make me strong. We're perfect for each other."

He nodded, then bent his head to hers.

She melted against him as his mouth covered her lips. This was what she wanted. What she needed. She could live without her mother's approval. But she didn't want to live without Roan.

Juan Pascual didn't have to enter the building to know what had happened inside. The place reeked of blood and death.

He kicked the bodies out of the way as he paced the floor, unable to believe that the woman was gone and Leblanc and four of his men were dead.

Five against one, and Cabrera still lived.

He drove his fist into the wall. How had Cabrera gotten so strong? Years ago, his old enemy had been the weaker of the two, as he should have been. Pascual was older; with age, came added strength. But now, somehow, Cabrera was the more powerful. How had it happened?

Pascual stormed out into the night, where he vented his rage and his frustration on the first mortal he saw.

He needed an edge, he thought as he drained his victim dry and tossed the body into a ditch. Something that would make him more powerful than Cabrera—something that would greatly weaken the other vampire's strength.

But what?

The lead story in the morning papers was about five unidentified bodies found in an abandoned warehouse. A grisly drawing accompanied the story, along with several theories regarding the deaths. A smaller story concerned a wealthy young man who had been found dead in a ditch, along with some speculation as to whether all the murders were somehow connected, though it seemed unlikely that Arthur Jacobs, Jr., son of a prominent banker, would have been acquainted with the five dead men, all of whom were strangers in town.

Kathryn's stomach turned when she saw the drawing— five bodies sprawled on a dirty floor. Four of them had broken necks. The fifth lay on his back, the two tiny puncture wounds in his throat drawn clearly.

Roan had done that.

He had killed before. She had seen it with her own eyes. Why was this any worse?

Her appetite gone, she pushed away from the dining room table. He had killed those men to save her mother, she reminded herself. Not in cold blood. Not for pleasure. Killed them as he had killed the highwaymen who had attacked her.

But even as she justified the killings, a little voice in the back of her mind whispered that, with his preternatural powers, he very likely would have been able to rescue both her and her mother without snuffing out the lives of the men involved.

Then again, maybe she was wrong. Maybe she was crediting him with more strength than he actually possessed.

How was she to know?

On waking that night, Roan sensed Kathryn's agitation. A quick brush of her mind with his revealed the source of her unease. For perhaps the first time, she had fully realized what he was. Of what he was capable. She was wondering if it had been necessary to kill the men who had attacked her and kidnapped her mother. She was right to think he could have subdued them instead. But the thought had never crossed his mind. They had attacked what was his and the penalty was death.

He dressed, then went out to satisfy his hunger. Sitting on the edge of one of the beds in the hospital, he spoke to the old woman's mind, then allowed her to relive the happiest time in her life—the birth of twin daughters when she thought she would never have a child. And all the while he was thinking of Kathryn, wondering if what he had done would cause her to look at him differently, to finally see him as the monster he was. To rethink her desire to be his wife.

After leaving the hospital, he stalked the town's underbelly, where harlots prowled the dark streets, where petty thieves lingered in shadowy doorways waiting for a mark. This was where he belonged, he mused, with the rest of the town's undesirables. He might live in comfort, dress in fine clothes, pretend he was equal with the town's gentlefolk, but, in truth, he was a monster who preyed upon others, no better than the footpads and whores.

He was in a foul mood when he returned home. He paused at the front door, his senses probing the interior. Nan was carrying a pot of tea up to Victoria's room. Mrs. Shumway sang in the kitchen as she kneaded a ball of dough.

Kathryn waited for him in the library. He frowned as his mind brushed hers. She was still thinking about the men he had killed, trying to convince herself the deaths had been unavoidable even though a little part of her conscience kept insisting killing them hadn't been necessary.

He grunted softly. As far as he was concerned, sparing their lives would have been risky and unwise. Doing so would only have given Leblanc and his cronies another chance to endanger those under his protection. He had long ago learned the hard way that the only way to survive was to strike fast and strike hard.

He had done the smart thing, but apparently not the right thing as far as Kathryn was concerned. Not when it had her rethinking their relationship. She loved him. She wanted him.

But was that enough?

He wasn't sure.

And neither was she.

Kathryn glanced up when Roan entered the library. She smiled uncertainly, unable to shake the feeling that he knew just how confused she was.

"Have you changed your mind about us?" he asked, his voice impassive.

She looked away, unsettled by the question. "I don't know."

He moved to stand in front of the fireplace, one arm braced on the mantel. "I know you're upset about recent events. Do you want to talk about it?"

Twisting a lock of hair around her finger, she said, "I don't know what to say. I'm not even sure what's bothering me. I know what you are. I know that you've killed people. I saw you drink the blood of one of the highwaymen who held up my coach." She took a deep breath. "There was a drawing in the paper of the hunters you killed when you rescued my mother." She made a vague gesture with her hand. "I don't know why it upset me so much."

"Are you afraid I might hurt you or your mother?"

"No. Not really. It's just . . ."

"That I'm a vampire."

"I thought I could handle it. But now . . ."

"Now you're not so sure."

"I love you, Roan. Truly, I do."

"But you're wondering if love is enough. The same thought crossed my mind."

"What do we do now?"

His brow furrowed and then, moving slowly, as though he feared he might frighten her, he drew her to her feet and into his embrace.

"I guess that's up to you," he murmured, and kissed her.

Kathryn leaned into him, her body yearning to be closer as her arms crept up to circle his neck. She moaned low in her throat as his kiss grew more intense. He had treated her with nothing but kindness and respect, this man like no other. How could she even think of letting him go? Of spending the rest of her life without him? He loved her. She knew it with every fiber of her being.

Lifting his head, he searched her face. "Think about it, Kat. Because once I make you mine, I'll never let you go."

Chapter Twenty-Eight

Farrin Leblanc sat hunched over a pint at a small tavern on the outskirts of town.

Gilen was dead.

Farrin had read the story in the newspaper, seen the lurid picture of his older brother's body. The telltale puncture wounds in the side of his neck.

He had warned Gilen not to go after Cabrera. The vampire was old, more powerful than any they'd taken before. As always, Gilen had refused to listen to reason.

And now he had paid the ultimate price for his stubbornness.

Farrin downed his drink and ordered another. He should have been with Gilen when he went after Cabrera. But no, he'd finally put his foot down and said he was through with bounty hunting. They had enough money to live in luxury for the rest of their lives. It was time to quit. He had been threatening to do so for months. But Gilen wouldn't give up. *Just one more head,* he had promised. Just like he'd been doing for over a year. Always one more. And one more after that. And now, because he'd been so bloody stubborn, Farrin was honor-bound to avenge his brother's death.

Just as soon as he found the courage to do so.

Chapter Twenty-Nine

A few days later, Victoria decided she needed a change of scenery and went to stay with Essie Cadwell, an old friend whose husband had recently passed away. The morning her mother left, Kathryn felt a guilty sense of relief. The constant tension between them had been wearing on her nerves.

Kathryn passed the morning helping Mrs. Shumway chop vegetables for stew. Later that day, she spent an hour working in the gardens, and another hour riding Bianca. Returning to the house, she went into the library looking for something to read.

Later, while she ate a solitary meal, she thought how nice it would be if Roan could dine with her. When Mrs. Shumway appeared with a basket of freshly baked bread, Kathryn invited her and Nan to join her.

Taken aback, Mrs. Shumway murmured, "'Tisn't done, the help eating with the family."

"Well, it's going to be done tonight, unless you'd rather not."

With a smile creasing her face, the cook hurried downstairs to fetch Nan. They returned moments later with their dinner.

Nan seemed ill at ease, but Mrs. Shumway was delighted and quickly broke into an amusing tale of going fishing with her father when she was a girl that soon had them all laughing.

"Thank you for keeping me company," Kathryn said, when supper was over. "We must do this again."

Nodding shyly, Nan cleared the table while Mrs. Shumway went downstairs to set out the dough for morning.

Humming her favorite hymn, Kathryn went back to the library, where she soon fell asleep while reading. The touch of Roan's hand on her shoulder woke her. Seeing him made her heart skip a beat.

"Would you like to go out this evening?" he asked.

She nodded enthusiastically, then frowned. "Do you think it's safe?"

"Safe enough. Are you ready?"

She glanced down at her dress—a simple green and gold frock with a square neck and fitted sleeves. "Do I look all right?"

The dress emphasized her figure; the color deepened the emerald shade of her eyes. He preferred her hair down and she wore it that way tonight, pulled back with a pair of tortoiseshell combs. "Perfect."

He lifted her to her feet and put his arm around her waist. "Hold on."

She gasped as the world spun out of focus. She had a sense of movement, of speed, of weightlessness.

When the world righted itself again, she found herself standing beside Roan in front of the Charing Cross Theatre where *Romeo and Juliet* was being performed.

Taking her by the hand, Roan led her inside. No one stopped them or questioned their presence. No one asked to see their tickets. The play had just begun. He paused a moment, his gaze moving through the auditorium until he found two empty seats. Again, no one paid them any attention.

Kathryn watched, mesmerized, as the story of star-crossed lovers unfolded. She blinked back her tears at the tragic ending. She felt less foolish when she noticed several other women wiping their eyes.

Outside, she took a deep breath. "That was . . . was beautiful. But so sad!"

"You enjoyed it, then?" he said, taking her hand in his.

"Oh, yes. But . . . why didn't anyone notice us?"

"A little vampire magic." Giving her hand a light tug, he started down the street. "Your mother left today."

"Yes. I feel guilty for being so happy about it, but she's never going to approve of our marriage."

"Isn't that why we're eloping?" he asked with a wry grin.

"We never really agreed that we were."

His fingers tightened around hers. "It's up to you, Kat. Whatever makes you happy."

"You make me happy," she murmured.

At her words, he drew her into his arms. "Do I?"

"I want to try one more time to win my mother to our side. If that fails, then we'll run away. Is that all right with you?"

"As I said, love. Whatever you want is fine with me." His gaze searched hers and then, heedless of the passing crowds, he kissed her long and hard. "Mine," he whispered fervently. "One way or another, you will be mine."

The next two weeks passed peacefully. There were no more murders. No mysterious disappearances. And life in the manor gradually returned to normal.

One day, feeling bored, Kathryn picked up paper and pen and began sketching—something she hadn't done in a while. A vase of flowers, a chestnut tree, a bowl of fruit. As always, there was something immensely satisfying about letting her imagination guide her hand.

Suddenly excited about pursuing whatever talent she might or might not have, she asked Mrs. Shumway to buy her an easel, paints, chalk, and a new sketchpad when she went into town the next day.

The following afternoon, Kathryn hurried down to the stable, eager to try her skill at painting Bianca.

Later in the day, she did a quick drawing of Nan.

That night she showed her work to Roan.

"I think you have a real talent," he said. "This one of the mare is quite good, as is this drawing of Nan. You have a genuine feel for capturing the essence of your subjects."

"Really?" Kathryn exclaimed. "You truly think so?"

"I do."

"Would you pose for me?"

He started to refuse, but, on reconsidering, he discovered a sudden desire to know what Kathryn saw when she looked at him. He hadn't seen his image in hundreds of years. Truth be told, he scarcely remembered what he looked like.

"Roan?"

He nodded. "If you wish."

"Why don't you sit in the chair beside the fire?" she suggested.

He did as she asked. "Any particular pose?"

"No. Just sit still."

He watched her as she worked, her brow furrowed in concentration, her pen making soft scratches on the paper—the way she blew a wisp of hair away from her face.

She had delicate hands, slender fingers. His gaze moved to the pulse in her throat. Would she grant him a taste later? Lost in thought, he found himself wondering what it would be like when they were wed. What it would be like to share his life with her. Would she agree to sleep with him in his lair? Or would she want to keep her own room? He didn't like the idea of leaving her bed every night just before dawn. But would she like waking up next to a man who was literally dead to the world?

It took him a moment to realize she had stopped drawing and laid her pen aside. He was surprised at how quickly the time had gone by.

"Roan?"

"Finished already?"

She nodded.

"Are you going to let me see it?"

"I don't know." She twisted a lock of hair around her finger. "It's not very good."

"Come, now, I'm sure it's fine."

Kathryn glanced at the sketch. She felt she had captured his image well enough—his wide forehead, the straight brows over an aristocratic nose, full lips that hinted at sensuality, hooded eyes with secrets behind them, a strong, square jaw. "All right," she decided, passing the drawing to him. "But be kind."

Roan stared at the image on the page. "I've not seen my likeness in centuries."

"You're disappointed?"

"No," he said, slowly. "Not at all."

"What's wrong?"

"Nothing. It's quite good." He looked pretty much the way he remembered, except for his eyes. He had seen cruelty in all its forms in his long existence, seen things and done things that could never be forgiven or forgotten. She had somehow managed to convey that in her drawing.

"I can do another one if you like."

"May I keep this one?"

"Of course." She smiled, incredibly pleased that he wanted it. "I'm glad you like it."

They spent the rest of the evening in front of the fire, locked in each other's arms, making idle conversation, sharing kisses and caresses. When Kathryn dozed off, he carried her up the stairs and put her to bed. After kissing her brow, he left the manor to wander the dark night.

A week later, sitting across the breakfast table from her mother, Kathryn could see that the trip had done Victoria a world of good. The color had returned to her mother's cheeks. She seemed to have gained a little weight and she smiled often as she reminisced about her visit with Mrs. Cadwell.

Kathryn didn't mention Roan or their plans to wed, and her mother seemed content to avoid the subject.

With her mother back in residence, Roan stayed away from the manor until after Victoria retired for the night, although he did come by one evening a few days later to take them out to see the progress on the new house.

In deference to Victoria's feelings, he stayed in the buggy while Kathryn and her mother went inside.

The house was much bigger than Kathryn had expected. In addition to the three bedrooms, there was a large front parlor for guests, a smaller parlor for the family in the rear, a dining room, kitchen, and a separate room for bathing and doing the laundry.

"It's wonderful!" Victoria said enthusiastically. "So much better than I imagined. I know we'll be happy here."

The following afternoon, Kathryn took tea with her mother. They discussed colors and drapery fabrics for each room and decided to go into town one day next week to look at furniture. Kathryn felt a twinge of guilt for allowing Victoria to think they were going to live in the house together.

It was late that night when Roan appeared in her bedroom. Kathryn went eagerly into his arms, all thoughts of the new house forgotten as his mouth claimed hers.

"Tomorrow night," he murmured, his hands skating up and down her spine.

She looked up at him, a question in her eyes.

He brushed a kiss across her lips. "We're going to be married."

"We are?" Her heart skipped a beat at the thought of being his wife at last.

Cupping her face in his hands, he said, "I love you, Kathryn. Please don't make me wait any longer." He kissed her again, deeper and more intimately this time. "I thought we'd be married in Paris and take our honeymoon there."

"Paris sounds wonderful. And I can't wait to be your wife. But . . . my mother . . ."

"We'll leave her a note, telling her of our plans. She can stay here, if she likes. If that doesn't suit, she can move into the new place and take Nan and Mrs. Shumway with her. I've made arrangements for Victoria to receive a monthly allowance. She'll never want for anything as long as she lives."

Kathryn nodded. "How long will we be gone?"

"As long as you wish." He smiled at her. "If you get homesick, we can be back here in the blink of an eye."

Of course, she thought, grinning. He was a vampire. Time and distance meant nothing to him. "I'll need a dress."

"I'll buy you one in Paris."

Kathryn tossed and turned all that night and woke in the morning feeling as though she hadn't slept at all.

While awake, she had thought of all the reasons why she shouldn't marry a vampire. But the love she had seen shining in Roan's eyes, the feelings of her own heart, could not be ignored. Deep inside, she knew being his wife was the right decision. The only decision.

Her dreams had been filled with scattered images of Roan. She relived the night he had saved her from the highwaymen, saw him bending over the dead man's neck. Saw the blood on Roan's mouth. She saw the drawing of the dead men in the newspaper and knew he had killed them all.

But she had also dreamed of the nights he had come to her in the hospital, easing her fears, saving her life. Taking her into his home because she had nowhere else to go.

Sitting up, she stared out the window. He was at rest now. Did he dream when he slept? Or was he merely trapped in the darkness until the sun went down? Was he aware of time passing while he rested? Or was it really a sleep like death? Not for the first time she wondered where he spent the daylight hours.

She was about to get up when she heard rapid footsteps in the hallway, a frantic pounding on her bedroom door. "Miss Kathryn! Miss Kathryn! Come quick! The barn is on fire!"

Kathryn flew out of bed and nearly knocked the maid over in her haste to get downstairs. She flung the back door open, her heart in her throat when she saw the flames and heard Bianca's shrill whinnies.

Running to the stables and grabbing an old towel she often used to dry the mare, she soaked it in the water barrel beside the entrance.

A hand on her arm stayed her. "You can't go in there!" Mrs. Shumway cried. "'Tis suicide!"

"I can't just let her burn!" Kathryn cried as she shook

off the cook's arm and dashed through the barn door, the towel over her head.

The fire had not yet spread to the right side of the barn, but the left side and a portion of the roof were in flames. The heat was overpowering.

Bianca paced restlessly in her stall, nostrils flared, her eyes wild.

"Easy, girl," Kathryn crooned, trying to force a note of calm into her voice. "Easy now." Kathryn lifted the latch on the stall door and held it open, hoping the mare would run for the outside. But Bianca continued to pace in a restless circle.

Praying that the roof wouldn't collapse, Kathryn grabbed the mare's headstall, snapped on a lead line, then wrapped the towel around the mare's head, covering her eyes. "Come on," she urged, relieved beyond measure when the mare followed her out of the barn.

Her mother and Mrs. Shumway waited outside, their expressions anxious.

Kathryn had no sooner reached safety than a corner of the roof collapsed, sending sparks flying everywhere.

Kathryn led the mare to the back of the house and tethered her to the iron bench beside the back door. There was no way the three of them could extinguish the fire; it would just have to burn itself out, which it seemed to be doing rather quickly. Fortunately, there was no wind to fan the flames. For a moment, she considered riding into town for help, but by the time she got there and back, the fire would likely be out.

Her mother and Mrs. Shumway came to stand beside her. "'Tis a good thing the barn isn't close to the house," the cook said, sliding a small pistol into her apron pocket.

Kathryn stared at the gun, thinking she couldn't have been any more shocked to find the woman holding a snake.

"What on earth are you doing with a pistol?" she asked, then recalled that the cook had told her that her husband, Nate, had taught her how to shoot.

"Better safe than sorry, don't you know?" Mrs. Shumway remarked sheepishly.

"Well, I don't think you'll be needing it today," Kathryn said. "Why don't you go inside and fix breakfast? I'm going to stay out here and keep an eye on the fire."

With a nod, Mrs. Shumway made a half turn toward the house when three burly men burst out of the shed brandishing weapons.

Victoria screamed.

Galvanized to action, Mrs. Shumway reached for the gun in her apron pocket, but before she could bring it to bear, one of the men lunged forward, and struck her across the back of the head with the butt of his rifle. The cook tumbled to the ground and lay still. The pistol skittered across the hard-packed earth.

Kathryn darted toward the gun, but before she could reach it, a man twice her size grabbed her arm and twisted it painfully behind her back. His other hand curled around her throat.

Victoria let out a cry as the third ruffian caught her, lifting her off the ground. Screaming "Let me go!" she kicked and fought, but she was no match for a man of his size and strength.

"Mama! Mama!"

Muttering "Shut up!" the man holding Kathryn dragged her into the house and out the front door. The second man followed with Victoria in tow. The third brought up the rear. An enclosed wagon drawn by a team of black horses waited at the end of the walkway.

Kathryn fought against being put into the wagon as hard as she could but to no avail. Her captor tossed her inside as if she weighed nothing at all. Moments later, her mother was pushed in beside her and the door was slammed shut, leaving them in utter darkness.

Kathryn took a deep breath as the wagon lurched forward. "Mama, are you all right?" Kathryn took her mother's hand in hers and gave it a squeeze. "Mama?"

"What? Oh, just a bit bruised."

"Did you see Nan anywhere? You don't think they hurt her, do you?" Kathryn shook off morbid visions of the maid lying dead somewhere in the house.

"I don't know," Victoria wailed. "Who are these men? Oh, Lord, where are they taking us?"

Kathryn had no answer, but she was sorely afraid that Juan Pascual was responsible. She stared into the darkness, praying that Mrs. Shumway would recover, that Nan was unhurt. Hours until dark. "Roan will find us. He's good at that," Kathryn said, forcing a note of confidence she was far from feeling. "Do you think Mrs. Shumway is . . . dead?"

"I don't know. She wasn't moving."

Kathryn blinked back tears as she recalled the day she had spent making custard tarts with the cook. The woman had always treated her kindly. Closing her eyes, she sent a silent prayer to heaven, praying that the cook wasn't as badly hurt as she feared, that Nan was safe somewhere in the house, that Roan would find them before it was too late.

The wagon bumped and jolted for what seemed an eternity. They had most certainly left Newberry Township far behind. Except for her brief stay in the city, Kathryn had never been away from Newberry, had no idea what lay beyond the town limits or how far it was to the next village.

* * *

She must have dozed because she came awake with a start. The wagon had stopped. She heard the rasp of metal scraping metal as the door was unlocked.

Night had fallen.

A man she had never seen before ordered them out.

Holding tightly to her mother's hand, Kathryn inched toward the door, suddenly reluctant to step outside. A second man appeared beside the first. She shuddered when she saw him. Pascual. Even in the dark, she recognized the vampire by the shock of his white hair. There was no sign of the three men who had abducted them.

Pascual smiled wolfishly when he saw her. And then, before she had time to react, he grabbed her by the shoulders, his fingers digging into her flesh as he sank his fangs into her jugular. Terror trapped the screams in her throat. She clawed at his face. It had never hurt when Roan drank from her. But then, he had never taken more than a sip or two.

Pascual took more. He drank and drank, until the world around her faded and went black.

Until he had taken it all.

Chapter Thirty

Roan woke from the Dark Sleep, roused by the sound of Kathryn's silent scream echoing in his mind. He bolted upright, his senses searching for her presence, for the reassuring beat of her heart. But he found nothing. He had no sense of her at all . . .

A thought took him to the parlor, where he found Nan slumped in a chair, shoulders hunched, fingers restlessly worrying the folds of her apron. Quiet sobs wracked her body. The strong scent of smoke and ash lingered in the air. There was no one else in the house.

"What is it?" he demanded, glancing around the room. "What's happened? Where's Kathryn?"

The maid looked up at him, her eyes wide with fear. "There was a fire . . . in the barn. Miss Kathryn ran outside to . . . to save her horse . . ." She took a deep, shuddering breath. "Mrs. Shumway and Mrs. Victoria went after her . . . I watched from the window . . ."

Pain like nothing he had ever known knifed through Roan as he imagined Kat running into the barn, being consumed by the flames. Death by fire. It was his worst nightmare.

"She got the mare out safely . . . but . . . but . . ."

Grabbing her by the shoulders, Roan shook her. "Where is she? Tell me, dammit!"

"Some men . . . three of them . . . they took her and her mother away in a wagon that was parked out front. I saw them from the window upstairs. Mrs. Shumway . . ." Another sob wracked her body. "She's in the backyard. I think she's . . . dead."

Swearing under his breath, Roan ran out the back door. The night was dark, quiet under a blanket of stars, as if the whole world had gone to bed. Bianca whickered softly, drawing his attention. He stroked the mare's neck as he glanced at the carnage. The barn lay in ruins. The scuffed ground told him what had happened. Kathryn and Victoria had struggled against their captors, then been dragged into the house. The cook lay on the ground. She was unconscious. Dried blood matted the hair at the back of her head and stained the high collar of her dress. Her breathing was shallow and uneven.

Anxious to go after Kathryn, he debated leaving the woman to her fate. Then, cursing the delay, he lifted Mrs. Shumway over his shoulder and transported her to the hospital. He gave the charge nurse the cook's name and requested she be given a private room. After thrusting a handful of bills at the nurse, he assured her that he would be responsible for any further costs, then ran out the door.

Returning to the manor, he followed the wagon's tracks, which took him several leagues out of town and ended in the middle of nowhere. The horses had been taken, the wagon abandoned. Skeletal trees and withered shrubs stood in stark relief against the skyline.

Lifting his head, he opened his senses. Pascual's scent hung heavy in the air, and with it, the unmistakable smell of blood.

Kathryn's blood.

A rustle in the bushes to his left caught his attention and he whirled around, lips drawn back in a snarl.

"He took her. He took my baby."

"Victoria!"

She staggered toward him, then dropped to her knees.

Roan knelt beside her, his gaze moving over her face. She seemed unhurt except for a few scratches and a large bruise on one arm. "Where? Where did he take her?"

"I don't know." She stared up at him, her face devoid of color, her eyes haunted. "He drank from her. He drank until . . . until she went limp in his arms. She was so pale. I thought she was dead. And then . . ." She made a visible effort to continue. "He forced her to . . . to drink his blood. I should have tried to stop him, but I was so afraid . . ." Her voice trailed off as shudders wracked her body.

"Go on."

"When she was done, he picked her up and . . . and they . . . they just disappeared. Is she . . . did he turn her into a . . . ?" Victoria stared at him, unable to say the word aloud. Roan nodded. Too upset to sugarcoat it, he said, "If she survives the day, she'll wake tomorrow night as a new vampire." Groaning softly, he closed his eyes. He had done this to her. It was all his fault. He never should have involved her in the hell that was his life. Juan Pascual was her master now. For as long as Pascual lived, he could compel Kathryn to do whatever loathsome thing he wished and she would be helpless to resist.

It was beyond bearing. Throwing back his head, Roan howled his anguish, his fury, while Victoria cowered beside him, her hands clapped over her ears.

His mournful cry was picked up by a wolf, and then another, until the whole world echoed with the sound of Roan's anguish.

* * *

Roan stood in the parlor, head down, one hand braced against the mantel. He had given Victoria a cup of tea heavily laced with brandy, then carried her up to her room. He had stayed with her until she fell asleep. He had also prescribed a cup of strong tea for Nan, assured her Mrs. Shumway would be home soon, and sent the maid off to bed.

Knowing how much Kathryn loved Bianca and certain she would never forgive him for not taking care of the animal, he fed and watered the mare, then turned her out into the pasture. The fence had been singed in the fire but was, thankfully, still standing.

When the maid and Victoria were safely bedded down for the night, he returned to the hospital to look in on the cook. The nurse at the reception desk advised him that Mrs. Shumway was in the last room at the end of the corridor.

Before the nurse could ask any questions, he hurried down the hallway. Mrs. Shumway had been sedated. A wide bandage swathed her head. Her face was pale, her breathing shallow.

A doctor arrived as Roan was preparing to leave and advised that his patient was in a coma and that they were doing all they could for her. Roan thanked the doctor and left the hospital.

Returning home, he went into the parlor and poured himself a glass of wine and downed it in a single swallow.

Kathryn had been turned by Pascual. The act had severed Roan's blood link with her as cleanly as a scalpel through flesh, making it next to impossible to locate her or speak to her mind. His only hope now was to find Juan Pascual, but he had vanished, leaving no trail behind.

Where would the other vampire go? Would he leave the area now that he had avenged himself on his age-old enemy? Or would he find a way to make Roan's life even more miserable?

Filled with impotent rage, he hurled the goblet into the fireplace, then paced the floor in long, angry strides until, frustrated beyond bearing, he slammed his fist against the wall, hard enough to crack the plaster.

"Damn you, Pascual!" he snarled as the sun crested the horizon. "I will hunt you to the ends of the earth if it's the last thing I do!"

Victoria sat in front of the fireplace in the parlor, a blanket wrapped around her shoulders, the breakfast tray beside her untouched. She had no appetite, could think of nothing but Kathryn. Every time she closed her eyes, she saw that dreadful creature forcing his blood down her daughter's throat.

Her daughter was a vampire now.

She should have done something. Anything. Grabbed a branch and hit him over the head, begged him to take her instead. Even animals defended their young. But no, she had dragged herself away and hidden in the bushes, praying that the monster wouldn't come after her. What kind of mother was she? How could she have been such a coward? And now Kathryn was a vampire, and it was all her fault.

She blinked back hot tears, sorely afraid that she would never see her daughter again.

Vampire. Victoria stared into the flames, the word repeating itself endlessly in her mind.

Now that it was too late, she realized Cabrera was nothing like the monster who had kidnapped Kathryn. As Kat had so often reminded her, Roan had taken them in, fed them, clothed them, offered to rebuild their ruined home, and asked for nothing in return.

And he loved her daughter. He would have provided for Kathryn for the rest of her life, cared for her, cherished her.

Victoria blew out a sigh of regret. She had let her fear of Cabrera, her prejudices, blind her to the truth. And to the love she had seen in his eyes whenever he looked at her daughter.

And now Kathryn was at the mercy of a true monster.

A flood of tears burned her eyes and spilled down her cheeks. Victoria made no effort to wipe them away. Wailing softly, she buried her face in her hands and sobbed until her throat was raw and she had no tears left.

Chapter Thirty-One

Kathryn woke in complete darkness, with no recollection of where she was or how she had gotten there. She felt strange, different, as if she was in someone else's body. There was a foul taste in her mouth, a curious ache deep inside.

She sat up, wondering why she felt so peculiar, why she could see so clearly when there were no lights visible and no windows, why she could hear whispered voices coming from beyond the closed door. Not just the sound, but the words, as well, as if the people speaking were in the room with her.

Rising, she tried the latch, somewhat surprised to find it unlocked. A short hallway led to a larger area. A single candle flickered in the middle of a square wooden table. The taper's soft glow cast dancing shadows on the walls. It hurt her eyes to look directly at the flame. Two men sat at the table. One of them was a stranger. He smelled human—and yet different—as if he was more than human.

The other was the vampire Juan Pascual.

Seeing him pricked her memory. "You! What have you done with my mother?"

He shrugged. "I've done nothing. She was fine when last I saw her."

"You left her? Where?" She doubled over, clutching her stomach as a sharp pain knifed through her. "Where . . . ?" she gasped. "Where is she?"

"I told you. I don't know."

Kathryn looked up at him, panting through the pain in her gut. "What have you done to me?"

He barked a laugh, though she failed to see what was so funny. Had he poisoned her? Was this his revenge again Cabrera?

"You're hungry, that's all."

She shook her head. She had never felt hunger pangs like this before.

Pascual grabbed the arm of the man sitting across the table, rolled up his shirtsleeve, then bit into the man's left wrist. Bright red blood welled from the twin puncture wounds.

And Kathryn's stomach clenched tighter. She stared at the blood as if she had never seen anything like it before. Stared at it and hungered for it as she had never hungered for anything in her life.

Before she realized what she was doing, she staggered forward, grabbed the stranger's arm in both hands, and lapped up the blood. It was strong and bitter on her tongue and yet undeniably desirable.

She drank until the man jerked his arm away.

Lifting her head, Kathryn bared her fangs and growled at him, then clapped her hand over her mouth. What had she done?

She stared at Pascual, at the smug expression on his swarthy face, and she knew.

He had made her what he was.

She was a vampire now.

Like Juan Pascual.

Like Cabrera.

She murmured Roan's name, and Pascual laughed again.

"Forget him," the vampire said. "You are mine now."

"I'll never be yours, you . . . you monster!"

"I guess that makes *you* a monster, too," he said with a cruel grin. "Just remember, it was I, Juan Diego Pascual, who turned you. That makes *me* your master, and *you* my fledgling. You are bound to me now, *mujer,* blood to blood for as long as I let you live. Whatever I command, you will obey."

"No!" Stunned by his words, she shook her head. "No. No, I don't believe you."

"Kathryn, sit down."

She tried to resist, but his voice ran through her, sharp and cold as shards of ice, stealing her will. Unable to help herself, she pulled out the third chair at the table and sat down, then stared at him in horror as she realized she was no longer in control of her own actions, nor would she be as long as she lived.

Stunned by the knowledge that her life was no longer her own, Kathryn slumped in the chair. "What are you going to do with me?" she asked, remembering that she had asked Roan the very same question not so long ago.

A wicked grin spread across Pascual's face. "What do you think?"

She shook her head as a number of possibilities, each worse than the last, flitted through her mind.

He cocked his head to the side, eyes narrowing thoughtfully. "To tell you the truth, I've not yet decided which will hurt him more—keeping you alive and by my side . . . or compelling you to walk into the sun's light."

Kathryn shuddered. Death by fire. She could think of nothing more agonizing for mortals or vampires.

"You're a very pretty woman." Pascual's gaze moved

slowly over her face, lingered on the swell of her breasts. "Very pretty indeed."

Springing to her feet, she backed away from the table, her hands clenched at her sides. "I'll kill myself if you touch me!"

"No, you won't." He sat back, fingers drumming on the tabletop. "What did Cabrera tell you of vampires? Didn't he tell you that master vampires can compel their fledglings to do anything and everything they desire?"

She nodded. Then, feeling suddenly sick to her stomach, she slid down to the floor, praying that Roan was searching for her, that he would soon find her and take her away from this dreadful creature.

Pascual slammed his hand on the table. "Bowen, go find me something to eat. Something young and fresh and female."

With a grunt, Bowen left the room.

"Is he your slave?"

"More or less. Many of our kind keep humans in their thrall. Someone to run errands during the daylight hours, or to watch over our lairs while we rest. But Bowen is more than that," he confided with a sly grin. "And I pay him well to serve me."

"Do you drink from him?"

"No. I need him to stay strong. Feeding on a human too often weakens them."

"So you've sent him out to find . . . ?"

"I believe *prey* is the word you're looking for." He smiled, displaying his fangs. "I'll gladly share it with you."

Bowen returned a short time later with a street urchin in tow. She was just a child, no more than two or three, with dirty brown hair, a twice-patched dress, and a look of terror in her eyes. Too frightened to scream or speak, she simply stood there, like a lamb waiting for the wolf to strike.

Kathryn stared at her in horror, then looked at Pascual. "You can't mean to . . . ?" She clamped her lips together. Anything she said would just scare the child more.

"The young ones are the sweetest." Pascual patted the girl's cheek. "So, fledgling, will you go first, or shall I?"

With a shake of her head, Kathryn backed away from the child, fully intending to return to the other room and shut the door. She wanted nothing to do with preying on children.

But Pascual had other ideas. "Sit, Kathryn! You will stay and you will watch. This is what you are. This is how you survive."

She sank back down on the chair, arms wrapped around her waist, unable to look away as Pascual pulled the urchin toward him and lifted her onto his lap. He mesmerized the girl with a glance so that she sat quiescent in his arms, her expression blank.

"You need to put your human emotions aside," Pascual said, stroking the child's hair, "and embrace what you are."

And then he sank his fangs into the toddler's throat and drank.

And drank.

To her utter horror, Kathryn watched avidly, unable to tear her gaze away. It was just a child. Innocent. Helpless. And yet the scent of the little girl's blood twisted Kathryn's gut. Had she been able to move, she feared she might have wrested the girl from Pascual's grasp and drained her dry. How had Roan lived with this insidious hunger for centuries without going mad?

As though sensing her thoughts, Pascual met her gaze over the child's head. "Would you like a drink?"

She shook her head, afraid he would try to compel her to prey on the little girl, and more afraid that she lacked the willpower to resist.

When Pascual was finished, the girl lay limp and unmoving in his arms.

Bowen took the body away to dispose of it.

Just another ragged, homeless child who would not be missed.

The streets were full of them.

The next two weeks were the worst of Kathryn's life. Pascual seemed determined to go out of his way to shock her, to prove to her that he was, indeed, the monster she took him for—to convince her that she was no better than he. His cruelty knew no bounds. As Roan had said, the vampire was merciless, with no hint of humanity. He killed indiscriminately and reveled in the pain and terror he caused.

Being with him, watching him, was torture of the worst kind. There was only one saving grace, one she could not explain. He could not force her to do anything she found truly abhorrent. Kathryn didn't know why, and neither did Pascual.

The first time his compulsion failed, he beat her until she was black and blue. She cowered beneath his attack, her arms covering her head. The pain was terrible but not unbearable. The bruises were gone when she woke the following night.

The second time he whipped her until she bled. This pain was worse but, because she was a vampire, the lacerations healed almost immediately, which only made him angrier. She knew he wanted to cow her into submission, but his abuse only served to make her more determined than ever to defy him even as it increased her hatred.

The third time she refused to obey, he locked her in a cellar, bound with heavy silver chains, and left her there for three days. This was the worst punishment of all. The silver not only burned her skin, it left her feeling weak. The pain of not feeding was excruciating.

On the fourth day, he brought her a little boy with big blue eyes and curly blond hair. It took every ounce of willpower Kathryn possessed to keep from falling on the child and draining him dry.

When she refused, Pascual broke the boy's neck. And in that moment, Kathryn vowed that one day she would destroy Juan Pascual even if she died in the attempt.

At the end of the week, he took her hunting with him. He found an elderly couple out strolling hand in hand in the rain. The woman held an umbrella, the man carried a cane.

Pascual mesmerized them both, pushed the man toward Kathryn, and bent his head over the woman's neck.

Murmuring, "Please forgive me," Kathryn took the man in her arms. Without quite knowing how, her mind brushed his and she knew that the cane he carried had a sword sheathed inside.

Before she could second-guess what she was doing, Kathryn pulled the sword and drove it into Pascual's back with all the strength she possessed.

Howling in pain, he fell to the ground.

She didn't wait to see if the blow destroyed him or not, just turned on her heel and fled.

Chapter Thirty-Two

Roan spent the week after Kathryn's disappearance searching the town from one end to the other. Every empty house and building, every barn and deserted shed and shack. Every possible place where a vampire might hole up, but he found no trace of Pascual or Kathryn.

He cursed long and loud as he prowled the town's outskirts. If Pascual had left town—or worse, the country—he would never find Kathryn.

But he couldn't stop looking. Not now. Not ever.

During the following week, he scoured every surrounding town and village, his search spreading outward, ever outward.

And still there was no trace of Pascual.

He spent little time in the manor with Victoria, unable to bear the anguish in her eyes, knowing that he was the one to blame for what had happened.

Victoria had broken down in front of him one night, sobbing that it was her fault Pascual had turned Kathryn. He had been stunned to learn that Victoria felt guilty because she had run away instead of trying to defend Kat and that she blamed herself for everything that had happened to her daughter. He had assured Victoria that trying to fight Pascual would have been useless and that, had she tried to interfere, Pascual would likely have killed her.

After that night, he made sure Victoria and Nan had everything they needed, but he shunned their company.

With the rising of the sun, he sought refuge in his lair. As he closed his eyes, his last conscious thought was always for the woman he loved. Murmuring, "Please let her be alive," he tumbled into oblivion.

Roan woke as he always did. One minute he was adrift in utter darkness, the next he was awake and aware. And on this night, as always, his first thought—like his last— was for Kathryn.

He rose, his preternatural senses expanding. Was he imagining it, or was she here, in the house? He had no sense of her other than the remembered scent of her skin and hair.

Dissolving into mist, he drifted to the manor's upper floor and there, in one of the empty storerooms off the kitchen, he found her huddled on the floor under a pile of old blankets.

Hunkering down beside her, he tossed the blankets aside. And cursed softly. Her hair was matted, her dress stained with old blood, hers and someone else's. It was obvious she hadn't bathed since being abducted. "Kathryn?"

Her eyes snapped open. For a moment, she didn't move, didn't speak. Then, with a mingled cry of joy and relief, she threw herself into his arms.

Murmuring her name, he stroked her hair, her back, unable to believe she was really there, alive and well and in his arms at last.

Holding her close, he showered her with kisses, until

they were both breathless. It took him a few minutes to acknowledge the changes in her—the way she moved, the fact that she was comfortable in the complete darkness that surrounded them, the faint scent of fresh blood on her breath, the slower beat of her heart.

Holding her at arm's length, he said, "He turned you." Victoria had told him what had happened, but he hadn't wanted to believe it. But there was no denying the proof of his own senses.

Kathryn's gaze slid away from his. "Does it matter?"

"Damn right! You're bound to him now."

She started to rise, but he grabbed her arm. "Where is he?"

"I'm not sure. I might have killed him. I hope I killed him!" she exclaimed, her eyes flashing fire.

"What happened?"

"You were so right about him! He is a monster, Roan. You can't believe what he's done, what he's capable of."

"I know exactly what he's capable of."

"He took me hunting last night. He chose an elderly couple for his prey. The man had a sword in a cane. I drove it into Pascual's back and then I ran. I don't remember how I got here but I must have transported myself. Everything that happened after that is just a blur."

"Unless you took his head, or that sword was silver and you drove it through his heart, you only wounded him."

She didn't want to believe Pascual still lived, but she knew it was true. "Then I'll just have to try again! He tried to force me do terrible things, things I can't even repeat. But I refused."

Roan frowned at her. "You refused? How?"

"What do you mean, how? I just said no."

"I've never heard of a fledgling being able to resist her master's compulsion."

"I couldn't at first. But I kept trying. Maybe it's because you gave me your blood."

"It's doubtful you have any left." But there was no way to know for sure. On the one hand, it was possible she had retained some small amount of his blood and that it had given her enough power to resist Pascual. On the other hand, if his blood still ran in her veins, why hadn't he been able to find her? "Where did he take you? I looked everywhere."

"He has an underground lair about two hundred miles from here." She shuddered with the memory. "It's like a dungeon."

Roan took a deep breath before asking, "Did he hurt you?"

She lowered her gaze. "I don't want to talk about it."

He didn't like the sound of that, but when he tried to read her thoughts, he couldn't get past the barrier she had erected, which only made him more certain that she had been through hell. And more determined than ever to destroy Pascual. "Could you find his lair again?"

She nodded. "But not tonight. Roan?"

"What's wrong?"

"Do you still feel the same about me?"

"Ah, Kat." Drawing her into his arms again, he rained featherlight kisses on her cheeks, her brow, the sweet curve of her neck. "My feelings for you will never change, love." Tilting her chin up, he gazed into her eyes. "What about you?"

"I still love you as much as ever. But . . ."

"Go on."

"How can we be together when Pascual is my master?"

"You've defied him before. You can do it again."

She nodded, though she didn't look convinced.

"He's a master vampire," Roan said quietly. "But so am I. I'm thinking if you and I exchange blood, it might dissolve the link between you and Pascual. At the least, it might weaken it, giving you the ability to ignore all of his commands."

"I'm willing to try anything to get him out of my head!"

"Vampires don't normally feed on each other," Roan remarked, "but since my blood once saved your life . . ." He shrugged.

"Let's do it. Now. Tonight."

"I'll drink from you first."

Closing her eyes, she tilted her head to the side, giving him access to her throat. With the brutality of Pascual's bites still fresh in her mind, she tensed when she felt Roan's fangs brush her skin. But there was no pain when he drank from her and she relaxed against him. This was Roan. He would never hurt her.

He drank deeply, taking more than he ever had in the past. She felt light-headed when he lifted his head.

"Your turn," he said.

"How will I know when to stop?"

"I'll tell you."

Feeling a little self-conscious, she put her arms around him and lowered her head to his neck. Pascual's blood had turned her stomach with disgust, but Roan's was sweet, just as she remembered from when he had visited her in the hospital. She felt its power flowing through her, filling her, warming her. To her relief, she felt Pascual's power over her gradually growing weaker.

"Kathryn, enough."

She lifted her head reluctantly.

"How do you feel?"

"I'm not sure. I don't think his link to me is completely gone, but my link to you is stronger." She threw her arms around Roan's neck. "Thank you!"

Roan hugged her close. He sensed Pascual's presence in her blood, but it was weak, almost nonexistent. Roan rested his forehead against hers. Kathryn was his again. The blood link burned bright and strong between them.

"Pascual's blood tasted horrible," she remarked, her brow furrowed. "His companion's was bitter. But yours is sweet. Why? I thought all blood was the same."

"No. Blood type, age, gender, your prey's health. I've heard witch blood is bitter. As for my blood," he said with a smile, "I'm sure love made the difference."

Kathryn reflected on that a moment, then pulled away, her expression troubled. "Are you my master now? Will you have the same power over me that Pascual had?"

"I don't know. But even if I do, you must know I would never use it. I don't want a slave or a zombie as my wife. I want a woman with her own thoughts, her own ideas." He pulled her back into his arms, his gaze caressing her face. "I want you."

"And I, you." For a few minutes, she sat there, content to be in his embrace. Then, with a sigh, she said, "My mother knows what I am, doesn't she?"

Roan nodded. "She's the one who told me what happened."

"How does she feel about me, now that I'm not me anymore?"

"You are still Kathryn."

"Am I?"

He nodded again. "Your mother blames herself for what happened to you. She's wasting away with guilt because she didn't try to defend you against Pascual. But she's not to blame," he said. "I am."

"You? Why?"

"This never would have happened if I hadn't brought you into my life. I knew the risks and I ignored them. I'm surprised you don't hate me."

Murmuring his name, she stroked his cheek. "I could never hate you. Maybe this was meant to happen."

He snorted.

"How do you know it wasn't?" she asked. "If I'd remained human, I would have grown old. This way, we can be together forever. If that's what you want."

"Is it what you want?"

"You know it is."

"You should probably get cleaned up and then go see your mother."

"I don't know."

"She'll be glad to see you, no matter what."

"All right," Kathryn agreed with a sigh. "Let's get it over with."

Taking her by the hand, he lifted her to her feet. "Come on, I'll show you where I rest. Where *we'll* rest."

She shivered as an image of that wooden coffin sprang into her mind.

"What's wrong?"

"That casket in the cellar. Is that where you really spend the day?"

"Not for centuries."

"The book said vampires had to sleep in their coffins with the soil of their homeland."

"Another myth."

"Thank goodness!" She couldn't bear the thought of climbing into a wooden box and closing the lid. And then she frowned. "If you don't need it, why do you keep it?"

"I'm not sure. Gyorgy told me I needed to rest in a dark place during the day. He rested in a coffin, so I assumed that meant I had to." He shook his head. "Some vampires might be comfortable in a dark, cramped place, but I wasn't. Come on, let's get you cleaned up. We've kept your mother waiting long enough."

Roan's lair was located below the wine cellar. At his word, dozens of candles sprang to life, illuminating a large, rectangular space. Oriental carpets covered the hard-packed earthen floor. An overly large bed and a small, square table were the room's only furnishings.

The walls narrowed and then formed a natural arch. The sound of running water reached her ears. Curious, Kathryn stepped through the arch and found a small pool surrounded by lacy ferns and a scattering of flowers.

"Milady, your bath awaits," Roan said, coming up behind her.

"Is it cold?"

"No." He handed her a towel and a bar of scented soap. "Take your time." He kissed her lightly. "I'll go upstairs and find you a change of clothes and let your mother know that you're home and you're safe."

Roan left clean clothes, a pair of shoes, and a hairbrush on the bed for Kathryn before going up to confront Victoria. He found her sitting on the sofa in the parlor, a blanket draped over her lap. She looked like she had aged ten years since Kathryn's disappearance.

He took the chair across from her.

She listened intently as he told her about Kathryn. "Is she all right?" Victoria's hands twisted in her lap. "Does she hate me for running away? What should I say to her?" She leaned forward, her brow furrowed. "Is she very different?"

"She's fine." Roan stretched his legs out in front of him. "She has no reason to hate you, nor does she think you're responsible for any of it. Everything that's happened to her, and to you, is my fault. Luckily for me, she's not casting any blame. As for being different . . ." He shrugged. "She is and she isn't. She's a little nervous about seeing you, about what you'll think."

Victoria fell back against the cushions. "I'm just so relieved that she's still alive . . ." Her gaze searched his. "Is she? Alive?"

"Yes, and no."

Victoria's face paled. "What does that mean?"

"It means she's alive but not human anymore."

"And she'll have to drink . . . blood? To survive?"

"Yes. You'll both have to make adjustments in your relationship. We all will."

"I owe you an apology," Victoria said, not quite meeting his gaze. "I thought you were a monster, but I realize now that . . . well, that I was wrong about you. But not wrong in wishing you and Kathryn had never met."

"Had we never met, Kathryn would have died in the hospital," he reminded her, his voice cool. "No matter what you think, I love your daughter with all that I am. I cannot be sorry I met her. But I am sorry for the pain and misery it has caused you both." He cocked his head to the side. "She's here."

Out in the hallway, Kathryn took several deep breaths. She didn't know why she was so nervous. Her mother loved her, she mused, then frowned. Her mother had loved a Kathryn that no longer existed. She didn't feel the same, didn't even know if she looked the same.

Kathryn clenched her hands. The only humans she had been near since Pascual had turned her had been prey. What if she couldn't control her hunger? What if she bit her mother? Attacked Nan? Or turned into some kind of ravening, uncontrollable monster?

"I can't do this," she muttered. "Not now." She ran out the back door into the backyard.

Bianca let out a joyful whinny when Kathryn approached the corral; then, with a toss of her head, the mare flattened her ears and backed away.

"Even my horse doesn't love me anymore," Kathryn muttered. "She's probably afraid I'll bite her on the neck!"

"She'll adjust." Coming up behind her, Roan slipped his arms around her waist. "And so will your mother."

"Are you sure about that?"

"I'm sure."

Kathryn shook her head. "I can't face her. It's too soon. I'm not ready."

"I'll be with you."

She turned in his arms, her gaze searching his. "Do I look the same?"

"Your skin is more translucent. Your hair is thicker, your eyes a little darker, your movements are more fluid, but I don't think your mother will notice any of that. All she'll see is her daughter."

Kathryn closed her eyes and took a deep breath. "All right, let's go."

Victoria threw the blanket aside, stood on trembling legs, and hurried forward to embrace her daughter. Tears rolled down her cheeks as she murmured Kathryn's name and begged for her forgiveness.

Kathryn tensed as her mother held her close, all too aware of the beating of her mother's heart, the scent of her blood. She was vastly relieved—if puzzled—that it didn't stir her hunger.

Taking a deep breath, she patted her mother's back. "There's nothing to forgive, Mama. You couldn't have done anything to help. Had you tried, you might have been killed. Or worse."

"That's what Roan said."

"And he was right," Kat said, smiling at him. "I'm home now and we're all together. That's all that matters."

Victoria shook her head. "How can you say that? You're a . . . a vampire, and . . ." Her voice trailed off as her body went limp.

"Mama!" Kathryn wrapped her arms around her mother and carried her to the sofa, then glanced over her shoulder at Roan. "What's wrong with her?" Kat asked, even as she marveled at her ability to lift her mother so effortlessly.

"She hasn't been eating. The lack of food, the excitement of seeing you again—I think it all just caught up with her."

Sitting on the floor, Kathryn took her mother's hand in hers. "She's all the family I have left."

"I think she'll be fine, now that you're home again."

Kathryn nodded. She hoped he was right. He had to be right.

Roan slipped his arm around Kathryn's shoulders. They had put Victoria to bed an hour ago, then retired to his lair. "How are you doing, love?"

"I'm not sure. Sometimes I'm filled with so much energy, I think I'm going to jump out of my skin. Roan, I picked up my mother as if she weighed no more than a child."

"Added strength comes with the territory," he said with a shrug. "You'll get used to it."

"Did it take you a long time to adjust to being a vampire?"

"It took a hell of a long time to control my hunger." His gaze probed hers. "How are you handling it, really?"

"All right, I guess," she said with a rueful grin. "At least I haven't killed anyone yet."

"Then you're way ahead of me," he said dryly.

"I was afraid I'd want to prey on my mother, but I didn't feel any need to do so. Isn't that odd?"

"You've been turned by two master vampires. I'm thinking that our blood—old blood—has tempered the hunger most fledglings experience. As for the rest, becoming a vampire doesn't drastically change who you are, once you adjust to your new life. If you weren't prone to evil and violence when you were mortal, becoming a vampire won't change that."

"Who turned you?"

Roan shifted on the bed. "His name was Gyorgy. He was Romani. A Gypsy. He had a voice like an angel and the soul of a devil. But he was a likable guy. He turned me on a cold winter night, told me what I needed to know, and left me."

"How old were you?"

"Twenty-seven."

"Were you married?" Funny, she had never thought to ask about that until now.

"Not at the time."

"What does that mean?"

"I was married briefly before I was turned. Her name was Lynette. We were both very young, less than twenty. We ran away together late one summer night." He smiled at the memory. "We had nothing, but it didn't matter. We were in love. Madly, deeply, in love. We settled in a small village. I found work. We lived in a rented room. We had nothing," he said again. "Nothing but each other. And it was enough. We'd been married five years when she got pregnant. And then the plague came and wiped out most of the village. It took her, too—and the child."

"I'm so sorry."

"It was centuries ago. Two years later, Gyorgy turned me."

"And you've lived alone ever since?"

He nodded. "More or less." Vampire or not, he was still a man. There had been women since Lynette and Varinia—he had lost count of how many—but he had never again given away his heart. Until Kathryn.

"Did you ever see Gyorgy again?"

"No. I've often wondered if he's still alive, just as I've wondered why he turned me instead of draining me dry."

Kathryn looked up at him, her eyes shining with love. "I'm glad he didn't kill you."

"So am I." He drew her closer, reveling in the womanly scent that was hers alone, the soft silk of her hair against his cheek. "I missed you more than you can imagine."

"Do you think Pascual will leave us alone now?"

"No. But now it's two against one," Roan said, his voice hard. "Next time we meet, I'll destroy him."

"Unless I beat you to it," Kathryn said, her voice as determined as his.

Roan chuckled. "It's not a contest, Kat."

"I want him dead as much—no, more—than you do!"

"Forget Pascual. When are you going to marry me?"

"As soon as my mother gets better, I promise."

In a move so swift only another vampire could have seen it, Roan had her flat on her back. Rising over her, his gaze burned into hers. "If you want to be a virgin on your wedding night," he growled with a roguish grin, "it had better be soon."

Chapter Thirty-Three

Pascual tossed the body of the first whore he had preyed on into a roadside ditch before sinking his fangs deep into the throat of the second. And all the while he cursed Cabrera's woman, even as he wondered where she had found the strength to defy him. No other fledgling he had ever heard of had been able to resist their master's compulsion. It was impossible. Yet she had defied him at every turn. It had amused him at first, but not for long.

He drained the blood from the second woman and tossed her body into the ditch on top of the first.

He had tried on numerous occasions to home in on his link to Kathryn. He could sense it but it was no longer strong enough to follow. There was something blocking his connection, something stronger, almost as if . . . He swore long and loud. Of course! Roan had drained her and then reclaimed her by giving her his own blood, as if turning her for the first time.

"Nice try," Pascual muttered. He didn't need a blood link to find the woman. He had no doubt she had run back to Cabrera's lair. It wouldn't be easy to lure Kathryn or her mother away a second time.

For a brief moment, he considered leaving town and

forgetting his vow to avenge himself on Cabrera. There was little excitement in this dreary place. Small towns offered scant shelter for vampires. It was far easier to lose oneself in more populous cities like Paris or London. Not to mention having access to a wider variety of prey. The blood from one country to another varied in taste and texture, a matter of importance to someone whose diet was severely limited.

The thought of moving on was tempting. He'd had some rollicking good times in Paris, dallying with pretty *mademoiselles* who smelled so damn good and tasted even better.

But then he remembered Varinia and how she had chosen Cabrera over him and how, in his rage, he had killed her.

As far as he was concerned, Varinia's death was on Cabrera's hands. And for that sin alone, his enemy had to pay.

After a prolonged recovery, Mrs. Shumway was discharged from the hospital. Roan had arranged for someone from the hospital to see her safely home and she arrived at the manor late in the afternoon.

Victoria noted with some distress that the cook had lost considerable weight but seemed to be in good spirits.

With a shy smile, Nan welcomed Mrs. Shumway home with a hug.

Victoria had noticed that the maid never had much to say but seemed quite attached to the older woman.

Patting Nan's back, Mrs. Shumway asked after Kathryn's whereabouts.

"She and Mr. Cabrera went off to spend the day together, but they should be back by nightfall," Victoria said, using the lie Cabrera had suggested. "How are you feeling, Mrs. Shumway?"

"A wee bit under the weather still," she said, lifting a hand to her head. "The doctor said I'll be right as rain in no time at all."

"That is good news," Victoria said, smiling.

Mrs. Shumway nodded. "Is Miss Kathryn all right? Poor lamb. Sure, and I thought we were all goners when those horrid men attacked us, though I don't remember much after that."

"She was badly scared, but she wasn't hurt," Victoria said, shading the truth. "Mr. Cabrera found her and brought her home. Why don't you rest a bit now?" she suggested, hoping to avoid further questions she wouldn't or couldn't answer. "Nan and I will look after things today."

"Oh, no, missus. I don't think I should. Mr. Cabrera isn't paying me to lay about."

"I'm sure he'll understand. After all, you were injured trying to save Kathryn."

Mrs. Shumway frowned uncertainly, but in the end, she agreed and went up to her room.

Nan went down to the kitchen to see about dinner, leaving Victoria alone in the parlor with too much time on her hands to think about things she would rather forget. How were they going to explain Kathryn's continued absences during the day? It was easy to promote the fallacy that Roan spent his days at work, but they couldn't use that excuse for Kathryn.

Victoria blew out a sigh. One thing was certain. Life had definitely become more complicated. She still didn't know what to make of her daughter. Kathryn seemed the same—looked much the same—and yet she was different. Of course, that was to be expected, now that she was a vampire.

Feeling a chill, Victoria scrubbed her hands up and down her arms. She knew nothing about vampires. Was Kathryn truly immortal now? Did she thirst for blood? Would she turn into some kind of monster? Were any of them safe in the house with two vampires?

She sighed again, wondering how long it would be until the danger posed by that other vampire was past and she could move into the lovely house Cabrera had had built to replace her old home.

Wondering if she would ever again feel comfortable around her own daughter.

Kathryn woke gasping for breath. For a moment, she lay there, hands fisted at her sides. It was disconcerting, waking from the nothingness of the Dark Sleep to full awareness. It always caught her by surprise. She imagined it must be like being brought back from the dead, if such a thing was possible. It was always a bit of a shock, emerging from the complete and utter blackness of the Dark Sleep into the darkness of the night. To know she would never see the light of day again.

She glanced to her right. Roan's side of the bed was empty. Being a master vampire, he was able to retire later and rise earlier in the evening than she.

It seemed odd, sleeping in the same bed with a man who wasn't her husband, she mused, and then grinned. They weren't really "sleeping," at least not in the usual sense. Still, she enjoyed waking beside him, knowing he would soon be hers in every way.

Opening her amazing new senses, she immediately

located everyone in the household—her mother was in the library, doing a bit of embroidery. She could hear the needle moving through the cloth. Nan was helping Mrs. Shumway prepare the evening meal.

Kathryn sighed. Never again would she taste Mrs. Shumway's roast beef and potatoes, or her heavenly cherry tarts, or enjoy a thick slice of her freshly baked bread, or indulge in any of Cook's other delightful culinary creations. For the rest of her life, she would be restricted to existing on a warm, liquid diet. With a frown, she realized that although she had once loved meat and potatoes and all the rest, she had no true longing for any of it, no real regret that she couldn't go upstairs and share the meal.

Sitting up, she focused on the blood link between herself and Roan. He was far from home, his thoughts closed to her.

But she knew what he was doing.

He was hunting the rogue vampire, Juan Pascual. She wished he had taken her with him, because she was sorely afraid it would require both of them to bring Pascual down.

Cabrera stared at the remains of the two young prostitutes sprawled facedown in the ditch, their bodies still warm. The blood at their throats glistened blackly in the faint light cast by the moon. Juan Pascual's familiar scent wafted from the dead, but there was no lingering scent to follow. The trail started and ended here. How was that even possible? What kind of vampire magic did Pascual possess, Roan wondered, that enabled him to vanish so completely?

And then he frowned.

Pascual had always had an affinity for witches.

Roan swore under his breath as he recalled Kathryn mentioning the bitter taste of the blood of Pascual's companion.

Perhaps it wasn't vampire magic at all.

Chapter Thirty-Four

Victoria was still in bed when someone knocked at her door. Sitting up, she called, "Who is it?"

"Nan, miss."

"Come in."

"I took Miss Kathryn's cocoa to her room, but she's not there."

"She and Mr. Cabrera had an early appointment this morning," Victoria said. "It's likely they won't be back until after supper tonight."

"Very well. I'll let Mrs. Shumway know." The maid bobbed a curtsy and shut the door.

Victoria stared after her. How long could she keep making up excuses for Kathryn's absence before the household staff grew suspicious?

Victoria put the question to Roan that evening.

"I'll take care of it."

"What will you tell them?" Kathryn asked.

"The truth. Kat, send them to me in the library. Victoria, please go with Kat. I'll speak to them alone." —

* * *

Roan was standing with his back to the window when Nan and Mrs. Shumway shuffled into the room, their eyes downcast. Mortal thoughts were easy to read and theirs came through loud and clear. They feared he was going to dismiss them.

Victoria had gone to her room, but Kathryn lingered in the hallway near the door, curious to hear what he had to say.

Roan sat behind the desk as a way to put some distance between himself and the help. The last thing he wanted to do was intimidate them. "There's something I need to tell you. Something you may find hard to believe. A little frightening perhaps."

Nan moved closer to Mrs. Shumway and reached for her hand.

"Kathryn and I have been very pleased with your service," he went on. "So much so that I'm giving you both a raise."

"Bless you, sir," Mrs. Shumway said, obviously relieved that she would be maintaining her position.

Nan smiled and nodded.

"Is that all, sir?" the cook asked.

"No. You may have wondered why I've never taken my meals with Kathryn, and why she's spending her days elsewhere."

Nan glanced at Mrs. Shumway, leading him to believe that the maid had informed the cook of all that had happened in her absence. Sensing Kathryn's presence in the hallway, he spoke to her mind. *Don't let them run away.*

With a nod, she stood in front of the doorway.

"The truth is, Kathryn and I are vampires."

Nan gasped, the color draining from her face as she moved even closer to the cook.

Head high, voice trembling, Mrs. Shumway said, "I suspected as much."

"I thought you did," Roan said.

Mrs. Shumway nodded. "Sure, and there were stories of the undead in the village where I grew up. I was certain the old carriage maker who lived down the road was a vampire, but no one believed me."

"And now that you know about us?"

"I don't understand what you mean."

"Are you going to tell anyone about us, or can we depend on you to keep our secret?"

"My loyalty lies with you and Miss Kathryn," the cook said, obviously offended that he would think otherwise.

"And you, Nan?"

She stared at him, wide-eyed. "I . . . I won't tell a soul."

Roan swept his gaze over the two women, his mind probing theirs. Both were telling the truth. "Very well. Go along, now. And thank you."

Stepping into the room, Kathryn said, "Wait."

Nan and Mrs. Shumway turned to face her.

"Roan and I are to be married soon. I should very much like for the two of you to stand up with us. If you've no objection."

"Why, it would be our pleasure, I'm sure!" Mrs. Shumway said, beaming. "You're like my own daughter, God rest her soul."

Nan smiled shyly at Kathryn, and then frowned. "I've nothing to wear."

"I'm confident we can find you something," Kathryn said. "Both of you."

"That's most kind of you," Mrs. Shumway acknowledged. "Will that be all, sir?"

Roan nodded.

Nan bobbed a curtsy. Still clinging to the cook's hand, she followed her out of the room.

Kathryn stepped into the library and closed the door behind them. "How do you know they won't tell anyone?"

"I read their minds, of course. They were both telling the truth."

"And if they'd been lying, what would you have done?"

"Either wiped the conversation from their minds and dismissed them or hypnotized them to believe that we took our meals with Victoria. But that's a difficult illusion to sustain over a long period of time."

"I can't believe Mrs. Shumway knew and never said a word. Of course, I guess you did save her life by taking her to the hospital the night we were attacked."

"Gratitude is a wonderful thing."

Smiling, Kathryn rounded the desk and sat on his lap. "I'm very grateful you came after us."

"Are you?" he asked, his lips twitching.

"Very."

"Care to give me a small expression of your gratitude?"

"I thought you'd never ask." Wrapping her arms around his neck, she kissed him, just a light peck on the cheek.

"You call that a proper thank-you for saving your life?" he growled.

"I'm sure I can do better." She kissed him again, longer, deeper, laughed merrily when she felt the evidence of his desire stir to life. Sliding off his lap, she said, "I think I'd better go now."

Roan glared at her as she skipped out of the room, leaving him to suffer alone and in silence.

A week later, Mr. Hastings sent word that the new house would soon be ready for occupancy. Roan took Kathryn and Victoria to see it that night.

Victoria clapped her hands in delight when she stepped through the front door. Roan and Kathryn trailed behind her as she hurried from room to room, admiring the carpets on the floors, the drapes at the windows.

"It's all so wonderful!" she exclaimed as they returned to the parlor. "So much more than I imagined! Roan, how can I ever thank you for all you've done for me, for us?"

Taking Kathryn's hand in his, he said, "By giving us your blessing."

Victoria dropped down on one of the plush chairs near the fireplace.

"Mama?"

"Of course you may have my blessing," Victoria said. "It's just that . . ."

"That you had something else in mind for your daughter," Roan said quietly. "Someone else."

"Yes." She looked at Kathryn. "I always dreamed of seeing you wed in a church, of being there when your children were born . . ." Her voice trailed off and she blinked rapidly.

"We can still be married in a church," Roan said, "if that's what Kathryn wants."

"You can enter a holy place?" Victoria asked. "I mean, you won't burn up?"

Roan shook his head. "I can assure you that neither Kathryn nor I will go up in flames. Although we will have to be wed after the sun goes down."

"And as soon as possible," Kathryn said, smiling up at him.

In the morning, Victoria went to the dressmaker to arrange for an evening meeting so Kathryn could look at samples and patterns for a wedding gown. And then she went to the church to speak with the vicar. The modiste had informed her that she would need two weeks to make a dress, so Victoria and the vicar settled on a Saturday night, two weeks hence.

That evening, Roan accompanied Kathryn and Victoria to the dressmaker's.

"I'll wait out here," he said, handing the women out of the carriage. "Take as long as you need. And don't worry about the expense."

"Are you sure?" Kathryn asked.

"You will only get married once, love. Order the very best she has." He turned to Victoria. "And buy something for yourself as well."

Kathryn shook her head as she laid a pattern aside. "They're all so beautiful. How will I ever decide?"

Madame Fontaine, the modiste, picked up one of the many porcelain dolls she used to display her wares. "This gown will look wonderful on you, *ma petite*."

Kathryn ran her fingertips over the dress. Made of fine silk and lace, it was the prettiest one she had seen. And by far the most expensive.

"She's right," Victoria said. "It is the best one."

"We'll take it," Kathryn decided, even as she wondered how Roan could afford it. To her knowledge, he had no employment, no source of steady income. An inheritance, perhaps? Though it would have had to be quite large to last so long.

"What color would you like? Blue is very popular this season, as is this pale yellow," Madame Fontaine said, pointing at another doll. "White is always a good choice. Or maybe a pale pink—"

Victoria shook her head. "'Married in pink, your fortune

will sink,'" she said, quoting a popular saying of the day. "'Married in brown, you will live out of town.'"

"White, I think," Kathryn decided. It would be a nice contrast to Roan, who would likely be in black. "And the green taffeta for my mother. Oh! What about Nan and Mrs. Shumway?"

"I could bring them in tomorrow afternoon," Victoria said, "if that's all right with you."

Kathryn nodded, then turned back to Madame Fontaine. "Are you sure you can have four dresses ready in two weeks?"

Madame Fontaine nodded. "I will begin your wedding gown in the morning. My girls will see to the others."

Later that night, after everyone else had gone up to bed, Kathryn and Roan sat on the sofa. She snuggled against his side, thinking how drastically her life had changed in so short a time. Sometimes, as now, sitting in front of the fire, with Roan's arm around her, she felt like she was living in a fairy tale.

She looked up at Roan, admiring his profile, his strong jaw, his broad shoulders. He was the dark prince, tall and mysterious, the man of her dreams. And she was his princess.

Thinking about their wedding, she could almost forget that she was no longer the woman she had once been. She regretted that she would never have children, that the daylight hours were forever lost to her, that she would never again indulge in her favorite sweets. And yet, secure in the circle of his arms, feeling his lips against her cheek, the things she had lost seemed a small price to pay for eternity with the man she loved.

They would have decades together, perhaps centuries.

The thought gave her pause. Would Roan still love her in a hundred years? Two hundred? Would she still love him?

She sighed when he began nuzzling her neck. "I'm trying very hard not to read your mind," he said, his breath cool against her skin. "But your thoughts are too strong to ignore."

"What if we stop loving each other?"

"Do you really want to worry about that now?" He leaned back, though he kept his arm around her. "Even I cannot predict the future, Kat. But I know that I will love you as long as I live. And if you stop loving me . . ." His gaze darkened and his voice dropped to a whisper. "If that happens, I will let you go."

The pain in his voice made her heart ache. She was being foolish, she thought. He was right. No one could foresee the future. She loved him now, deeply, completely. Why was she ruining the present by worrying about something that might never happen?

"Two weeks," she murmured. "Right now, that seems like forever."

He nodded, his gaze burning into hers. "Darling, you have no idea."

Feeling suddenly playful, she batted her eyelashes at him. "I guess it's a good thing you have a lot of self-control."

"If you keep looking at me like that, my love, it might not last much longer."

Laughing softly, she ran her tongue across his lower lip, gasped when she suddenly found herself flat on her back beneath him.

"Still think it's funny?" he growled.

She took a deep breath. He was all vampire now, his eyes glowing with that faint red gleam, a hint of fang visible in his feral grin.

"Are you going to make my white gown a lie?" she asked with a saucy grin. "It stands for purity, you know."

"Kathryn, you're playing with fire."

Lifting her hand, she caressed his cheek. "Burn me, then. I've waited long enough."

She never knew what he might have done if her mother hadn't chosen that moment to come downstairs. Victoria uttered a wordless cry when she saw the two of them entwined on the sofa.

Kathryn let out a startled shriek of embarrassment.

Roan rolled off her and stood, his hands clenched at his sides.

"I'm . . . I'm sorry," Victoria stammered. "I . . ." Cheeks flushed dark red, she turned on her heel and ran back up the stairs.

"You'd better go, too," Roan said. "Before I lose what little self-control I have left." Muttering, "Only two bloody weeks," he closed his eyes and fought for restraint as his future bride left the room with her virtue still intact. On the one hand, he was glad for the interruption. He didn't want to take what was not yet truly his. On the other hand, the painful ache in his groin made him wish Victoria had never come down those stairs.

Roan didn't come to bed that night, nor was he there when Kathryn woke the following evening.

Opening her senses, she called his name. *Roan.*

I hear you.

Where are you?

On the front steps. Waiting for you to wake up. Get dressed and I'll take you hunting.

Hunting. The word sent a shiver of unease down her spine. She hadn't quite grown accustomed to thinking of herself as a predator. But there was no denying the hunger sizzling through her veins. *Five minutes.*

Take your time. We've got all night.

But she couldn't wait that long. Scrambling out of bed, she found a pair of black trousers, a black shirt, and boots on the chair near the door. Since they were her size, she tried them on. They fit like a glove.

Four minutes later, she joined Roan on the porch steps. She grinned, thinking they looked like a pair of Grim Reapers, which she supposed was what they were.

"Ready?" he asked.

"I always thought you wore black just because you liked it. But now I'm thinking it's so you can blend into the night."

"Finally figured that out, did you?"

"I'm guessing it doesn't show the blood, either."

Roan grinned at her. "No point in being morbid."

"But it's true, isn't it?"

He shrugged, but she didn't miss the amusement in his devil-black eyes.

"Let's go," she muttered.

"You'll feel better after you've fed."

"Do you ever miss real food?" It surprised her that she hadn't so far, though she felt like she should.

"Not for a long time." Taking her by the hand, he willed the two of them to a nearby town.

It took only minutes to find suitable prey—a young couple standing in the shadows, locked in each other's arms.

Roan mesmerized them both with a look. "Male or female?"

"Male."

Nodding, he gave the man a gentle push in her direction. "Do you ever feed on men?" Another question she had never thought to ask.

Roan shook his head. "Rarely. I find women are sweeter and smell better."

Kathryn took a deep breath. "He smells all right to me, kind of woodsy and . . . and I don't know how to describe it."

"Opposites attract, whether you're looking for a mate or a meal," he remarked as he cupped the young woman's chin in his hand and tilted her head to the side.

Kathryn watched, fascinated as Roan's tongue swept along the side of the woman's neck before he sank his fangs, very gently, into the tender skin beneath her left ear.

Pascual hadn't been gentle with his prey. Male or female, he had attacked them viciously, leaving nothing behind but an empty shell with terror-filled eyes.

But she could see that Roan made it pleasant for the woman. He held her for a moment, speaking quietly to her mind to ease her fears before he lowered his head to her neck.

Taking the man in her arms, Kathryn tried to do the same for him.

They decided to walk home. With her hand clasped in his and her hunger appeased, Kathryn studied the night, thinking she had never truly appreciated it before. She had never seen so many stars, though she knew the number hadn't changed. It was only her enhanced vision that made it seem like more. Flowers looked as bright and colorful in the dark as they did in the light of day. She was aware of sounds and scents she had never noticed before. Oddly, she felt as if she was a part of the night itself. It seemed to wrap itself around her, a palpable thing, whispering secrets in her ears that mortals would never know.

Roan tugged on her hand. "Come on."

Before she could ask where they were going, they were racing through the darkness. It was magical, she thought. Her feet barely touched the ground. She sailed effortlessly over obstacles in their path, vaulted lightly over hedges whether high or low. Her laughter trailed behind them as they sped toward home.

It was near dawn when the walls of the manor came into view. "That was exhilarating!" she exclaimed.

"Being a vampire isn't all blood and hunger, you know."

"It was amazing! I'm not tired or winded or anything." She twirled around, her arms outstretched. "I have so much to learn."

"And I'll be happy to teach you anything you want to know."

"I hate to see the night end," she said with a sigh. "I never knew it could be so beautiful."

"We'll have many more nights, love." Drawing her into his arms, he kissed her, a long, slow exploration of her lips with his. And then, abruptly, he lifted his head. "Go inside."

"What's wrong?"

"Just go. Now."

He was her master and there was no refusing that tone of voice. Inside, she hurried to the front window and pulled the curtains aside.

Roan stood in a shaft of waning moonlight, arms at his sides, hands clenched, as Juan Pascual stepped out of the shadows. She had no trouble hearing their conversation.

"So," Pascual drawled. "We meet again."

Roan nodded. "Shall we make it the last time?"

"I want my woman back."

"She was never your woman. She never will be."

Rage flared in Pascual's eyes. "I turned her. That makes her mine. And I will have her!"

"Not as long as I live."

Pascual took a step forward, then hesitated as the first faint rays of the rising sun crept over the horizon. "Next time we meet, I will destroy you, and the woman will be mine," he hissed and disappeared from sight.

Muttering an oath, Roan willed himself into the manor, threw his arms around Kathryn, who was already succumbing to the Dark Sleep, and willed them both down to his lair.

After putting Kathryn in bed, he slid in next to her and gathered her close to his side.

"He will not have you," he whispered. "The next time he crosses my path will be the last if I have to follow him into hell and back."

Chapter Thirty-Five

Kathryn couldn't help noticing that Roan was on edge the next few nights. He insisted she stay inside, and when she reminded him that she needed to feed, he let her drink from him.

It was an amazing experience. Roan's blood satisfied her as nothing else and tasted sweeter than any other. "Why can't I just drink from you all the time?"

"My blood won't sustain you over a long period of time. You need to feed on mortals to survive."

"But your blood is so much better. It makes me feel powerful. Invincible. And it tastes so good!"

"As does yours, love."

"How much longer do I have to stay in the house?"

"Until I know you're out of danger."

"And when will that be?" It was a foolish question. She knew the answer.

Roan nodded. "Not until Pascual is destroyed," he said flatly. *Or I am.*

Kathryn had expected some tension between herself and Nan and Mrs. Shumway now that they knew the truth, but both the maid and the cook seemed to have no qualms about working for a pair of vampires. Then again, with jobs hard to find—especially ones with good wages—maybe they were just happy to have steady employment. Their duties were light, since only Victoria was up and about during the day. And Roan had promised them a raise, leaving Kathryn to wonder, yet again, about the source of her future husband's income.

Roan had taken Kathryn and Victoria to see Madame Fontaine so that Kathryn and her mother could try on their gowns. Victoria had taken Nan and Mrs. Shumway to visit the modiste several days earlier, in the company of a hired bodyguard. Nan had chosen a pale yellow silk; Mrs. Shumway had selected a subdued mauve.

Kathryn sighed. Her mother was anxious to move into her new home and fretted because Roan deemed it unsafe for Victoria to live alone as long as Juan Pascual was a threat.

Everything came back to Pascual, she thought bitterly.

Thoughts of Pascual faded as her wedding night grew closer. Roan took her and Victoria to see Madame Fontaine for Kat's final fitting.

"It's beautiful," Victoria said, wiping the tears from her eyes. "And you look beautiful in it!"

"I feel beautiful," Kathryn murmured. She wished with all her heart that she could see her reflection in the full-length mirror. Unfortunately, Roan had neglected to teach her how to project an illusion, so she quickly changed back into her own clothes and stepped out of the dressing room before the modiste came in to see how she was doing.

"We'll take it," she said, handing the gown to the modiste, who assured them that all the gowns would be delivered the day before the wedding.

* * *

"Everything all right?" Roan asked as they emerged from the shop.

"I suppose so," Kathryn said.

"Why so sullen?" he asked, handing her into the carriage. "Doesn't your dress fit?"

"How would I know? I can't see myself."

"It fits beautifully," Victoria said. "And you look lovely in it."

Roan nodded as he helped Victoria into the carriage, then ducked in behind her. Not being able to see his reflection had never been much of a problem for him, but then, he was a man and not overly concerned with his appearance. But he could readily understand Kathryn's disappointment. She was about to be a bride for the first time. Of course she wanted to see how she looked.

And on their wedding night, he would use a little vampire magic to make it happen.

Victoria hung Kathryn's wedding gown in the wardrobe in the bedroom where Kathryn no longer slept.

Her daughter was getting married. It should have been an occasion for celebration, a happy gathering of friends and family all coming together to wish the bride and groom a long and happy life.

Of course, even if Kathryn had been marrying an ordinary man, there still would have been no family to help them celebrate. There were only the two of them, now that Basil was gone.

Sighing, she went down to the parlor. How she missed the days when Kathryn was a little girl, when they read stories to each other at bedtime, picked wildflowers in the spring and took long walks together—those halcyon days when her little girl needed her.

She sighed again as she looked around the room. She even missed tidying up her own house. There was nothing for her to do here. Nan did the cleaning and the laundry, made the beds, scrubbed the floors, washed the windows. Mrs. Shumway did the cooking and the baking, which in itself was a full-time job, even with only the three of them to cook for.

Sinking down on the sofa, Victoria gazed into the fireplace. Where did Kathryn and Roan spend the day? Had they been intimate yet? Was Kathryn happy as a vampire? Victoria shook her head. How could anyone possibly be happy with a life bereft of children? A life lived only at night?

Kathryn woke abruptly. Would she ever get used to being completely unaware one moment and suddenly awake the next? Even though she didn't need light to see, she was grateful for the candle beside the bed. A thought brought the flame to life. For a moment she stared at it in amazement. She really had no idea how her new powers worked, only that they did.

She turned onto her side, her gaze sliding over Roan. Candlelight flickered on his face, his bare chest, his muscular arms, and broad shoulders. He really was beautiful, she thought, and tomorrow night he would be hers forever. She ran her fingertips over his chest and flat belly. Tomorrow night she would be able to explore every inch of him.

"If you keep looking at me like that, we won't make it until tomorrow night," he warned, and in the blink of an eye, she was on her back and he was poised over her, every muscle taut, his eyes blazing.

Kathryn stared up at him, hardly daring to breathe.

Lowering his head, he ran his tongue along the side of her neck. His bite was gentle, at odds with the fire she had seen in his eyes. Pleasure flowed through her, warmer and sweeter than ever before.

She writhed beneath him and the next thing she knew, he was under her. She blinked at him. How had *that* happened?

Roan burst out laughing at the surprised look in her eyes.

"How did I do that?" she asked. It was one thing to light a small candle, another entirely to move a man of his size and strength.

"If you think something hard enough and it's within your power, you can make it happen."

"Really?" She smoothed the hair from his brow, then cupped his face in her hands, lowered her head and licked the soft skin beneath his ear. And then she bit him. His blood ran hot and sweet over her tongue and she lost herself in the pleasure it gave her.

"Enough," he said after a moment.

"Never enough," she complained.

"Sorry, love."

He rolled her over, then sat up and drew her into his arms. "Before this gets entirely out of hand, why don't you go upstairs and take a bath, and then I'll take you"—he sent her a wicked grin—"to dinner."

Kathryn made a face at him. Dinner, indeed. No prey in the world would ever taste as good or be as satisfying as that of her very own master vampire.

They hunted in a neighboring town, then took a leisurely stroll toward home. Once, walking several miles would have tired her, Kathryn mused. Now, she had energy to spare.

Roan unleashed his preternatural senses, searching the night for any sign of Pascual's presence. Detecting nothing out of the ordinary, he pulled Kathryn into the shadows to steal a kiss.

"Tomorrow night," he murmured, nuzzling her neck. "No doubts? No second thoughts about tying your life to mine?"

"Not one. We'll be happy, won't we?"

"That sounds like second thoughts to me."

"No," she said with a sigh. "I'm just hoping that our marriage won't be like my mother's second one."

"Why did she marry Darlington?"

"We didn't have anything after my father passed away. He was a wonderful man but not much of a provider. Basil offered my mother a home, security. It was only later that we learned his true nature. He was a cold, cruel man. Selfish. We would have been better off in the streets."

"Why didn't she leave him?"

"She tried. But he always found us and brought us back." Kathryn drew a deep, shuddering breath. "He beat her. And no one cared. She was his wife, after all. His property. The last time she ran away, he threatened to beat me if she left again."

"I'm sorry, love."

"Thank you for taking such good care of us."

His hand cupped her nape and he kissed her lightly, tenderly. "I love you, Kat. I will always be here for you and your mother."

"Can I ask you something?"

"Of course."

She hesitated. "Never mind."

"What do you wish to know, love? I want no secrets between us."

"I was wondering . . . I mean, you live in a manor house, you have servants. You built my mother a new home. Paid for my wedding gown and a dress for my mother . . . How? You don't work."

He was suddenly sorry he hadn't let the matter drop.

She looked up at him, waiting for his answer.

His hand slid away from her nape. "You won't like it."

"No secrets," she reminded him.

He stared past her, a muscle throbbing in his jaw. "When I was first turned, before I learned to control my rage and my hunger, I killed my prey."

She nodded. He had told her that before.

"And then I robbed them. I had acquired a small fortune by the time I learned to control my nature. I couldn't return the money, so I invested it. And now I live off the interest. I'm not proud of what I did . . ." He shrugged. "My wants and needs are few, but I quickly learned that having a permanent, secure lair was safer than resting in a cave or holing up in some abandoned building. Of course, I have to move every so often before people start to notice that I don't age."

She nodded again. That made sense. "So, do you have other lairs?"

"One in Italy. One in France." His gaze probed hers. "Does this change anything between us?"

"No. What's past is past. It's what you are now that matters. And I like who you are now."

He kissed her again, more deeply this time. "I'm happy to hear you say that," he said, reaching into his pocket. "I think it's time you had this."

Kathryn's eyes widened when he handed her a small, velvet box. Hardly daring to breathe, she opened it. Inside, nestled on a bed of black satin, was the most beautiful ring she had ever seen. The biggest diamond any girl could ask for was mounted on a wide gold band, surrounded by tiny rubies that, she was embarrassed to say, reminded her of drops of blood.

"Oh, Roan."

"You like it?"

"I love it. And you."

He kissed her again, wondering what he had ever done to deserve her trust and her love. And how he would survive the pain if he ever lost her.

Chapter Thirty-Six

Kathryn woke to the fragrant scent of roses. Sitting up, she saw the bed was covered with hundreds of dark red petals. A crystal vase of pure white roses sat on the bedside table. She picked up the card propped against the vase, smiled when she read the rhyming lines, written in a bold, scrawling hand:

> *Happy Wedding Day, my love*
> *Your tub awaits*
> > *I'll meet you at the church at 8*
> > *Don't be late!*
> > *RC.*

Still smiling, she went upstairs.

"Good evening, miss," the maid said with a shy smile. "Your bath is ready."

"Thank you, Nan."

"I'll be back in half an hour to help you into your gown."

Kathryn nodded as she went behind the screen to undress. She was getting married in an hour, she thought. Tonight she would be Roan's wife. Mrs. Cabrera.

Giggling like a schoolgirl with her first crush, she stepped into the tub.

Nan arrived thirty minutes later to help Kathryn into her gown. She oohed and aahed over Kathryn's ring.

Victoria entered the room a short time later. Clad in the green taffeta and wearing a pair of matching shoes, her hair upswept and pinned with a pair of glittering combs, she looked as if she didn't have a care in the world. "What's going on?" she asked when she saw Nan hovering over Kathryn. "Are you hurt?"

"No." Kathryn held out her hand, noting how the diamond reflected the candlelight.

Victoria's eyes widened. "My, that's . . . that's . . . it must have cost a fortune. Well," she said candidly, "at least we know he can look after you properly."

Laughing, Kathryn said, "Mama, you look beautiful."

"Thank you, Kat. So do you. How do you feel?"

"Fine. A little nervous. I've never been married before."

"Nan, if you don't mind," Victoria said, "I'll take over now."

"Yes, ma'am." The maid dropped a curtsy and left the room.

"Is something wrong?" Kathryn asked.

"No," Victoria replied, smiling as she picked up Kathryn's brush. "But as you said, you've never been a bride before. And I don't want to share these precious moments with anyone else." She ran the bristles through Kathryn's hair. "Will you wear it up?"

"No. Roan likes me to wear it down."

When Kathryn's hair lay in soft waves over her shoulders, Victoria picked up the veil and set it in place. It fell in graceful folds down Kathryn's back to the floor.

"You look like an angel," Victoria said, blinking back her tears. "I can't believe my little girl is getting married."

The words *to a vampire* hung unspoken in the air between them.

"I love him, Mama. Please don't worry about me. I've never been happier."

Victoria held out her arms and Kathryn went into them. She remembered all the good times they had shared before her father died—birthdays and Christmases, making cookies, reading stories, playing make-believe. Dozens of sweet traditions she had hoped to carry on with her own daughter someday.

She shook the thought aside as another took its place. She and Roan could be married for centuries. What did vampires do with all that time?

Taking a deep breath, Victoria wiped the tears from her eyes. "Are you ready? It's almost eight."

Kathryn nodded. "How do I look?"

"Perfect. I've never seen a happier or more beautiful bride. Let's go."

Nan and Mrs. Shumway were waiting for them in the parlor, each looking quite stylish in her new gown, hat, and shoes.

"The carriage Mr. Cabrera hired to take us to the church is waiting outside," the cook said. "And a lovely thing it is."

Eager to see Roan, Kathryn hurried outside, the butterflies in her stomach fluttering wildly as the driver—a burly man with hands as big as hams—opened the door. A second man sat on the bench, a shotgun across his lap.

"Miss Kathryn," the burly man said. "I'm Falcone. Mr. Cabrera sent us to drive you to the church."

She nodded. "The dove cries at midnight."

"And the rooster crows at dawn."

She smiled as Falcone murmured the countersign Roan had given her.

The driver handed Kathryn inside. She scooted over to make room for her mother. Nan and Mrs. Shumway climbed in after Victoria, chattering excitedly, admiring the interior of the carriage, which was plush indeed.

Falcone closed the door. The carriage swayed as he climbed up on the bench. A crack of the whip and the team moved out.

They hadn't gone far when the coach rocked violently back and forth. For a moment, Kathryn thought something was wrong, but when there was no cry of alarm and the horses didn't slow, she settled back in her seat.

A moment later, she shivered as a peculiar ripple moved over and through the interior of the coach. Dismissing it as a gust of wind, she settled back once again.

Unable to stop smiling, she lifted the curtain and glanced out the window. She was on her way at last. Soon, she would be a married woman. Mrs. Roan Cabrera, mistress of her own home, wife to the most wonderful man she had ever known.

She was so lost in daydreams, it took her a moment to realize her mother was trying to get her attention. "What is it, Mama? Did you forget something?"

Looking worried, Victoria said, "This isn't the way to the church."

"What?" Kathryn looked out the window again, expecting to see the church steeple ahead. Instead, she saw only darkness. She reached for the hand strap to steady herself as the horses broke into a gallop. The carriage rocked dangerously from side to side. Nan let out a hoarse cry of alarm as she was thrown against Mrs. Shumway.

Kathryn pulled the curtain back, intending to lean out and tell the driver to slow down, only to find that she couldn't. It was as if an invisible barrier prevented her from reaching beyond the window.

She recalled the odd wind that had blown over the carriage. Too late, she realized it hadn't been an errant breeze at all. It was magic, wrought by Pascual's man, Bowen. She had experienced it before. But tonight, caught up in the excitement of marrying Roan, she had let her guard down and it had passed by her unnoticed.

Fearing it was useless, she tried to open the door. It remained stubbornly closed.

She fought down the terror that threatened to engulf her. If Bowen was here, could Juan Pascual be far behind? The thought of seeing that monster again filled her with a cold and bitter rage. She had accepted what he had done to her because it couldn't be undone. Instead of spending the rest of her life railing against fate, she had chosen to make the best of her circumstances. But she wouldn't let Pascual hurt her mother, or her friends. Brave thoughts for a vampire who was still a fledgling. And then she smiled. She had defeated Pascual before and she could bloody well do it again. And this time would be the last time.

Victoria tugged on her arm. "What's going on?"

Kathryn shook her head. This couldn't be happening, not again. Her gaze darted from her mother's face to Nan's and Mrs. Shumway's. All were staring at her, eyes wide and scared, faces pale. She blew out a deep, shuddering sigh. Until Roan realized they were missing, she was their only hope. Where was Bowen taking them?

And what did Pascual plan to do with her and the others once they arrived?

She straightened her back and squared her shoulders, determined that this would be the last time Juan Pascual interfered in her life. She wasn't helpless and afraid this time. She might be a lowly fledgling, but she could feel Roan's blood thrumming through her veins, giving her strength and courage. Their link would lead him to her.

Hands tightly clenched, she watched the countryside speed by.

Roan arrived at the church, expecting to find Kathryn and the others waiting for him. Deciding to wait for her outside the beautiful old edifice, he stood in the shadows, enjoying the sounds of the night—the flutter of an owl's wings, the soft susurration of an errant breeze, the distant call of a night bird.

One minute passed. Five. Ten. And still no sign of Kathryn.

Something was wrong.

Opening his senses, he searched for the link to his woman. At first there was nothing. For a moment, panic threatened to engulf him, but then the blood bond between them quivered to life, stretching between them like an invisible tether.

All he had to do was follow it.

Just when Kathryn thought Bowen intended to drive all night long, the carriage slowed. A glance out the window showed they had entered a walled keep of some kind. The plants and trees around it were dead. Weeds flourished.

When the carriage came to a halt, Nan and Mrs. Shumway huddled together in a corner, looking scared half to death. Not that Kathryn could blame them. Now that they seemed to have arrived at their destination, her own courage wavered a little. Who knew what evil waited inside that dark abode?

Victoria gasped when Pascual's face appeared at the window on her side.

Bowen stood at the other. He murmured words Kathryn couldn't decipher, but when Nan and Mrs. Shumway suddenly slumped forward, she had no doubt it was a magical incantation. She was relieved to see they were still breathing.

Pascual tossed a pair of handcuffs through the window. They landed in Kathryn's lap. "Put those on." Seeing the rebellion in her eyes, he added, "Your mother will pay for any disobedience on your part."

Mouth set in a firm line, Kathryn did as she was told. The silver burned her skin like hellfire.

Bowen muttered another incantation and Kathryn felt the spell that imprisoned them inside the coach dissipate.

Pascual opened the door on her mother's side, grabbed Victoria by the arm, and hauled her, none too gently, out of the carriage. Victoria let out a cry when his fingers dug into her arm.

Bowen opened the door on Kathryn's side. "Get out."

Kathryn noticed he was careful to stay out of reach as she alighted. She glanced around, searching for some sign of Falcone and found none. She had little doubt that he and his companion had been killed and thrown off the coach.

"Start walking," Pascual ordered.

Kathryn sent her mother a reassuring glance, then struck out for the manor house.

Pascual stepped in behind her, followed by her mother and the warlock.

"What are you going to do with Nan and Mrs. Shumway?" Kathryn asked.

"I'll send Bowen back for them once you're settled."

Settled. She didn't like the sound of that.

"Bowen," Pascual called over his shoulder. "Get up here and open the door and invite Kathryn inside."

The man came running, dragging Victoria behind him. A word from the warlock had the front door flying open. Once inside, he shoved Victoria out of the way and said, "Kathryn, welcome to my home."

When she made no move to enter, Pascual gave her a push. Kathryn felt an odd sensation as she stumbled into the room. Thresholds had the power to resist vampires. She recalled reading that in Roan's book. "Mama, are you all right?"

Victoria nodded though she was visibly shaken.

Kathryn took a quick look around. From the outside, the place looked like it hadn't been occupied in decades, but the inside, reasonably well-kept, was furnished with ornate tables and sofas and chairs covered in rich fabrics. Shelves held expensive-looking vases and porcelain figurines. Paintings that appeared costly adorned the walls. Heavy velvet drapes covered the windows. She couldn't help wondering if Bowen had stolen every item in the house.

Sneering, Pascual tugged on her gown. "Nice dress, but I'm afraid there won't be a wedding tonight." He leered at her, then licked the side of her neck.

Stifling the urge to cringe at his touch, she glared at him.

Grabbing her forearm, Pascual said, "Let me show you to your bridal chamber. Perhaps instead of a marriage, we'll have a honeymoon."

"I'd rather die!"

"I can arrange that!" he snapped. "Bowen, bring the old lady along with us."

Kathryn tried to escape Pascual's grasp, but the silver

was doing its work, leeching her power, leaving her feeling weak and vaguely disoriented.

He dragged her down a narrow hallway and two sets of stairs. An iron-barred door waited at the bottom. It opened with a shriek of metal against metal.

Kathryn stared into the murky darkness beyond. Was it a dungeon?

Bowen locked her mother in the first cell while Pascual forced Kathryn to the end of the corridor, shoved her into the last cage, then slammed and locked the door with a flourish.

"I'll have to leave you now," Pascual said, with mock regret. "But don't worry. I'll be back soon. Bowen, go get the other two. All this excitement has given me a hell of a thirst."

Chapter Thirty-Seven

Roan materialized beside the carriage. At first, he thought it was empty, but then he heard slow, steady breathing, the beating of two hearts. Peering in the nearest window, he saw Nan and Mrs. Shumway slumped against each other. The lingering signature of a witch's spell hung in the air.

But it was Kathryn's scent that called to him. Dissolving into mist, he circled the house, but there was no way inside, not without an invitation from the owner. More likely Bowen than Pascual, he thought. Not that it mattered. Neither one was likely to ask him in.

Roan returned to the carriage, wondering what to do about Nan and Mrs. Shumway. They were obviously under an enchantment of some kind. Would they come out of it on their own, in time, or did Bowen have to remove it?

Grunting softly, he shook the maid's shoulder gently and then a little harder. When that failed to rouse her, he slapped her. She jerked upright, her gaze slightly unfocused.

"Nan?"

She stared at him a moment, her expression blank, and then she burst into tears.

"It's all right," he said gruffly. "Get hold of yourself. We've no time for tears."

Nan let out a startled gasp when Roan slapped Mrs. Shumway, sobbed her relief when the cook came awake with a start.

"Kathryn!" Mrs. Shumway exclaimed. "That monster has taken her again!"

"I know," Roan said dryly. "At least this time you didn't get hit on the head. Come on, let's get the two of you out of here." It wasn't the best decision he had ever made, he thought, wrapping one arm around the maid and the other around the cook. Their absence would alert Pascual to his presence, but leaving two women who were under his protection at Pascual's mercy was out of the question. There was little chance they would survive the night.

A thought carried the three of them to the parlor at Cabrera Manor.

"Keep the doors and windows locked," Roan instructed, his tone brusque. "Don't let anyone—friend or stranger— inside the house. And don't go outside under any circumstances. Understand?"

Nan nodded vigorously. The scent of fear coming off her skin made her smell like prey, arousing his thirst.

"I understand," Mrs. Shumway said. "Don't be frettin' about me and Nan, sir. Just bring Miss Kathryn back home. I've grown to love her like she was my own."

"Don't worry about us," Roan said. "You just stay safe." He made a slow turn around the room, taking it all in. Until Kathryn had entered his life, it had been no more than four walls and a roof, a place to hide from the rest of the world. She had made it seem like home. "If we don't come back, the manor is yours."

He was gone before either of the women could reply.

* * *

Pascual frowned when Bowen returned empty-handed. "Where are they?"

"Gone."

"Gone?" Pascual cursed. "That means *he* was here."

Bowen nodded. "He took the two women and left the horses and carriage behind."

Pascual paced the floor with long, angry strides. He had been looking forward to satisfying his lust and his thirst on the young one.

"You knew he would come sooner or later," Bowen remarked.

Pascual glared at him. "Of course I knew it! Why else would I have taken the girl?"

"I can think of a couple of reasons," Bowen said with a wicked grin.

"She's mine!" Pascual snapped. "And don't you forget it!" He swore again. "I need to feed. I won't be gone long. Stay here until I get back. And keep your hands off the women."

Kathryn paced the floor of her cell, her thoughts chaotic. The constant burn of the silver shackles made it hard to concentrate on anything else. Her mother was crying softly at the other end of the dungeon. What had happened to Nan and Mrs. Shumway? Had Pascual drained them dry and tossed their bodies in a ditch? How was she going to get her mother out of here before it was too late? Where was Roan? She had felt him through their link, knew he had been on his way. What was taking him so long?

She stopped pacing at the horrible realization that even if Roan knew where she was, there was nothing he could do, no way to get past the threshold without Bowen's invitation.

The thought sent a cold chill down her spine.

Pascual could keep her and her mother here indefinitely, subject to his every desire.

It took only moments for Roan to follow his link back to Kathryn. Dissolving into mist once again, he drifted around the perimeter. There was no one outside. Kathryn, Victoria, and the witch were inside the house. He had no sense of Pascual's presence, though the scent of vampire hung in the air.

Resuming his physical form, Roan tried the front door. It yielded at his touch, but the threshold's magic prevented him from going inside.

Cursing softly, he returned home.

Mrs. Shumway looked up, her expression worried, when he entered the parlor.

"Where's Nan?" he asked.

"She's gone to bed. I fear the night's events weigh heavily on her mind." She paused a moment. "Kathryn's not with you?"

"No. I can't get inside the place where she's being held. It's warded against vampires."

Mrs. Shumway took a deep breath, then said in a rush, "I can get inside."

He had been certain she would say just that, though he had been prepared to compel her if necessary. "I have to warn you that you'll be going up against a vampire and a warlock."

Her eyes widened. "A witch *and* a vampire. Oh, my."

"Exactly."

"I'm not afraid." Her words were bold, but she couldn't disguise the slight tremor in her voice. Lifting her hand to the pale scar near her hairline, she muttered, "Besides, I owe the bloody blackguard a little payback for this."

Roan reconsidered his options. He could wait and hope Kathryn found her own way out of the witch's lair. He could try to take Pascual and Bowen unawares and force Pascual to release Kathryn, but the odds of getting both men outside at the same time were slim. And he didn't want to leave Kat and her mother at Pascual's mercy a minute longer than necessary. Hence his plan to get Mrs. Shumway into the house.

He dragged a hand over his jaw. If she failed, he would have the death of one more woman on his conscience.

"Sure, and we're wasting time," Mrs. Shumway reminded him with asperity.

Roan nodded. "Sure, and we are," he agreed.

Dressed all in black, her hair tucked beneath a black cap, her husband's pistol in one pocket of her long coat and a sharp wooden stake in the other, Mrs. Shumway crept toward the entrance of the keep. Holding her breath, she lifted the latch. To her surprise, the door opened quietly at her touch.

Roan waited behind her.

Keeping one hand on her pistol, she inched forward, her gaze sweeping right and left the way Nate had taught her. When she saw no one, she turned toward Roan. "You are welcome here," she whispered. "Enter."

Praying it would work, and sorely afraid it wouldn't, Roan tried to enter the house, but once again, the threshold's power repelled him. As he had feared, only the owner of the manor could invite him inside.

"I'll find her," Mrs. Shumway declared, "or I'll bloody well know the reason why."

Roan stifled the urge to laugh at her bold words. "You can't go wandering around in there alone."

"Sure, and I can," she retorted, and melted into the darkness of the entryway.

An oil lamp burned on the mantel. Lifting it, she moved forward cautiously, checking each room. All were decorated with what looked like expensive furniture and priceless works of art. Who lived here? she wondered. The vampire or the warlock? And where were they?

Leaving the last room, she stumbled onto a narrow hallway that led down two sets of stairs. An iron-barred door waited at the bottom. It creaked loudly when she pushed it open, revealing a yawning black maw. Praying for courage, she tiptoed into the dungeon. The lamp cast flickering shadows on the damp gray walls, revealing a large ring of keys on a rusty hook.

"Mrs. Shumway! What are you doing here?"

"Miss Victoria! You're alive!"

Hearing the cook's voice, Kathryn called, "Is Roan with you?"

"Yes, but he can't get inside." Taking the key ring, Mrs. Shumway hastened toward Victoria's cell. The third key opened the lock.

Victoria hurried out of the wretched cage. Giving the cook a quick hug, she said, "We have to get Kathryn out of here."

Kathryn?

Relief washed through her at the sound of Roan's voice. *I'm here.*

Are you all right?

Yes.

Tell Mrs. Shumway to get out of there now. Bowen is inside.

"Mama, Mrs. Shumway, run! Bowen is somewhere in the house!"

"Not without you!" Victoria exclaimed.

"There's no time!" Kathryn insisted. "Go! Hurry!"

Victoria grabbed the key ring from Mrs. Shumway's hand and ran toward Kathryn's cell. Forcing herself to be calm, she tried one key after another, but none fit the lock.

Seeing it was hopeless, Mrs. Shumway grabbed Victoria by the arm and hustled her up the stairs. She let out a shriek when a man stepped out of a hidden alcove. She didn't stop but darted toward the front entrance, still dragging Victoria behind her.

They burst out through the open door.

Roan immediately stepped between the house and the women. "Mrs. Shumway, get the hell out of here!"

The cook didn't argue. She forced Victoria into the carriage and slammed the door, then scrambled up onto the driver's seat and cracked the whip, sending the horses into a gallop before Victoria had time to protest.

Bowen ran outside, then slid to a stop when he saw Roan blocking his path.

The air vibrated with preternatural energy as witch and vampire faced off.

Gathering his own power, Roan thwarted the warlock's magic, striding forward as he did so.

Bowen pulled a wand from inside his jacket, but Roan was on the witch before he could utter whatever incantation he had in mind. Grasping the man's shoulders, Roan buried his fangs in the man's throat.

The blood of witches was notoriously bitter, but Roan drank with gusto and then tossed the empty husk aside.

The threshold's power died with its owner. A thought carried him swiftly to Kathryn's cell. He grabbed hold of the door and gave a mighty yank. There was a deafening screech of metal against metal as the hinges broke free.

Stepping into the cell, he wrapped his arms around Kathryn.

"Cabrera!" Pascual's angry cry sounded from the stairway.

Flashing his fangs at his enemy, Roan willed himself and Kathryn home with Juan Pascual's promise of retribution ringing in their ears.

Roan and Kathryn were waiting in the stable when the carriage arrived. Roan had managed to break the chains binding Kathryn's wrists and assured her that the burns and the pain would be gone by morning.

Laughing and crying at the same time, Victoria flew out of the carriage and wrapped her daughter in a bear hug that surely would have bruised Kathryn's ribs had she still been mortal.

Roan helped Mrs. Shumway from the driver's seat. Lifting her hand to his lips, he murmured, "I am forever in your debt. Ask anything you wish of me and it is yours."

Chapter Thirty-Eight

Juan Pascual stalked the darkening shadows of the night. He preyed viciously on anyone who crossed his path until he was drunk on the blood of his victims. And all the while he cursed Cabrera.

Cabrera, who had won the beautiful Varinia's heart.

Cabrera, who had won the love of another woman, something Juan had never done.

Cabrera, who had killed Arwel Bowen, the only friend Juan had made in centuries.

Cabrera, who thwarted him at every turn . . .

After leaving another body in his wake, he willed himself to his new lair on the outskirts of the next town.

There had to be a way to destroy Cabrera once and for all and take the green-eyed woman. But how?

His own preternatural power seemed inadequate.

Bowen's dark magic had been ineffective.

What the hell else was there?

Chapter Thirty-Nine

After assuring her mother that she was unhurt, Kathryn hurried upstairs to change her clothes.

Roan made sure the house was secure, strengthened the wards on the walls and gates surrounding the grounds, then made his way up to the master bedroom.

He found Kat sitting on the bed, her cheeks stained with tears. "What is it?" he asked anxiously. "Are you hurt?"

"My dress," she wailed. "It's ruined. And I don't know where my veil has gone."

Lifting her to her feet, he drew her into his arms. "I'll buy you a dozen dresses."

Sobbing, she buried her face against his shoulder. "I'm sorry I'm being such a ninny."

He laughed softly. "You're the second bravest girl I know."

"Who's the first?" she asked, sniffing back her tears.

"Mrs. Shumway. She marched into the lion's den bold as brass with a pistol in one pocket and a wooden stake in the other."

"She was brave, wasn't she? Did you know her husband was a soldier? She told me they went on adventures all around the world and he taught her how to shoot."

Roan laughed softly. Sitting on the edge of the bed, he drew her down beside him. "You just never know about people, do you?"

"I guess not." She huffed a sigh. "We should be married now. On our honeymoon."

He brushed a lock of hair behind her ear. "Fate seems to be against us."

"It's not fate." Suddenly restless, she rose to pace the floor from one end to the other. "It's that horrid Pascual."

"Indeed. We'll never have any peace as long as he walks the earth."

Pausing in midstride, Kathryn looked at him sharply.

"It's time to put a stop to this," he said quietly. "I'm tired of worrying about what he might do next. There are people who are dead because of his hatred for me—Dudley's niece. Elsbeth. Tim. And who knows how many others? It's time to end it once and for all."

Kathryn laid her hand on his arm. "What are you saying?"

"It's time for the hunted to become the hunter."

"Do you think that's wise?"

"Wise? Maybe not. But I'm tired of playing his games. He's kidnapped you and your mother twice. He almost killed Mrs. Shumway. He's taken lives indiscriminately in my territory. Enough is enough!" Standing, he slid his arm around her waist and pulled her close to his side. "I love you. Never forget that."

"Wait!" She grabbed his arm when he released her. "You're not going now?"

"It's as good a time as any, don't you think?"

She shook her head vigorously. "No."

He smothered her protest with a kiss that curled her toes and left her breathless.

And then he was gone.

* * *

Outside, Roan opened his senses. "Where are you, Pascual? What loathsome hole are you hiding in?"

Where, indeed? It was doubtful the vampire would return to the witch's lair. Or was it? Maybe that was the last place Pascual thought he'd look. Or maybe his old friend didn't think he would come looking for him so soon.

Roan grunted softly. Whether Pascual was there or not, it was as good a place as any to start. Pascual had always been keen on getting rich on other people's money, and Kathryn had said the warlock's house was filled with statues and works of art worth a small fortune.

Muttering, "I've got to start somewhere," he willed himself to the outskirts of the keep, swore an oath when he found Kathryn waiting for him near the front door. "What the hell are you doing here?" he exclaimed. "Haven't you had enough of this place?"

"He's here," she said.

"I thought he might be. Now, go home."

"No. I want him dead just as much as you do. Maybe more, after all he's done to my mother. To me." Her fangs descended as her anger grew. She knew her eyes had gone red, that she probably looked like a crazy woman, but she didn't care.

"Dammit, Kathryn . . ." The words died in his throat when Pascual stepped out of the house. The white streak in his hair seemed to glow in the moonlight.

Pascual's gaze raked over Kathryn from head to foot. "Well, look who couldn't stay away," he drawled. "Saves me the trouble of going after you."

Kathryn glared at him.

"Leave her out of this," Roan said. "Just you and me. Right here. Right now."

Pascual shrugged and then, in a blur of movement, he was on Roan.

Kathryn darted out of the way as they came together, fangs bared, fists driving into preternatural flesh, clawed hands seeking to rip the heart from their opponent.

For a time, it seemed as if neither man would emerge victorious. Until Pascual fell back.

Eyes red as flame, Roan moved in for the kill. He let out a sharp cry of pain as Pascual uncorked a bottle and hurled the contents—acid mixed with holy water—into his eyes. He reeled back, temporarily blinded, as the liquid splashed over his face.

With an exultant shout, Pascual lunged at Roan, his fingers delving through cloth toward Roan's heart.

With a harsh cry of her own, Kathryn grabbed the stake she had tucked into the waistband of her skirt. Summoning every ounce of power she possessed, she flew at Pascual and drove the stake through his back.

And missed his heart. In desperation, she yanked it free.

Snarling, he turned on her, hands clawing for her throat. Panic lent her added strength. Twisting away from him, she drove the stake into his chest, praying she would strike his black heart this time.

He let out a hideous shriek, then stumbled toward her, his hands outstretched.

Kathryn backed away, felt the bile rise in her throat as she watched the life drain out of him. Almost in slow motion, he toppled to the ground. For a moment, he writhed in agony and then his body disintegrated, leaving nothing behind but a pile of cold gray ash that was quickly carried away by the wind.

"Roan!" She hurried toward him. The skin on his face was badly blistered. Patches of flesh were gone. His eyes were red and swollen shut. "Roan, are you all right?"

"Kathryn!" He held out his arms and she went into them.

She cupped his cheek, then jerked her hand away when he recoiled from her touch. "Is that going to heal?"

"I hope so," he muttered. The pain was excruciating. With luck, he would heal while he slept. "Think you can get the two of us home?"

"Yes." Slipping her arm around his waist, she willed the two of them to his bedroom in the manor.

A short time later, bathed and wearing a pair of loose trousers and a shirt of fine lawn, Roan sat on the edge of the bed, hands resting on his thighs.

Kathryn hovered over him. "What can I do?" He looked awful, his face raw and blistered, his eyes still red but no longer swollen completely closed.

Swallowing a groan, he said, "I need blood."

"Take mine."

"Human blood."

Nodding, Kathryn said, "I'll be right back."

Wiping the sleep from her eyes, Mrs. Shumway opened her bedroom door. "Miss Kathryn," she mumbled.

"I need your help."

"Oh. What can I do?"

"Actually, it's Roan who needs your help and we've no time to waste. He needs blood. Human blood."

The cook took a wary step back. "My blood?"

"Yes. I know it's a lot to ask, but . . . I'm begging you."

For a moment, Kathryn thought the woman would refuse. Then, taking a deep breath, the cook drew herself up to her full height.

"'Tis the least I can do. Sure, and he saved my life. Twice. I owe him for that. But . . . will it hurt?"

"No."

"Just let me grab my robe."

Mrs. Shumway's eyes widened when she saw Roan. "Stars above, what's happened?"

"There's no time to explain now," Kathryn said. "We need to hurry."

"Oh, aye." Rolling up her sleeves, Mrs. Shumway sat in the chair Kathryn dragged over to the bed.

"Kat, don't let me take too much."

She nodded.

Muttering, "I'm sorry," he grasped the cook's forearm. The cook tensed as he bit into the soft skin of her wrist. Earlier, he had promised to grant her anything she wished, and now he was feeding on her. The thought sickened him.

Mrs. Shumway let out the breath she'd been holding. "'Tis a wonder!" she exclaimed. "It doesn't hurt at all."

Kathryn kept an eye on Mrs. Shumway. When she judged he had taken enough, she said, "Roan, no more."

When he didn't respond, she shook his shoulder, then slapped him when he growled at her. "Roan, stop! Now!" Relief washed through her when he dropped the cook's arm.

Falling back on the bed, he closed his eyes. "Get out," he hissed. "Both of you."

Kathryn helped Mrs. Shumway to her feet.

"Did I do something wrong?" the cook asked.

"No," Kathryn assured her. "I think he's just ashamed that he had to drink from you and a little embarrassed because he didn't want to stop." Patting the woman's shoulder, she said, "Thank you so much."

With a wave of her hand, Mrs. Shumway said, "All in a night's work."

Kathryn stood in the hallway for several minutes. She was debating whether to return to Roan or give him a few minutes alone when she glanced at her hands, still covered with Pascual's blood.

Hurrying into her room down the hall, she lifted the pitcher, filled the ewer on the dresser, and scrubbed the blood from her hands. Then, moving with preternatural speed, she filled the tub in her room, warmed it with a glance, stripped off her bloody garments and sank into the blessedly hot water. Her brow furrowed as the events of the night replayed in her mind. She had killed a man. Yes, he'd been a monster. Yes, he'd killed numerous men and women through the centuries. Perhaps thousands. Yes, he had been trying to destroy Roan. But he had still been a living creature and even though she had washed away the stains, she would always have his blood on her hands.

Closing her eyes, she wondered if she would ever feel clean again.

Roan stared up at the ceiling. Kathryn had called it right, he thought. He had been ashamed of his need to prey on Mrs. Shumway and embarrassed by his lack of self-control. Had Kathryn not been there, he feared he would have drained the cook dry. The little he had taken had eased his pain so that it was no longer excruciating, but it still hurt like the fires of an unforgiving hell. A taste of his future, he mused, for if anyone on this earth had ever deserved damnation, it was he. Had he never interfered in Kathryn's life, she wouldn't be a vampire, nor would she have had to take Pascual's life to save his own. And that was the most bitter thing of all, that the woman he loved with every fiber of his being had risked her young life to save his worthless hide.

The best thing he could do for her, the kindest thing, would be to get out of her life and stay out.

And this time, for good.

Half an hour later, Kathryn stepped out of the tub. Slipping into her favorite nightgown, she opened her mind, trying to read Roan's thoughts, but he had shut her out. She tried not to feel hurt. She knew the events of the night had upset him even more than they had upset her. As she brushed out her hair, she smiled, thinking they could console each other.

Her remorse at destroying Pascual had faded. Why should she feel guilty for what she had done? He had been a monster, with no regard for human life or any other. He would never have stopped hunting them as long as he lived. But for him, she would be Roan's wife now, locked in his arms.

Maybe she should suggest they just forget the wedding. After all, they were vampires. Maybe the laws of society and the Church no longer applied to them. Did she really care what anyone thought about her relationship with Roan? If she did, she would never have moved in with him in the first place, or stayed this long. Of course, with her mother now living under the same roof, she had the perfect chaperone as far as the outside world was concerned.

Barefooted, she padded down the hallway to the master bedroom. Whispering Roan's name in case he had already succumbed to the Dark Sleep, she opened the door. The bed was empty. She knew a moment of alarm, then shook her head. No doubt he was waiting for her in their lair.

She smiled as she hurried downstairs. One nice thing about being a vampire was falling asleep at his side.

Only, the lair was empty.

Crawling into bed, she closed her eyes.

Where was he?

It was her last thought before she tumbled into oblivion.

Kathryn woke, reaching out for Roan. Only, his side of the bed was still empty. She fought down her rising panic. He wouldn't leave without telling her. No doubt he had just risen early this evening. He was probably waiting for her upstairs.

Yet even as she tried to convince herself all was well, she knew he wasn't in the house.

Nor was he anywhere in the vicinity.

His guilt had driven him away. She knew it in the deepest part of her being, knew his thoughts as if he had written them all out in a letter of good-bye. He blamed himself for the times that her life and the lives of her mother and the household staff had been in danger. Pascual had turned her, but Roan carried a load of guilt for that, as well, blaming himself for what had happened. He felt he had ruined her life and now, with Pascual dead and the danger gone, he was certain she would be better off without him.

Her hurt quickly turned to anger and then rage. After all they had been through, he had decided to leave her. No matter that they were engaged to be wed. No matter that she had given him her heart, her very soul. No matter that she loved him more than life itself. He had decided she would be better off without him!

Well, so be it!

If he didn't want her, then she didn't want him!

Leaping out of bed, she paused when she saw the sheet of paper on the nightstand. So, he had left a letter, after all. She stared at it as if it might blow up in her face, took a deep breath and picked it up. It was short and to the point.

Kathryn, I have added your name to
all of my accounts. Please draw funds
as needed to furnish the new house
and provide sustenance for your mother
and the others. I know you will hate me
for leaving, just as I know you
will undoubtedly move out of the manor.
Please don't let your anger or your pride cause
hardship for yourself and the others.
RC

No word of returning. Just the offer of cash, as if she were some trollop he had bought for the night! Filled with pain, she tore the note to shreds.

He had been right about one thing. Tomorrow night, they would leave Cabrera Manor and move into their new home.

And she would never look back!

Chapter Forty

Drowning in despair and regret, Roan went to ground. In four hundred years, he had never done it, never considered it, though he knew many ancient vampires, weary of their long existence, often buried themselves deep in the earth—sometimes for a month, sometimes for a year, sometimes for decades or more.

A new adventure, he mused, as he arrowed down, down, meeting no resistance.

Mother Earth welcomed him, cradling him in her arms as if she knew it was where he belonged.

Murmuring Kathryn's name, he closed his eyes and dived into the endless black void of oblivion.

Chapter Forty-One

Weeks after burying his brother, Farrin Leblanc found the courage to go searching for Roan Cabrera. It hadn't taken much effort to discover where the vampire lived. Surprisingly, Cabrera was well-liked by all those who knew him. Even more amazing, none of the men and women Farrin had spoken to in the last few days even suspected the man was one of the undead.

Now, lurking in the shade of a tall tree outside Cabrera Manor, he wondered if Cabrera or anyone else currently resided in the house. According to his sources, a young woman, her mother, and two female servants lived here, but he had been watching the house day and night for the last week and he hadn't seen anyone going in or coming out.

Squaring his shoulders, he walked boldly to the front door and rang the bell.

No answer.

Thinking the bell pull might be broken, he rapped his knuckles on the door.

Still no answer.

Frowning, he sauntered back down the path and took up his place beneath the tree.

He would give it another week, maybe two, before he gave up and went home to tell his mother and his ailing father that their eldest son was dead.

Chapter Forty-Two

Hands fisted on her hips, Kathryn stood in the center of her bedroom in the new house. What with choosing furnishings for each room and stocking the kitchen cupboards and shelves with new pots and pans, dishes, silverware and towels, the nights had flown by.

Now, almost two weeks later, she was mostly settled in, except for putting away the box of clothes sitting on the floor by the door. Roan had bought them for her and she felt guilty for keeping them now that the two of them were no longer together. She would have felt guilty about moving into the house, too, but it had been his idea to burn down the old one. It had seemed like a good plan at the time.

Nan and Mrs. Shumway shared the third bedroom. They had asked, somewhat hesitantly, if they could move in with her and Victoria, since they were uncomfortable staying in the manor alone. Kathryn didn't blame them for not wanting to stay there.

She was glad for the company of the other women, and grateful for the many tasks that needed doing to make the house a home. She hadn't minded the hours spent unpacking and arranging furniture. She loved caring for Bianca; she didn't even mind the fact that she had to ride in the dark. Fortunately, the mare didn't seem to mind, either.

When she had nothing else to do, Kathryn sketched countless pictures, anything to keep her hands and her mind busy.

Anything to keep from thinking about Roan.

It didn't work, of course. She missed him dreadfully. He was the first thing she thought of when she woke, his face the last image in her mind when the Dark Sleep claimed her. Where was he? What was he doing? Was he somewhere in Newberry, shielding his presence from her, or had he left town for good? Had he met someone else?

The pain of losing him didn't lessen with time. Her anger faded away, leaving her with a sense of emptiness that grew deeper and stronger as time passed. The coming of each new dawn found her looking forward to the Dark Sleep. For those few hours, there was no pain, no hurt, just oblivion.

Farrin Leblanc shifted from one foot to the other. He had been watching the Cabrera place for two weeks. If nothing happened tonight, he would abandon the hunt.

Overcome with weariness, he closed his eyes.

When he opened them again, there were lights on inside the manor. He checked his coat pockets—wooden stake, silver blade and cross, flask of holy water.

Murmuring, "This is for you, brother," he marched up to the front door.

Kathryn wandered through the manor, much as she had during her first days there. Strange, how empty it felt. It wasn't just that no one lived here now. It was as if the spirit of the house had died when Roan left. She recalled how she had always felt his presence, always known when he was there, even before she had been turned.

Going down to his lair, she sat on the edge of the bed. "Roan, where are you?" she wailed softly. "Why did you leave me? I never blamed you for anything that happened. You must know that sooner or later I would have asked you to turn me so we could be together forever . . ."

Her voice trailed off when she heard someone at the front door. Roan! The thought sent her running up the stairs, and then she stopped. Why would he wait outside for someone to let him in?

Blowing out a sigh of disappointment, she opened the door. A strange man clad in a pair of black trousers and a dark gray shirt stood on the steps, his hands jammed into the pockets of a long black coat.

"May I help you?" Kathryn asked.

Too late, she caught the scent of hunter.

He saw the recognition in her eyes at the same time he realized she was a vampire.

He moved first. Before she could slam the door, he grabbed her arm and yanked her outside with one hand while his other hand jabbed a stake into her chest. Stumbling back, she fell to the ground.

The hunter swore in frustration when he realized he had missed her heart.

Leaning down, he reached for the stake, no doubt intending to stab her again, but a hand curled around his neck, lifting him up until his feet dangled in midair.

"Kathryn," Roan asked, "are you all right?"

In spite of the pain in her chest, she smiled up at him. "I am now," she said, gaining her feet in a single, fluid movement.

Roan shook the man in his grasp as if he were a sack of wheat. "Who the hell are you?"

"Farrin . . . Leblanc," he gasped, trying to loosen Roan's hold on his throat.

Roan grunted softly. "Come to finish what your brother started, did you?"

"Damn . . . right."

"Good luck with that." He tightened his grip on the hunter's neck. "I don't expect you to believe this, but I killed your brother in self-defense. I let him go once with a warning not to come back. If he'd listened, he would still be alive." Lowering his arm, Roan set Farrin on his feet. "I'm giving you the same chance. Walk away and don't come back. If I see you again, I'll kill you."

"Believe me, you won't. As of tonight, I've given up hunting for good." As if to give weight to his words, Leblanc reached into his pockets. Withdrawing a flask and a silver crucifix, he threw them on the ground along with a wooden stake. "I'm done."

Nodding, Roan watched Leblanc run down the path and skitter around the corner before turning toward Kathryn. "What are you doing here?"

"What are *you* doing here?"

"I knew you were in trouble." His gaze moved over her. How he had missed her. How good it was to hear her voice, even if she now hated him. "Are you all right?"

She lifted a hand to her chest, surprised to find the wound already healing. "It hurts a little."

"That's not what I meant." He jammed his hands into his pockets and balled them into tight fists to keep from reaching for her. "Are you all right?" he asked again, his voice gruff.

"No."

"Neither am I, without you," he said quietly. "I'm sorry, Kat. So sorry for all the pain I've caused you."

"None of this is your fault. I chose to stay with you

because that's where I wanted to be. There's no point in wishing things were different. They are what they are. I have no regrets, and I don't want you to have any, either."

"How can you say that, after what that wretch Pascual did to you?"

"I could handle being a vampire," she said with asperity. "I could handle anything, as long as you were with me."

"And now?"

"Now I hate it."

"Kat . . ." He raked his fingers through his hair. "I've been a selfish fool. Can you ever forgive me?"

"Only if you promise never to leave me again."

"I promise. I swear it." He held out his arms, felt the sting of tears in his eyes when she moved into his embrace and wrapped her arms around his waist.

"You still owe me a wedding." Blinking back tears of her own, she rested her cheek against his chest. "Do you think it would be all right to have the honeymoon first?"

The words were barely out of her mouth when she found herself flat on her back beneath him on the bed in their lair. Looking up at him, she laughed with the sheer joy of being near him again, of seeing the love in his eyes as he lowered his head to hers.

How she had missed him. His touch. His scent. The way her heart pounded when he was with her, the way her blood ran hot for his touch.

"I love you, Roan," she whispered. "More than you'll ever know."

"And I, you, my sweet Kathryn."

"Where did you go?"

"I went to ground."

"You what?" She stared at him, certain she had misheard him.

"It's something a lot of the old vampires do."

"Why?"

He shrugged. "When they miss all that was once familiar and they can't accept the changes in a world that seems alien to them, they bury themselves deep in the earth and go to sleep. It revitalizes them somehow."

She looked at him in horror. "They bury themselves alive? On purpose?"

He nodded.

"But why did *you* do it?" He didn't seem to have any trouble fitting in to the world around him. "Did you need to . . . to revitalize yourself?"

"No." He lifted his hand as if to touch her, then lowered it to his side. "I just didn't want to face the world without you."

"Oh, Roan. I don't want to live without you, either!" Kathryn exclaimed. And then she frowned. "But . . . how did you know Farrin was here?"

"Through our bond, of course."

"How could you find me when I tried night after night to find you and couldn't?"

"Because I'm still your master, Kat. Have you forgotten that?"

She tilted her head to the side, a look of mischief dancing in her eyes. "Command me then, my lord."

"Kiss me, my love. Kiss me until the night is over."

Cupping his face in her hands, she drew his head down and kissed him with all the love and longing in her heart. Home, she thought, as his hands caressed her. She was home at last.

He rolled onto his side, carrying Kathryn with him. "I'm afraid our honeymoon will have to wait until tomorrow night," he murmured, his fingers threading through her hair. "The sun is about to steal you away from me."

Wishing she could hold back the dawn, she kissed him

again, and yet again, until she felt herself falling, falling, into darkness.

Roan held her close, one hand lightly stroking her back, sliding over her thigh, until he, too, surrendered to the Dark Sleep.

Kathryn woke to the scent of flowers. Lots of flowers. Opening her eyes, she saw vases of every size and shape sitting on every available surface, all filled with delicate purple orchids or dark red roses interspersed with baby's breath.

A sheet of paper on the bedside table caught her eye. Unfolding it, she read, "'Go upstairs to my chambers, my love. RC.'"

Flinging back the covers, Kathryn stepped into her slippers and ran up the stairs to the master bedroom. She had expected to find Roan waiting for her there, maybe in bed, she thought, smiling, so they could finish what they had started the night before.

Disappointment twisted her heart when there was no sign of him. And then she noticed the dress hanging from the door of the wardrobe. It was without doubt the most beautiful wedding gown she had ever seen, a froth of pristine white lace and shimmering silk. It looked like something fit for the Queen of England herself. And the veil! It was as light and delicately woven as a spider's web.

Shaking her head with wonder, Kathryn ran her finger-tips over the gown. Had her mother picked it out? No. An indrawn breath told her only three people had handled it. She didn't recognize one of the scents—that of the seam-stress, perhaps? One belonged to Madame Fontaine. And the other was Roan's. Her heart skipped a beat with the re-alization that he had chosen it just for her, though she had no idea when he'd found the time to shop. He must have risen today before the sun went down.

A second folded sheet of paper waited for her on the chest of drawers. She smiled as she opened it.

> *Nothing will stop us this time!*
> *Come hell or high water, tonight we wed!*
> *Nan has readied a bath for my lady fair.*
> *Be ready at 8.*
> *RC*

She hugged the note to her chest. Then, giddy with excitement and eager to try on the new dress, she pulled her nightgown over her head and kicked off her slippers. Stepping around the screen, she slid into the tub, which Roan had thoughtfully moved into the master bedroom.

At a quarter to eight, wearing her beautiful new gown and veil and feeling like a storybook princess, Kathryn went downstairs. Her mother, Mrs. Shumway, and Nan waited for her in the parlor.

Her mother wore a new dress; the one she had been wearing when Pascual kidnapped them had been ruined by her time in the vampire's filthy cell. Victoria had been loathe to spend the money on a new gown and thought to have the original one cleaned, but Kathryn was certain nothing could rid the green silk of the awful smell that clung to it.

"Mercy!" Mrs. Shumway exclaimed as Kathryn entered the room. "Sure, and I've never seen a gown as lovely as that one!"

Victoria nodded in agreement. "I thought the one you

had before was beautiful, but this one is exquisite. When did you have time to shop?"

"I didn't." Kathryn ran her hand over the silk of her skirt. "Roan picked it out. And I love it!" She twirled around. "This one means even more than the last one, because he chose it for me."

Materializing beside her, Roan said, "I was hoping you'd like it." He glanced from Kathryn to the other women. "Are you all ready to go?"

"Are you sure it's safe to leave the house?" Victoria asked. "Remember what happened last time."

Roan looked pointedly at Kathryn. They hadn't told anyone about Pascual's demise. And now was not the time. "It won't happen again," he assured Victoria. "All right, ladies, I need you to stand close beside me, two on my left, two on my right, with your arms around each other." When they had done as he asked, his put his arms around the two who were closest. "Hold on tight to each other."

Looking frightened, Nan closed her eyes, as did Victoria.

Mrs. Shumway took a deep breath. She didn't look scared or worried, merely curious to see what would happen next.

Even though Kathryn knew what to expect, it was still a little daunting, being whisked through the darkness at such incredible speed.

When the world stopped spinning, they were standing outside a grand old church made of white stone set in a field of emerald green. Lights shone from behind the stained-glass windows. More light spilled from the open door. A pair of wrought-iron benches flanked the flagstone path to the entrance.

"Where are we?" Kathryn asked, glancing around. Nothing looked familiar.

"Scotland."

Victoria pressed a hand to her heart. "Scotland!" she exclaimed. "Oh, my."

"Scotland," Nan repeated, looking as if she might faint.

Grinning, Roan looked at Kathryn, who grinned back at him.

"I know this church," Mrs. Shumway said, her voice tinged with amazement. "Sure, and my grandparents were married in this very place. I remember my mother bringing me here when I was just a wee girl. We sat on that bench yonder while she told me stories about the fey folk."

Taking Kathryn's hand, Roan led her inside. He chuckled as he overheard Mrs. Shumway murmur, "How on earth did we get here so fast?"

Kathryn glanced at her surroundings, awed by the beauty of the chapel, the statue of the Virgin Mary. Colorful stained-glass windows lined both sides of the aisle, each depicting a moment in the life of Christ from His birth to His resurrection.

She smiled at the black-robed minister who waited for them at the altar. He was a tall, spare man, with short brown hair and twinkling blue eyes.

"Welcome, my children," he said. "I understand you wish to be married."

Nodding, Roan introduced Nan, Mrs. Shumway, Victoria, and Kathryn to the minister, who welcomed each of them with a handshake and a smile.

Victoria and the other two women took a few steps back, leaving Roan and Kathryn standing side by side in front of the altar.

"Roan and Kathryn," the minister began, "since you have both agreed to enter into the covenant of Holy

Matrimony, you will now declare your consent before God and these witnesses. Roan Cabrera, do you take Kathryn to be your wife? Do you promise to be faithful to her in good times and in bad, in sickness and in health, to love her and to honor her all the days of your life?"

Gazing deep into Kathryn's eyes, he murmured, "I do."

"Kathryn Marie Winterbourne, do you take Roan to be your husband? Do you promise to be faithful to him in good times and in bad, in sickness and in health, to love him and to honor him all the days of your life?"

Blinking back tears of joy, she said, "I do."

"Have you rings to exchange?"

Kathryn looked at Roan. She hadn't even thought of rings. Had he? Or would he think them unnecessary?

With a wink at Kathryn, Roan said, "We do."

Reaching into his coat pocket, he retrieved two gleaming gold bands which he handed to the priest, who blessed them, then handed the smaller one to Roan and the other to Kathryn.

"Roan, repeat after me," the minister said. "Kathryn Winterbourne, receive this ring as a sign of my love and fidelity. In the name of the Father, and of the Son, and of the Holy Spirit."

Repeating the words, Roan slipped the ring on her finger.

Kathryn murmured the same words, using Roan's name, then, unable to stop smiling, she placed the ring on the third finger of Roan's hand. He was hers now, finally and for always.

"Having exchanged vows and rings," the minister intoned, "I now pronounce you husband and wife. Mr. Cabrera, you may kiss your bride."

Kathryn's heart skipped a beat as Roan drew her gently into his arms. "I will love you and only you, as long as I live," he murmured. "And I will protect you with my life."

They were, she thought, the sweetest words she had ever heard.

His kiss, when it came, was exquisitely tender, filled with all the love in his heart and the promise of forever.

After returning to the manor house, Victoria, Nan, and Mrs. Shumway drank toasts to the bride and groom—champagne for Victoria, Nan, and Mrs. Shumway, vintage red wine for Kathryn and Roan.

After a few moments of small talk, Victoria announced she was going to bed. Nan and Mrs. Shumway said their good nights, as well, and followed her up the stairs. Due to the lateness of the hour, they had all decided to spend the night at the manor.

A million butterflies took wing in the pit of Kathryn's stomach when Roan reached for her hand. "Alone at last. Do you remember when you said you'd never seen a bed as big as mine?" he asked, his lips twitching in a grin. "And I replied that you were welcome to try it out?"

Kathryn nodded.

"I think the time has finally come."

She nodded again, her heart turning happy somersaults when he swung her into his arms and carried her swiftly up the stairs to the master bedroom.

Inside, he set her on her feet, then locked the door. "You are the most beautiful woman I have ever known," he said, his voice husky with desire. "If you don't believe me, see for yourself."

Opening the blood bond between them, he let Kathryn into his mind, allowing her to see herself as he did.

Her mouth formed an "O." Was that really her? The dress fit perfectly; the veil fell to the floor in graceful folds. Wearing it made her feel like a princess. Now she saw that she even looked like one. She frowned as she examined her features. She looked the same as she remembered and yet changed somehow. Her hair was thicker, more lustrous. Her eyes seemed a shade darker, her skin almost translucent. "I look different."

"It's part of being a vampire. One day soon, I'm going to commission an artist to paint your portrait dressed as you are now. I intend to hang it over the fireplace so that I never forget how beautiful you looked on this day, or how very lucky I am to have found you."

"Two portraits," she said. "One of the two of us together."

Murmuring, "As you wish," he removed her veil and carefully laid it aside. Then, turning her back to him, he unfastened her gown.

She shivered when his fingers brushed against her bare skin, sighed when he rained kisses along the side of her neck.

She stepped out of her dress and petticoat, blushed when she removed her undergarments. Then, feeling suddenly bold, she undressed him until, at last, they stood naked, only inches apart. Heat climbed into her cheeks when she saw him. She had never seen a naked man before and he was beautiful, his shoulders broad, his belly flat and ridged with muscle. And that part of him that made him a man . . . Knowing she was blushing furiously, she looked away.

"I love you, Kat," he said, his voice thick. "Only you, always and forever."

"And I love you," she replied tremulously. "And never anyone else."

Taking her hand, he led her to the bed. "Don't be afraid. I promise not to hurt you." Gathering her into his arms, he kissed her—a long, slow, deep kiss that sent shivers of anticipation coursing through every nerve and fiber of her being.

Somehow, they were in bed, mouths still fused together, bodies straining toward each other. Feeling his body pressed so intimately against hers—with nothing between them—was more wonderful than Kathryn had imagined. She watched his hand—that large, capable hand—slide ever so slowly up her thigh and thought the sight of his hand on her bare skin the most erotic thing she had ever seen.

Or felt.

Because of the bond between them, she knew what he was thinking, what he was feeling, as their bodies melded together, becoming one flesh. He whispered words of love to her in a language she had never heard before, and yet, miraculously, she understood every endearment. Perhaps expressions of love and desire needed no interpretation.

His touch kindled a fire inside her, growing hotter and hotter until she thought she might melt in his arms. And then, as he moved deep within her, she did melt, pouring herself over him as two became one in body and spirit.

Sighing, replete, she ran her fingers through his hair while he sprinkled kisses over her cheeks, her nose, her brow. She was his now, she thought, truly his, for now and for always. As he was hers.

She was surprised when he wanted her a second time. Surprised and eager. They took it slower this time, savoring each magical moment, drawing out each kiss and caress until Kathryn thought the very bed would go up in flames, and then he possessed her again.

* * *

Much later, she rested her head on his shoulder, thinking how wonderful it was to be able to make love all through the night. She felt sated, complete, and not tired at all. It was amazing.

All too soon, she sensed the sun's rising behind the heavy drapes of the master bedroom. Whispering, "I love you forever, my husband," she tumbled into the waiting darkness, secure in the knowledge that tomorrow night and every night she would wake up in the arms of the man she loved.

Cabrera rolled onto his side, carrying Kathryn with him, utterly content for the first time in his long existence. Waiting for the darkness to carry him away, he held her close, his fingertips tracing the curve of her lips, thinking how blessed he was to have such an incredible woman in his life.

Epilogue

Eighteen Months Later

Roan sprawled in his favorite chair in the parlor, his gaze resting on the painting of Kathryn in her wedding gown that hung over the mantel. Much had happened since that night. He had feared that, as time passed, his bride would grow to hate being a vampire. Though she never spoke of it, he knew there were times when it grieved her that she would never have children, but those times had grown fewer as the year went by. She had redecorated the manor from top to bottom and when that was done, she had insisted on a new barn for Bianca, and then his lovely wife had decided she wanted to raise horses.

To that end, they had built three enclosed paddocks in addition to the new barn, bought a blooded stud horse, a pair of quality mares, and hired Conal Matheson, Kathryn's former riding instructor, to run the operation.

And life was good. After the wedding, Victoria had decided to remain in the new house and had asked Nan to stay with her. To everyone's surprise, Victoria ran into a man she had known years ago. A widower now, John Kent had recently moved to Newberry Township. He and Victoria had met by chance in church one Sunday morning. A few months later, they had announced their engagement. And three months after that, they were married.

Mrs. Shumway had elected to return to the manor. Though Roan and Kathryn had no need for a cook, she took care of the housekeeping duties and ran whatever errands needed to be taken care of during the day. He and Kathryn had another surprise when they discovered that Conal Matheson was courting Mrs. Shumway. Six months later, the two were married.

Roan grinned at the memory. They made an unlikely couple, but you had only to see them together to know they were very much in love. Conal moved into the manor after the wedding. There was, after all, plenty of room.

Roan glanced over his shoulder at the sound of Kathryn's footsteps. As always, his heart lifted at the sight of her.

Alighting on his lap, she asked, "Did you miss me?"

"I always do."

"Mama sends her love. You won't believe this, but she's pregnant!"

Roan lifted one brow.

"I'm as surprised as you are," Kathryn muttered with a shake of her head. "Surprised and shocked. I never thought about my mother's age, but she told me she was only sixteen when I was born."

"Making her thirty-seven," he said. "Not a vast age for child-bearing."

"Just think," Kathryn exclaimed, eyes sparkling. "We'll have a baby in the family!"

Roan nodded. Perhaps this would ease her longing for a child of her own.

"I always wanted siblings. I used to ask Mama for a baby sister every Christmas. She always promised me one," Kathryn said, grinning. "It certainly took her long enough."

"Are you happy, Kat?" He knew she loved him, but the

fear that one day she would leave him lurked like a dark shadow in the recesses of his mind.

"Yes, of course." She kissed him. "Why are you asking at this late date?"

"You're not sorry you married me?"

Brow furrowed, she asked, "What is it, Roan? What's bothering you?"

"I know how much you wanted a family. How it must hurt, knowing your mother is with child and that you . . ."

She cupped his face in her hands. "Oh, Roan, I wouldn't trade what we have for all the babies in the world," she said fervently. "Don't you know that? I love you more every day." She grinned at him. "And now I can enjoy all the fun of loving a baby with none of the work or the responsibility. What could be better?"

Cradling her to his chest, he kissed her long and hard. "I love you, Kathryn Marie Winterbourne Cabrera," he declared, and whisking her up the stairs to the master bedroom, he made slow, sweet love to her until the sun came up.

Connect with Us

Visit us online at
KensingtonBooks.com
to read more from your favorite authors, see books
by series, view reading group guides, and more.

for sneak peeks, chances to win books and prize packs,
and to share your thoughts with other readers.

facebook.com/kensingtonpublishing
twitter.com/kensingtonbooks

Tell us what you think!

To share your thoughts, submit a review,
or sign up for our eNewsletters, please visit:
KensingtonBooks.com/TellUs.

Romantic Suspense from
Lisa Jackson

Available Wherever Books Are Sold!
Visit our website at **www.kensingtonbooks.com**